The Liar's Club

The Urbana Free Library

To renew materials call
217-367-4057

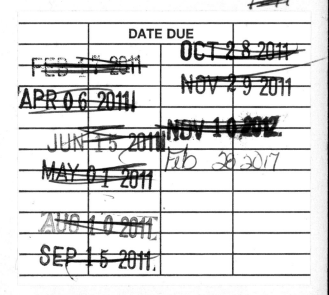

11-1

The Liar's Club

Layla Jordan

KENSINGTON PUBLISHING CORP.
www.kensingtonbooks.com

DAFINA BOOKS are published by

Kensington Publishing Corp.
119 West 40th Street
New York, NY 10018

ISBN-13: 978-0-7582-4703-2
ISBN-10: 0-7582-4703-6

First Printing: December 2010
10 9 8 7 6 5 4 3 2 1

Printed in the United States of America

This is dedicated to Jasmine, Jada, Jake and Julien.
I'll take you for that walk now.

ACKNOWLEDGMENTS

There are so many people to thank for this new adventure. First and foremost is our heavenly father who'd blessed me long before I had the common sense to realize it. To Granny, my baby Alice, who continue to inspire me though it's from up above now. My sister Channon "Chocolate Drop" Kennedy— you're still the best. My other sister, Charla Byrd, the funniest woman I know. My beautiful niece, Courtney—I love you. Kathy and Charles Alba-salt of the earth.

Brenda Jackson for being a good friend and inspiration. Marc Gerald for taking me under your wing. To Selena James for having the patience of Job.

PART I

O, what a tangled web we weave,
when first we practice to deceive!

—Sir Walter Scott, *Marmion*

1

Sinclair

Whoever said "money can't buy you love" has never so much as stepped a pinkie toe onto Rodeo Drive. Prada, Dolce & Gabbana, and Christian Dior, their mere existence is proof that there's heaven on earth. Every time I strut down the pristine three-block stretch of expensive boutiques, I feel and look like a billion bucks. And why shouldn't I? I'm a dime diva. Long locks (weave), even golden honey complexion (MAC), and coke-bottle curves that make even the white boys' tongues in this Barbie-doll-infested town roll out of their heads. Hell, I don't mind. My big tits, small waist, and round ass are about the only real things my momma gave me. My street smarts and hustler mentality are courtesy of my father, God rest his soul. Add all those wonderful attributes together, and you get a fierce bitch who has landed herself an insanely rich producer husband, Omar Fines.

Omar. The first thing that pops into my mind whenever I think about him is *cha-ching*. I mean the man has mad loot. None of that hood rich bullshit that's an epidemic in my hometown. I'm talking no limits. We have three homes in the States—Beverly Hills, Manhattan, and the Hamptons—and two homes in Europe—Paris and Spain. Not to mention the yachts, Learjets, and fleet of Italian cars. I'd like to say this is the lifestyle

that I've always dreamed of, but before I met Omar, I didn't
know people lived like this—let alone black people. I mean, I'd
heard of rich people, but you really have no idea what money
can buy unless you have it. Now, I know that may sound a bit
ignorant, but check it. I'm from the gutters of Detroit. My
mother, Felicia, crackhead extraordinaire, was so trifling that
we kept getting kicked out of the projects. Do you know how
hard it is to get put out of public housing? That takes a special
kind of fuckup. So for most of my teenage years, I didn't have
an address. We laid our heads down at whoever's friend of the
moment would take us in.

Now look where I am. So what if my head is a little blown
up? Let me kick back and enjoy the shit for however long this
is going to last.

Money can't buy you love. Puh-lease. I *love* my homes, jets,
boats, and cars. I love my apartment-sized walk-in closets that
look like mini-boutique stores. I love my jewelry. I *love* this entire lifestyle. But if the question is do I *love* my husband, Omar?
Well, that's a little more complicated. True, he looks a hell of a
lot like that actor in the old *Rocky* movies, Carl Weathers. Tall,
chocolate, and totally ripped from the hours he spends pumping iron in the gym—well, that and his extensive steroid use.
The latter left his dick so small that the first time I saw it I
thought about filing a missing dick report. Don't laugh. Marrying a small dick is a serious adjustment, and it's not something that a woman should do all willy-nilly without weighing
the pros and cons.

PROS: CONS:

Money   Sexually fuckstrated (that's not a typo)
Money   Sanity (Omar is more than a little anal retentive)

Okay. So there wasn't that much deliberation. I snatched
that five-carat, emerald-cut diamond ring before Omar's knee

hit the floor. Hell, in that moment, I thought, *I can do this. I'll just buy tons of sex toys.* Sheeiit.

I totally underestimated how much I love a good dicking down. If you don't agree, then I hate to be the one to tell you that you just ain't had a brother that hit it right. I *love* sex—and not just the standard three positions: missionary, cowgirl, and doggie style. I'm a certified freak and unrepentant dick addict who needs a helluva lot more than what my husband is working with. So . . . I creep.

Surprise, surprise, right?

And don't judge me. I hate that shit. All that finger-pointing and gossiping bullshit when you know damn well deep down inside that if you were dealing with a grown man with a dick a few inches bigger than your clit, you'd be doing the same thing. Hell, most of America creeps nowadays. Look at our politicians, movie stars, professional athletes—hell, look to some of your own family members. Chances are you know quite a few people on the creep, if you're not doing it yourself.

The trick is not to get caught, which is difficult in the age of camera phones, YouTube, and saved text messages. Pulling off a successful creep is equivalent to obtaining a PhD in neuroscience out here. But let me be real: As long as Omar's money is raining, I'm not going anywhere. I'm going to keep it right and tight, and play my position as the perfect Hollywood trophy wife for as long as the position is available.

Today is another sunny California day when I step out of my custom-made, white Bentley Mulsanne dressed in a Prada baby blue scoop-neck dress that hugs my hips and caresses my swaying black girl booty. My matching pumps add four inches on my 5'9" frame, while my wrists, neck, and ears are blinged out by that patron holy saint Harry Winston.

To look at me, one would make the mistake that I was born into the lifestyle of the rich and famous instead of the hard streets in the south side of Detroit, but what people don't know won't hurt them. All that matters now is that Beverly

Hills is my new playground and I have no intention of jumping out of the sandbox.

"Sinclair!"

Who in the hell is screeching my name out here? Turning, I remove my shades and flutter my mink lashes at Brijetta Hamilton's loud ass as she races down the sidewalk to catch up with me. Now, don't get it twisted. I love my girl. Ever since I first met her at a *Vanity Fair* Oscar party, I knew that she was, to coin the phrase, good people. Sure it's easier to detect that things aren't exactly what they seem to be between her and her action superstar, and recently ranked *People*'s Most Beautiful list, hubby Trey Hamilton, but I let her go on with her pretense because I live in a glass house my damn self.

"Oh, hey, Brijetta. I didn't even see you." I lean in for a quick hug and air kiss. When I feel my girl's tits brush against me, I jerk back, stunned. "Damn, girl. When did you get those?" I reach out and give her new silicone babies a soft squeeze right there in the middle of the sidewalk. Trust me, that's a compliment in this town.

Brijetta strikes a pose that thrusts her new DDs up high in the air. "You like? Trey bought them for my thirtieth birthday."

I sweep a critical gaze over my girl, who looks like she went two sizes too big and is in danger of tipping over. I don't have it in me to tell her that she looks like a stick with tits, so I take a dive. "Girl, if you like it, I love it."

"In that case, the jury is still out," she says. "I didn't know getting these babies would hurt so damn much. I'm popping Percocets like candy. But shit. Trey loves them. The bandages came off yesterday, and last night he wore me and these babies out."

I fight like the devil not to roll my eyes. As far as I can tell, her beloved Trey is never satisfied. He clearly views his wife as his blank canvas, because every time I turn around he's trying to get Brijetta to do one crazy, drastic surgery after another. Case in point, when I first met Brijetta at that Oscar party two years ago, she was a three-hundred-pound, fashion-challenged, lonely virgin who was still working as an RN at Cedars-Sinai. Now she weighs a petite hundred pounds, is a complete label whore, married, with her days of working nine-to-five firmly in her rear view.

The tabloids had a field day with her and her steady transformation. Trey Hamilton had broken a lot of hearts when he upped and married Brijetta sixty days after meeting her. Most headlines labeled him a chubby chaser and then speculated that Brijetta was just the rebound chick from his highly publicized and doomed relationship with supermodel Camilla. So it stands to reason that every week the rags report or make up stories about martial spats and pending divorce—they're like the darker versions of Brad Pitt and Angelina Jolie.

It's no wonder Brijetta is always fighting to prove her marriage is on solid ground. Nobody is buying it—including me. But in Beverly Hills, creating the perfect lie is important.

"You look like you were lost in your own world. Where are you headed?" Brijetta asks.

"Armani. I'm picking up a suit for Omar and then I have to head out to The Ivy to meet Jaleesa for lunch. You want to come?"

"Sure. Let me just text Trey where I'm going to be," she says, pulling out her cell. "I thought Jaleesa was still filming that Denzel thingy out in New York?" Brijetta starts walking and texting beside me. "She didn't get fired again, did she?"

"Don't know. She called me last night and said that she wanted to meet for lunch." Now, in truth, I wouldn't be at all surprised if that heifer did get fired. That girl put the D in diva. Once upon a time she might have been considered a good actress; now all the tabloids talk about are her drunken antics in the clubs and on movie sets. That old adage "there's no such thing as bad press" isn't true anymore. Bad press has killed many careers out here in the city of bright lights, and I'm afraid that all signs point to my girl being next on the chopping block.

"Honestly, I don't know how she keeps getting acting gigs," I say.

"According to her, it's because she has a mean head game on the casting couch," Brijetta snickers.

"Do you actually believe that?"

"What—that Jaleesa is a ho? Girl, I know it. I've known Jalessa since we were in junior high. The day she got breasts she was pushing them up on every guy that walked past her. And the night she realized the power she held in between her legs, forgetaboutit."

"Humph. Some women go a whole lifetime and never realize their power."

"Some misuse it," Brijetta volleys.

"And some try to conquer the world." I smile. "That would be me."

We crack up as we enter Giorgio Armani and, of course, buy more things than what we came in there for. Two hours later, Brijetta and I are escorted to our seats by The Ivy's white picket fence. Without a doubt, the restaurant is a celebrity magnet, drawing a list of who's who of the Hollywood elite. A lot of people hail the place as the best restaurant in Los Angeles—for its food and for the paparazzi accessibility that tend to camp out across the street.

We already know that Jaleesa's ass is going to be late, so we go ahead and order our usual Cajun shrimp salads and golden margaritas.

"So how are things with you and Omar?" Brijetta asks, taking her glass before the waitress has the chance to set it down. "I read in the trades that he'll be producing the Hughes brothers' film."

I instantly perk up as my husband's latest achievements inflate my own ego. "Yes, Lion's Gate green-lighted the deal. Omar is thrilled to have a strong contender for a summer blockbuster."

"Well, let's drink to that," she says cheerily, holding up her glass.

"Damn straight." I tap my margarita glass against hers and then moan aloud when the chilled alcohol slides down my throat. The first sip of alcohol is a euphoria like no other. "Ahh. Now this is how to spend an afternoon."

"Hello, ladies!" Jaleesa singsongs while strutting her stuff toward us. She's dressed in a strange combination of street casual and haute couture. Add in gaudy Mardi Gras beads and a pair of bumble-bee-styled Chanel glasses and you have the hot mess that is Jaleesa. The amazing thing is that despite the loud argument her clothes were having, Jaleesa is still a knock-out. "I didn't know you were coming, Brijetta." She leans down and gives both of us air kisses while pressing our cheeks together. "How are . . . ahhh. What are these?" She gropes Brijetta's silicone twins. "Nice. Nice. Who did your work?"

"Dr. Oxford on Rodeo Drive. Brilliant surgeon," Brijetta gushes. "I'll definitely be using him again."

"Again?" I hike up a brow. "Don't tell me that Trey already has you signed up for something else."

Brijetta shrugged her thin shoulders. "Just a little nip and tuck. Nothing major."

Bullshit. I can tell just by the sudden way she's avoiding making eye contact. But I gotta hand it to Trey, I'm curious what his final masterpiece will look like when he's finally finished with her.

"I hope you don't mind me playing tag with Sinclair. My afternoon was free."

"Don't be silly." Jaleesa waves her off and finally sits down. "I haven't seen you in ages. Well, at least since . . . did you get a new nose, too?"

Brijetta gushes as she strikes a couple of profile poses. "Well, you know I suffered from a deviated septum."

I have to speak up. "Child, please. That's what Jewish and Greek girls say around town to explain their nose jobs. Just admit you pulled a Lil' Kim and leave it at that."

Jaleesa laughs. "Ain't that the truth? No need to fake the
funk with us. Keep it real and we'll keep it real with you."

More bullshit. The last thing any of us do is keep anything
real. These little get-togethers only serve two purposes: to gossip and to brag. Let's face it, I like these girls, but I wouldn't call
either one of these heifers if I was in a real jam. They aren't like
the ride-or-die chicks I grew up with in Detroit. Telling either
one of these chicks the real 4 1 1 meant that it will be all over
Los Angeles before the eleven o'clock news came on. No,
what we have here in this sunny paradise is the Liars' Club. In
this town, there is no lie too big to fail; and in order to survive,
it's a prerequisite to be able to tell them with a straight face and
a sincere voice. As for me, Sinclair Fines, I'm probably the
biggest liar of them all.

2

Jaleesa

I love having lunch at The Ivy. It's absolutely the best way to guarantee my name in the hot gossip rags and blogs—well, at least a casual mention. A lot of celebrities like to pretend there's some made-up war between them and the paparazzi; but let me tell you, it's all bullshit. We love the paparazzi, we adore them. We lie awake at night dreaming up all these fantastic ways to get their attention. They are the life blood that feeds our vampiric thirst to be in the spotlight; which is why I'm sitting here wondering if this table is giving those snapping photographers my best angle.

"So what are you doing in town?" Brijetta asks, leaning back in her chair and sipping on a margarita.

I immediately wonder how many drinks the secret alcoholic has downed already before I arrived. I've known this vapid heifer since her Nell Carter look-alike days, and I think it's just some weird comic joke that she landed her big ass on the arm of Trey Hamilton instead of me. Really, what the hell does she know about this industry? How can she boost his image? I mean, really. Creating the perfect power couple is essential in any industry. Think Will and Jada, Jay-Z and Beyoncé, or heck, Barack and Michelle. Trey Hamilton needs to upgrade to someone like me.

"Jaleesa?" Brijetta presses, snapping me out of my wild musings about her man.

"Oh, girl, those assholes can kiss my ass. The script is bull-shit and is getting stupider with each daily rewrite. How the hell do they expect me to memorize my lines if they're chang-ing them all the damn time?"

Brijetta and Sinclair exchange looks.

"Well, fuck both of you, too, then," I snap, then glance around. "Where the hell did our waitress go?"

"All right. Calm down," Sinclair says. "Why don't you just tell us what happened?"

"Puh-lease. The same bullshit that always happens. The lead actor and director on some dynamic duo bullshit trip that leaves the rest of the crew feeling like we're just squirrels in their world trying to get a nut." I finally see the waitress who led me to my table. "Hey, honey, I need an orgasm over here!"

Every head turns.

"What?" I ask, laughing.

Brijetta and Sinclair crack up. I wink at them. "I love or-dering that drink in public," I admit, then laugh myself.

"So what really happened?" Sinclair asks. "Were you out partying every night again?"

"Ha-ha. A bitch can walk and chew gum at the same time, you know."

"I'm going to take that as a *yes.*"

"Believe what you want to believe." I reach for my purse and remove my lipstick and compact mirror. "I told those bas-tards what they could do with their stupid movie and I stormed off the set. The director is a major asshole, anyway."

"You stormed off a Denzel Washington movie? Have you lost your mind?" Brijetta asks. "Do you know how many ac-tresses would kill to be in a film with Denzel?"

"Don't you start in on me. My agent has been blowing up my phone for the last twenty-four hours. Fuck them. I have principles, you know. Those bastards snuck a nude scene in the script, and that shit ain't in my contract."

"Since when have you objected to showing your tits to anybody who wants to see them?" Brijetta asks, smirking.

"It'll cost an extra cool million to put my shit on the big screen. Believe that."

"A million? Girl, you're smoking something fierce. They don't pay that kind of money to see black titties. Are you crazy?

"Especially since they are running around wild and free in Africa, " Sinclair adds.

"They will if they want to see *these* titties. My shit is real. I'm not double bagging like you, sweetheart." That shuts the bitch up. She finally gets some titties and she's suddenly a fucking expert on the shit? Give me a fucking break. "Anyway, the whole thing is bullshit."

"Here's your drink, ma'am," my waitress says, smiling. It's a damn shame that you have to look like a model in this town just to get a waitressing job. "Would you like to place an order?"

"That won't be necessary. I'm on a liquid diet this week. Just keep the drinks flowing."

"I'll have another margarita," Brijetta says, then goes back to fluffing her lace front to make sure that her curls are holding steady. "So what are you going to do? You know that they're going to sue you for everything you got."

"Shit. Line up. Hell, if my own damn daddy is suing me, I don't know why I should give two cents in hell why some studio with its head up its ass should faze me." I down my drink in one long gulp, savoring the rich, creaming coffee flavor, and then smile at my two girlfriends. "This is how a bitch starts an afternoon."

Sinclair shakes her head. "I don't get you. You begged for this job and now you're just blowing it off. Pretty soon the only work you're going to be able to get is on *Celebrity Rehab* or . . . porno."

"Well, I'm sure as hell not going to any damn rehab. No. No. No. So you can forget that shit." I lay my best Hollywood smile on her. "But I did happen to thumb through the trades and read about Omar's latest project: *Defiance*. It's already generating quite a buzz around town about it being a possible summer blockbuster."

"Crossing our fingers and toes," Sinclair says.

"So . . . I was thinking that you have to know which dick I gotta suck to get my hands on a copy of that script. My agent, Maury, ain't worth shit." Sinclair gives Brijetta another one of her sneaky sideway looks before she bursts out laughing in my face.

"Please say your flaky ass is joking."

My heart and hopes drop. "I'm not flaky—just a little misunderstood." I shrug. "C'mon. Surely you can hook me up." Here I am giving my best sister-girl pitch and this heifer is looking at me like she doesn't know me from Adam. "Oh, you're just gonna play me to the left like that?"

Sinclair rolls her eyes. "I'm not trying to play you, but I don't get involved with Omar's business. You know that."

"But you can put in a good word with him." I smile. "You know, a little pillow talk here and there."

"I don't understand," Brijetta cuts in. "You and Spencer Reid had a thing a while back. Why don't you ask him for a part?"

"Please, that brother's casting couch is a dead end. He takes the pussy and just promises a callback that never happens. Slick bastard." I turn to Sinclair and pull on all my acting skills to keep my desperation out of my voice. No way am I about to let these two bitches know my real situation. So what if I didn't walk off my last movie but was instead fired. The most important thing is to get ahead of the story and to lock down my next gig before the studio's vow that I'll never work in this town again has a chance to take root. Damn it. I'm an actress—a damn good actress. I was nominated for a Screen Actors Guild

Award for my first film, *Blue Skies,* ten years ago. I was hot. The black *It* girl who was going to be the next Halle Berry. All these directors and producers gassed me up good with that shit. I have the looks and the talent. Every party I walked into, they were tripping over themselves trying to get at me. Now they play crazy and try to act like I have to audition or screen-test for D-list films. What the fuck?

Next thing I know I have to pull bullshit drunk stunts outside clubs and conveniently forget to wear panties in order to get any kind of love in the tabloids. But let's face it, that shit doesn't work as well as it does for blond, blue-eyed white girls. The truth, though this isn't the type of town that wants to talk about the truth, is that there's only a handful of African American women who even work steadily in this town. The other handful of working black actresses packed up long ago and moved to Atlanta so they can remain on heavy rotation with Tyler Perry.

Sinclair huffs, "I'm not going to make any promises, but I'll see what I can do."

I jump out of my seat and throw my arms around my new BFF. "Thank you, thank you, thank you."

"I *said* no promises."

"Understood." I *need* a part in *Defiance* like a crackhead needs a five-dollar hit, and I'm not afraid to do whatever it takes to get what I want. That includes me throwing myself on Omar's casting couch. Sinclair will just have to understand that the shit ain't personal. It's just business.

3

Brijetta

Jaleesa knows her ass is trifling. She's thinks that she's pulling the wool over muthafucka's eyes, but her game is whack as hell. Her ass up here trying to tell us that she just walked off a major movie set. C'mon now. Do we have "Boo Boo the Fool" stamped on our heads? Jalessa's ass has always been foul. It's one bullshit scheme after another, and she's not above using and abusing anyone to get what she wants. She thinks my ass is her friend, but nothing is further from the truth.

Yeah, we go back aways—junior high, in fact. Trust. She was just as trifling then; a backbiting, boyfriend stealing, ho is my middle name, daddy-tease bitch. Yes, I threw in daddy-tease because my mother claimed to have caught her more than once trotting her little ass in front of my dad in just panties and a bra when I'd foolishly invited her over for sleep-overs. My monogamy-allergic dad was practically nipping at the bit to get at her young pussy—so much so that my mother eventually had to ban the trick from coming back over to the house.

Admittedly, at first I didn't want to believe that shit. Me and my mother battled all the time back in those days. Typical teenage shit. Then Jaleesa set her sights on the boy she *knew* I had the biggest crush on: Darrin Savoy. Sure, I was a little chubby back then, and Darrin didn't know I was alive, but Jaleesa got me to admit my die-hard crush during a truth or dare game and then the very next day, she was rubbing her stank-ass titties all over Darrin. She got that boy so pussy-whipped that when she moved on to one of her other BFF's boyfriend, Darrin was so heartbroken that he put a .38 to his temple and threatened that he'd kill himself if she didn't take him back.

She didn't.

He blew his brains out.

That shit alone rocketed her to fame in Culver High. The girls wanted to know her secrets to get a boy to fall that deeply in love, and the boys wanted to sample what had hooked a brother so bad that he'd take his own life. Hell, it was a win-win situation for Jaleesa. She still used that whole tragic episode in her movie biography as some great triumph that she had to get over in order to become the great piece of shit actress she is today.

Foul.

No, I'm not a hater. I'm watching from the sidelines waiting for this bitch to finally get what's coming to her. It's coming. Karma is a bitch. Believe that. Don't think that I don't know that it's fucking killing her that I married one of the hottest actors in the business. Shit. Jaleesa stood as one of my bridesmaids at my wedding with her nose damn near ready to twist off her face. And she held that sour look in every picture the photographer snapped of her that day.

How did *fat* Brijetta hook someone like Trey Hamilton? Hell, that's what the whole world wants to know. My answer? I put up with a lot of bullshit. Anyone who's been in this town more than two seconds should know that not everything that glitters is gold. Dating actors, let alone marrying them, is like having a lobotomy . . . daily. Their vanity, their God complexes, and their constant need for love and attention is not for the faint at heart. But . . . I love my husband . . . just as I love the life being married to him has afforded me. And if I ever have to choose between one or the other, I choose Trey each and every time.

I grew up with nothing . . . less than nothing. A broken home with an alcoholic and constantly cheating father left me and my six siblings to deal with a deeply bitter mother. The kind of mother who never missed an opportunity to tell me how I was never going to amount to anything and not to bother with ever trusting a man. I get it. She was hurt, but her words battered my fragile self-confidence until I found myself repeating her hateful words to myself in the mirror.

It's no wonder I found comfort in food. A little pizza to smother the loneliness, a little ice cream to mute the pain of my dead-end career. Before I knew it, I was tipping the scales at 315 pounds and trying to convince myself that the pain in my back and legs was no big deal. Trey saved me, and in return I try each and every day to save him right back.

And don't think I'm foolish enough to ever leave Jaleesa alone with my husband. Not going to happen. Hell, I don't even invite this trick over to my house, and I certainly don't discuss what projects Trey is working on so she can beg me for a motherfucking job. This bitch could be on fire and I wouldn't bother to piss on her to put it out. Believe that.

I don't know Sinclair that well, but she's going to have to learn her own lessons when dealing with Jaleesa. I threw out a couple of hints and I'm going to leave it at that, because bitches in this town love nothing more than to shoot the messenger.

"Oh, look at the time," I say, glancing at my watch. "I gotta head back. We're doing some renovations on the west wing of the house and I have of a team of contractors coming."

Jaleesa frowns and pokes out her bottom up. "Aww, but I just got here."

"We'll just have to catch up next time." I stand and brush a brief kiss against her cheek and stretch my fake smile as wide as her own. "Take care and good luck with your audition."

"Oh, I'm not going to have to audition. My girl Sinclair is going to hook me up. Ain't that right?"

Sinclair's face twists. "I didn't say that. I *said* that I'd get you a copy of the script."

I shake my head, but then hug and kiss Sinclair good-bye. Like I said, she's gonna have to learn her lessons the hard way. "Check you later, girl."

A few minutes later, I'm in my blue Mercedes, flying up Santa Monica Boulevard, basking in the afternoon sun, and re-playing Jaleesa's desperation over and over in my head. Damn. I should have busted out my camera phone and taken a picture of her begging Sinclair for a script. It's not much, but I have the sneaking suspicion that it's just the tip of the iceberg.

I pull up to the gate of my estate and punch in the code. When the wrought-iron bars swing open, I get hit with that same wondrous disbelief that this is my place. My home. It's gorgeous. Emerald green lawn neatly manicured and land-scaped with blankets of flowers I don't even know the names of. Water fountains, Cupid statuaries, and sculptured hedges are nothing compared to the French chateau-styled mansion nes-tled on the three-acre estate.

My house. How you like me now, Momma?

After parking the car in one of the nine carports, I rush into the house certain that I have about twenty minutes before the first contractor gets here. Plenty of time for a quick wardrobe change.

"Ah, Mrs. Hamilton, thank God you're home."

I look up at the top of the winding staircase to see Amaya, our four-foot, husky build housekeeper, looking like she's in a state of panic. "What's wrong?"

"It's Mr. Hamilton. He no come out the room. I think that something may be wrong."

I'm already running up the stairs before she's even finished talking. "Where is he?"

"In the bedroom. That man came by again this morning." Amaya struggles to keep up with me while I run toward my bedroom. "I don't like that man. He scares me."

"Why didn't you call me?" I reach the door, and sure enough the damn thing is locked. "Trey?" I knock. "Baby, are you all right?"

KNOCK. KNOCK.

"Trey?" I turn to Amaya. "Find me a screwdriver."

"Yes, ma'am." She takes off.

KNOCK. KNOCK.

"Trey, baby. Open up." I press my ear against the door and I think I can just barely make out Trey moaning my name. Fear seizes me as I rattle the knob and bang on the door harder. "What did you do, baby?" Tears splash down my face because I'm already imagining the worst. "HURRY UP, AMAYA!"

"I'M COMING!"

My knocking is now a raucous bang. It doesn't do any good since the door is solid oak. "TREY, CAN YOU HEAR ME, BABY?"

BANG! BANG!

Amaya races back to my side, red faced and out of breath. "Here you go, Mrs. Hamilton."

Shakily, I snatch the screwdriver out of her hand and get busy dismantling the doorknob. "Hold on, baby. I'm coming." Shit. I'm so fucking nervous, I can barely get my hands to stop shaking.

"Do you think he's all right?" Amaya asks nervously over my shoulder.

I don't bother answering her because I really don't need my mind going there. I stab my fingers a couple of times, chip a nail, but I finally get the doorknob off and rush inside. My gaze instantly flies to the large mahogany bed where Trey is facedown with a needle still protruding out of his arm.

"Shit. Shit." Rushing over to him, I still try to push all negative thoughts to the back of my head. *He's okay. He's okay.* I desperately need to believe this. I snatch the needle out and, with Amaya's help, get Trey flipped over onto his back. I search for a pulse, but I'm having trouble and he's clearly turning a purplish color. "Help me get him into the bathroom."

Amaya starts to back away. "I dunno. Maybe we should—?"

"Don't argue. Grab his feet." I swear to God I'll beat the holy hell out of her if she bolts.

Amaya hesitates for just a second, but then hops to it. Together, we manage to carry Trey off the bed. Getting to the bathroom is more of a challenge. I even break a heel off my shoes, trying to lug Trey's dead weight. We make it to the king-sized tub and Amaya turns the shower on while I'm still sitting behind Trey and trying to slap him awake. The minute the cold water hits us, Trey springs to life, sputtering and gasping.

"What the fuck?" He roars and then sputters under the icy current. "Goddamn it. TURN THAT SHIT OFF!"

Startled, Amaya shuts off the water and then looks me dead in my face, and says, "I can't do this no more, Mrs. Hamilton. It's not right. I quit!" She turns and runs off.

"Amaya, please come back!"

"Let her ass go. Fuck!" Trey huffs and then eases back against my heaving chest; like us hanging out in the tub with our clothes on in freezing water is something we do every day. My clothes are ruined, I broke my favorite pumps and chipped a nail, but Trey is all right. *Thank God.*

How did I snag a man like Trey Hamilton?

I put up with a lot of bullshit.

4

Sinclair

"Ooooh, Jeeesus!"

I grab fistful of the hotel bed's silk sheets and sink my teeth in Clevon's hard chocolate shoulder while his ten-inch cock drills in between my legs. I pay no attention to how hard my head bangs into the headboard or how loud my screams and moans fill the hotel suite. The only thing that matters in the world right now is this nut I'm about to bust.

"You coming, baby?" Clevon whispers, and then starts nibbling on my ear.

To be honest, I don't know what I said back to him or even if it was in English. This chocolate god was doing things to my body that I know was a crime in a couple of states. Just looking at his magnificent, muscled body is usually enough to get me off. But to look this good *and* be swinging a Mandingo dick, are you kidding me?

I deserve this shit, too. Two years enduring nothing but my husband's pencil dick that can't find a G-spot even if I draw him a damn map has nearly driven me insane. And no amount of coaching will ever get Omar Fines to eat pussy the way I like it. Oh, he will kiss all around it, lick my clit for a few strokes, but then he'll wipe the juices from his mouth by rubbing it against my thigh.

What the hell is that?

When *I* go down, I get busy, sucking and slurping like my damn life depends on it. I've brought that man closer to God than a month of Sundays next to the pulpit, and he damn well knows it. When it comes to sex, I've always believed that to get, you gotta give, right?

Shit.

Clevon is an ex-Compton thug, who is now one of the most sought-after personal trainers in Beverly Hills. I took one look at him at the Sports Center and knew that I had to have him. The fact that he has a big dick and a skilled tongue and knows how to work *both* of those motherfuckers is just an added bonus. Creeping with his ass has been one of the best damn decisions I've ever made.

"Jesus! I'm fucking coming," I pant. My pussy muscles squeeze his thick shaft and coax him to come with me. Greedy, I lock my legs around his hips and then fill my hands with his strong ass cheeks as I match his thrusts pound for pound.

The hotel bed starts jumping. "Shit, this is some damn good pussy," Clevon growls.

Hot, trembling, sweaty, I call on the Almighty one last time before my body explodes and splinters into a gazillion glorious pieces.

"Damn, woman," Clevon pants, then flings himself to the other side of the bed. "I thought you were going to rip the skin off my back."

I cock a grin in his direction. "You complaining?"

"Hell, naw," he says, reaching in between his legs and gently rolling off the cum-filled condom. "If anything, I'm bragging."

I laugh at that shit. "I bet you say that to all your female clients."

Clevon hikes a brow up at me. "Do I detect jealousy?"

"Hardly. I'm just keeping it real." To prove my point, I

reach over to the side of the bed and grab my purse. I look him dead in his eyes when I spread ten one-hundred-dollar bills onto the nightstand. "I know a ho when I see one."

Smiling, Clevon pulls my body back against him so I can feel his double-digit cock stiffening again. "It takes one to know one."

I slap him so hard that my hand stings.

Clevon laughs while he effortlessly pins my hands down over my head. "My pussycat has claws."

"If you're smart, you'd remember that."

"Is that right?" His lips slope sideways while his heavy cock starts inching its way toward my pussy on its own volition. "Maybe if you made more time for a brother, I wouldn't be tempted to stray." I roll my eyes while he leans down and starts nibbling on my neck. "I don't know why you're tripping. You know I love you, girl. Despite all this unnecessary bullshit you're trying to put me through."

I look into his eyes and I think he means it, but in this town, you never know.

"Why don't you leave that limp-dick husband of yours? I make good money. I'll take care of you."

"Limp dick, huh?" Smiling into Clevon's chocolaty brown eyes, I reach for his thick, tree-trunk-sized cock and squeeze its large, mushroom head in between my thighs. "I'm not asking you for love, so just concentrate on your job, hustler."

Clevon's smile widens as he thrusts his hips upward. "You're a cold bitch, Sinclair. You know that?" I just smile while he leans forward and pops a nipple into his mouth and then suckles like a newborn baby.

"Ooo. Yeah." I sigh dreamily. This man is like the Energizer Bunny. He hooks my long legs over his shoulders and goes to town. After delivering two more orgasms, he peels open my creamed pussy and starts eating like it's a home-cooked meal.

Pumping and rotating my hips, I draw pleasure trying to

drench Clevon with as much of my juices as possible, but he sops it up like a starving child from a Third World country.

"Mmm, ma. Give it to me," he coaches.

And give it to him I do. All of it. I'm so wide open that my orgasms make me look like I'm having a series of epileptic seizures. One after another. Why can't Omar eat pussy like this? Mop the ceiling and the floor.

"Thank you, baby. Thank you, baby."

Clevon lifts his shiny face and crawls up my body to kiss and share my sweet taste.

"Mmmm," I moan, licking the insides of his lips.

Floating down from a cloud of ecstasy, I roll my body toward the nightstand just as my cell phone starts ringing. I lift my head and read the ID screen. It's Omar.

"Aren't you going to answer that?" Clevon asks, reading over my shoulder.

"Mind your own business," I say, tossing the phone back onto the nightstand. Every time I get to feeling good, Omar bubbles to the surface and ruins my orgasmic high.

Good sex isn't the only thing I've sacrificed for a life of luxury; my sanity is a close runner-up. My husband's obsession for perfection keeps me on edge. Our house, our clothes, our cars, and even our smiles have to be perfect to the watchful eyes of the gossiping public. He made it perfectly clear from the giddyap that bad press will not be tolerated. I'm to be on my p's and q's at all times.

In order to get away with what I'm doing, my lies and alibis have to be tight, and that's no problem for a slick bitch like me.

So far.

Two years down and five more to go if I ever hope to profit from this god-awful match. At least that's what my prenuptial agreement states. Omar may have been hypnotized by my tight pussy, but the brother wasn't taking any chances with his finances. Everything is stipulated in that damn 1,200-page document. Everything from the weight I must maintain to how many times I must sleep with him. Ain't that some shit?

I turn away from the nightstand and smile when I see Clevon has already nodded off. The true sign of dealing out some good coochie is how fast you can put a man to sleep. Just then, my own eyes start to droop—an equally good sign of me getting some good dick.

The only man who has ever rocked my body harder than Clevon was my first husband, Kwame Franklin. *That* mother-fucker always had me caught up. He'd tell me to jump and I never stopped to ask how high. I would just bounce my ass until he was satisfied. Hell, until we were both satisfied.

I was 17 when I met Kwame. We thought nothing of knocking over a convenience or liquor store to score some money for the latest clothes, cars, or even investing in the best weed rolling through town. Back then my name was just boring-ass Tracy Smith, daughter of the neighborhood crackhead, Felicia. My father? Hell, he'd been locked up years before I was born on a double homicide charge. Let Felicia tell it, she'd gotten knocked up during a rare conjugal visit.

People in my grandmother's congregation told Felicia I was special because I was born with a veil, a filmy membrane that looked like a shimmering coat of blood. They said I had a calling on my life. Whatever the hell that's supposed to mean.

The first eight years of my life, I was dragged up to the prison every Saturday before Father's Day, cheesing and acting like having a father behind bars was the most natural thing in the world. Well, maybe it was from my side of the tracks, but still. Thankfully, Felicia got tired of running up there every week playing wifey to a man who was never gonna come home and she simply stopped going.

Cold turkey.

For the most part, I've been hell on wheels since the moment I entered the world. Fast talking, fast acting, and always at the center of any and all trouble within a twenty-block radius. Hell, I had to do something to stick out and get noticed. Puberty was also around the time I started having strange dreams, the kind of dreams I could still recall after waking with the hairs on the back of my neck standing straight up. I don't get them all the time, but when I do, I've learned to start paying attention.

My first vision was about my high-school gym teacher, Mrs. Kraus. I'd dreamed some guy was beating and kicking the shit out of her. I thought it was strange that I dreamt about her because I couldn't stand her ass. I told my friend Fredricka about it and we had a good laugh all the way to school; but once we got there, we learned Mrs. Kraus was killed that night by her deranged husband.

At 15, I dreamed Fredricka was being raped by her father. The next day, Fredricka showed up at school black and blue. Nine months later, she gave birth to her own sister.

At 17, Kwame walked into my dreams. He was everything I could ever want: a 6'3" cinnamon brown thugalious brother with tats all across his back and arms. The hottest thing about him was his big-ass dick with a sterling silver ring pierced through the head of his cock.

Kwame knew how to sling dick like no other. He had me begging, crying, and praying all at the same time during sex. No doubt, the brother strung me out. He'd say jump and I'd ask how high. When that dick sprang up, it was my duty to ride until I got saddle sores.

Damn I miss him.

Good, hot, freaky-ass sex has and will always be my downfall. Looking back on my teenage years and early 20s, I regret nothing. I lived, hustled, and loved hard, and to be honest, those were the best years of my life.

The good times came to a crashing end when Kwame, after ignoring one of my dreams, got popped with a trunkful of drugs. He was sent to the federal pen to serve hard time. I sat in the first row of that courtroom until when the judge read out his sentence and I was forced to make a hard decision. The last thing I wanted was to turn into Felicia where I played wifey to iron bars.

In the end, I never wasted one Saturday visiting Kwame's hard-headed ass. I kept it moving. I ran through a line of stick-up boys, block hustlers, and even landed in the bed of the black Godfather in Detroit for a six-month stint, but none of those game players can hold a match to the *legal* Hollywood hustle Omar has on lock.

The minute I met his ass outside a Chicago nightclub, I knew I'd found my golden ticket. It took one minute to capture his attention, one evening to land him in bed, two weeks to get a brand-new shiny engagement ring, three months to change my last name.

I smile when I feel a pair of lips against my collarbone and I abandon my memories for the possibility for some more dick. Clevon slaps on another condom and we get busy for another hour. After bending and flipping into every position imaginable, I finally have to beg for a break. After which, I promptly fall asleep. Almost immediately I fall into a deep slumber where an angry voice barks out at me:

"What—you thought you were going to make a fool out of me?" Omar shouts, sliding his belt free from his waist.

I blink, but have no time to react before the first lash strikes me across my ass. A scream leaps from my throat while a sting of pain races across my skin.

"Woman, you got me confused," he roars, unleashing another blow against my thighs and legs.

Whap!

I bolt straight up in bed and blink in confusion at the darkened room. The hairs are standing up at the back of my neck as I quickly scramble out of the tangled sheets. "Shit. What time is it?"

To my right, Clevon moans and hugs the pillow.

I grab my cell phone and see that I've missed two more calls. "Shit!" I shoot out of bed and stumble my way to the bathroom. I can hardly get my mind right while I search through my mental Rolodex of excuses I can give Omar, who's waiting for me across town.

"Shit. Shit. Shit." I jump into the shower and after lathering up and rising off a few times, I hear Clevon's heavy feet slap the bathroom's linoleum.

"You want some company in there?" He peeks around the thin plastic shower curtain and licks his thick lips. "Looks like you could do with an extra set of hands. I can hit a few spots you're missing."

"No," I moan, knowing where his back scrubbing will lead us. "I really gotta hurry and get out of here."

"Well, I ain't gonna stop you," Clevon lies, stepping into the shower and taking the soapy mesh sponge and sliding it over my curvy body. "I'm just trying to help." He nibbles on my ear just as his heavy sex rubs against the crack of my ass as if begging for permission to enter.

"Clevon—"

"Hmmm?" His hand slides in between my legs; then his fingers dip inside to rub my swollen clit.

"I. Have. To. Go," I insist.

"Uhmm, hmm. Is that the reason why you keep rubbing your ass against this good dick?"

I blink, surprised that's exactly what I'm doing.

"You know you ain't gonna get fucked *good* for a couple of days, baby. Why the hell are you fighting it? We can get in another quickie before you go."

"You know I won't get shit if my husband divorces me."

"Yeah. Yeah. You have to be married seven years." His dick

continues to slide down the crack of my ass as if it's a hot-dog bun. "What happens if he's taken out of the picture?"

"What?" I glance over my shoulder. "You mean like an accident or something?"

"Yeah."

I just stare at him, surprised by the dangerous direction the conversation has shifted.

Hell. I hadn't thought about that shit. "Don't start talking crazy."

"Fuck that." The head of Clevon's thick dick teases the rim of my ass. "You know you want this."

Clevon is always trying to play with my ass, but that's just one hole I don't fuck with. Wiggling away, I throw the mesh sponge against his chest and climb out of the shower. "Cut it out."

"Fine. Your loss," he shouts, chuckling.

"Whateva." I laugh and search high and low for my black lace panties. Finally, I have to give up the search and throw on the rest of my clothes. Smiling, I leave two more crisp one hundred dollar bills on the bed and race out the hotel room with a smile as wide as the whole state of California.

5

Jaleesa

"Home sweet home," I declare as I breeze through the door of my two-million-dollar West Hollywood condominium. I toss my car keys on top of the antique Bombay chest in the foyer, kick off my black Christian Louboutins over into the corner, and I'm two seconds from diving onto my cluttered ten-thousand-dollar leather couch when my doorbell rings. "Who in the hell?"

I'm not really all that concerned that it's a burglar or a stalker given the amount of security here in the Sierra Towers. It's more likely to be a neighbor, if anybody. But as luck would have it, it's the one person I've been hoping to avoid.

"Maury," I declare with an over-the-top enthusiasm I don't feel. "How did you get in the building?"

Maury rakes back his mouse brown hair and hits me hard with an icy blue stare. "You're not my only client that lives here, you know."

"Oh. Well, I was just about to call you," I lie.

"Cut the shit, Jaleesa," he says, rolling his eyes and strolling into the condo without waiting to be invited. "What the fuck happened in New York?"

I shut the door behind him and draw in a deep breath for

a performance of a lifetime. "Those people are impossible, Maury. I had to quit."

"They said that they fired you."

"Of course *they* said that. I'm not surprised." I toss up my hands and head toward the kitchen. "Want something to drink?"

"No, I don't want anything to drink. Tell me what the fuck happened. The truth, if you can manage it."

"Hell, why don't you tell me? Since you have all the answers." I storm toward the kitchen in order to buy more time.

"Do you think this is some kind of joke?" Maury thunders as he dogs my heels. "Do you know what I had to do to get you on that picture? Do you know how many favors I had to call in because you swore that you were going to be on your best behavior?"

"I *was* on my best behavior. It was that damn director that insisted on humiliating me every damn time I turn around. One hundred and seventeen takes on my first scene. Give me a break. It was just *one* line."

"He said that you kept flubbing the line. Said that you were hungover."

"Bullshit." I jerk open my subzero freezer and pull out a Zima. "He had everyone snickering and laughing at me. He made it clear that I wasn't his first, second, or even third choice for the role, and he did everything he could to get me off that set."

"So you accommodated him? Where's the logic in that?"

"You don't understand, Maury! You weren't there." I pop the top to my drink and then storm past him to the living room. "I know you don't believe this, but I do have some pride."

Maury laughs. "You're right. I don't believe it, but that's neither here nor there. You're through—*we're* through. I can't work with you anymore." He starts toward the door.

My heart drops before I lunge after him. "Wait! What do

you mean we're through? You're not bailing on me, are you?"
I block him from reaching the door.

"Out of my way, Jaleesa."

"No, we need to talk about this."

"There's nothing to talk about," he insists, looking angrier
than I've seen him in some time. "You don't take any of this
shit seriously. And when you act up like this, you drag my
name and agency down with you. My word has to account for
something in this town, and I swore to the studios that you
wouldn't burn them on this." He rakes his hands through his
hair again and then jams them into his pockets to jingle the
change in there.

"Maury . . ."

"NO! It's over, kid. I wish you all the luck in the world, but
this is the end of the road for me and you."

He tries to move around me, but I throw myself up against
the door. "Maury, you don't mean that! C'mon, we've been together for ten years. How can you just dump me when I need
you the most?"

Maury rolls his eyes like he's dealing with an unruly child.
"Look, we had a lot of laughs. I made you a lot of money."

"Correction: I made *you* a lot of money."

He tosses up his hands. "See? I can't even talk to you."

"All right. All right. *You* made me a lot of money. Whatever. The point is that we need each other."

He cocks his head.

"All right. *I* need you." I toss up my hands. "Damn. C'mon,
Maury. Don't make me beg." Tears are burning the backs of
my eyes, but I'm doing my best to keep them at bay. My whole
life is crashing and burning around me. "I'm going to make it
up to you. I swear." I reach for his belt buckle on his blue suit
and am shocked and hurt when he pulls away.

"Jaleesa, don't. Desperation is not a good look on you."

"Then give me another chance," I beg. You're less than

nothing without an agent in this town. "I got an audition coming up."

"What audition? I didn't book you any audition."

"With Omar Fines," I lie. "That's why I was going to call you. I had lunch with his wife, Sinclair, today and she told me how much Omar wants me in his next film."

"*Defiance?* Omar Fines wants you in that film? For what part?"

I swallow. "I don't know."

"Jaleesa—"

"Sinclair is sending me the script over tomorrow. I swear."

Maury stares at me. "Why didn't he contact me—or the agency."

I shrug. "He knows me and Sinclair are good friends, so he just had her ask me if I'm interested. I told Sinclair that I'd take a look at the script and get back to him." When Maury doesn't respond, I throw up my right hand for good measure. "I swear."

"Please. Please. Whatever you do, don't swear." He moves me aside and then reaches for the door.

"Maury . . . please."

"All right. When you get the script, I want to know the date and time for this supposed audition."

"You got it."

Holding my gaze for a few more seconds, he looks like he wants to say something else. I try to help him out by reaching for his belt buckle again.

"Jaleesa—"

"All right. All right. I just thought—" Those damn tears are starting to feel like acid.

"Just call the office with the information." He shoves me away from the door again and this time succeeds in escaping from the condo.

However, once the door slams behind him, I'm left feeling like a big pile of shit. "Now how am I going to pull off this fucking miracle?"

6

Sinclair

Beyond late, I whip up to the security check point at Lion's Gate studios and flash the guard my best smile as I wait for my window to slide down. I'm more than an hour late for the private get-together Omar arranged to celebrate the studio green-lighting *Defiance*. It's not a huge deal. It's just the behind-the-scenes guys who put the deal together, but judging by the way Omar is blowing up my phone, you'd think I'm running late for the Oscars or something.

"Evening, Marcus." I hold up the guest badge Omar gave me early this morning.

The old guard is tall and skinny as a beanpole, but in the few times that I've come to the lot, I've found him to be funny and as adorable as a newborn puppy. "Now, aren't you a sight for sore eyes," he says, leaning into the car and cheesing at me. "We were all beginning to worry about you. Mr. Fines has been calling up here every five minutes to check whether we've cleared you at the gate."

I can't help but roll my eyes. This man would put a LoJack on my ass if I let him.

Just then the phone in the booth rings and Marcus rolls his eyes as well. "One guess who that is."

"This is embarrassing," I mumble under my breath.

"Yes, Mr. Fines," Marcus says, smiling. "I'm letting her through now." He hangs up the phone.

"I'm so sorry he's been bothering you," I say.

Marcus just waves off the comment. "Aw, don't worry about it. If I was married to a pretty thing like you, I wouldn't want you out of my sight, either." He tosses a wink at me and finally opens the gate.

"Thanks, Marcus, but something tells me that you were quite the ladies' man back in your day."

"What's with the past tense?"

We laugh and I ease onto the accelerator and cruise by the security booth and onto the studio lot. Parking is near impossible, especially for guests. And even as the day melts into evening, this place is still cram-packed. I loop around a couple of times until someone finally un-asses a parking spot. When I remove my cell phone from the car's charger, I see that I have twenty-seven missed calls.

This motherfucker here. I slip the straps of my purse over my shoulder and slam the car door before marching toward the building. The sheer size of the Hollywood studio has often left me bereft of speech. Tracy Smith has definitely arrived.

As the evening cool breeze whips across my face, I become more than aware that the tips of my hair are still sopping wet and I curse Clevon for popping off the top two buttons on my white blouse. That's just the kind of thing Omar will notice.

"Good evening, Mrs. Fines. We were just wondering if you were going to be able to join us."

I turn just as Omar's assistant Beverly Daniels approaches. She's 5'7", about two hundred pounds, a Loretta Devine look-alike. As long as I've known her, Beverly has never lost her Texas-size smile, and is always armed and ready to recite Bible quotes for any and all situations.

Simply put: The bitch gets on my last nerve.

"Car trouble," I lie, and keep it moving.

"Again?" Beverly's brows pinch together with either concern or disbelief, I can't tell which and I really don't give a damn. "It being a new car, maybe you should take it back to the dealership. You might have a lemon on your hands."

"I'll certainly look into it." I turn and head for the back entrance of studio B. I don't have to glance over my shoulder to know Beverly is dogging my heels. "Omar will be back in a minute. He took a call in one of the back offices from one of the studio heads. There's just a few of us still milling about."

"You mean I missed the whole thing?"

"Well, it was a small party—just twenty-five people."

Shit. I'm never going to hear the end of this.

"We were worried that maybe you'd been in an accident or something," Beverly says breathlessly. "We've been calling your cell phone."

"My battery died. It just finished charging when I pulled up." I cover with a rubber smile and march the rest of the way to the stage, my mind a whirling twister.

I step out onto a hardwood stage and catch the attention of Nelsan Reynolds, the screenwriter. His smile is instant and sexy as hell. If he were an actor, he would give Trey Hamilton a serious run for his money. He excuses himself from the small cluster of money men and makes his way over to me.

"We thought you weren't coming," he says. "I'm glad you could make it."

"It looks like I missed it," I say, looking around. "Any champagne floating around here?"

"C'mon. What's a party without alcohol?" He leads me over to a banquet table. While he pours the champagne, I pick over the cheese and grapes. "Here you go, madam."

I accept the drink from him and don't miss for a second how his hand lingers on the champagne flute before his fingers lightly brush against mine. It's a slick move that I haven't seen for a while and I can't help but blush at his subtle flirting.

"Congratulations," I say, lifting my glass in a private toast. "This is a big sale for you."

Nelsan clinks our flutes together while his sexy smile stretches wider. "It is. I might actually be able to afford a vacation this year." His eyes lock on to mine. "You wouldn't happen to have a single twin sister who'd like running on the nude beaches of Brazil, would you?"

My brows hike up. "Nude?"

"A woman's body is like a work of art that should be shared and enjoyed by the masses."

"Sounds like you're describing a hooker." His laugh is the sexiest thing I've heard in ages and my interest perks up even more. "Where are you from, Nelsan?"

"Detroit. South side. Born and raised."

"Oh." My smile quickly melts off my face. The idea of me running into someone from my hometown has been a nightmare of mine for sometime.

"Not a fan of Detroit?" he asks.

I glance around. For once, I'm looking for Omar to come and save me. "I don't have an opinion of it. I've never been there."

Nelsan instantly cocks his head. "Huh. I'm usually pretty good with accents, and I would've bet my paltry paycheck that you're a native."

Lie. Lie. "No, you're mistaken."

He nods, though his expression tells me that he sees straight through my bullshit. I need to change the subject. "So when do I get the chance to read this wonderful manuscript that has this town buzzing?"

"You'd like to read it?" he asks in clear surprise.

"Absolutely. I'd love to get an autographed copy."

His suspicion instantly vanishes at the idea of me interested in his work, which isn't surprising in this town. At least I'll be able to pass the script over to Jaleesa without having to go through Omar. He would ask way too many questions and be too afraid of the script leaking into the wrong hands.

"Consider it done," he boasts. "And I look forward to hearing your opinion."

I level another smile on him and drink him in again. He really is a magnificent piece of work, and I can't help but wonder how he might be in the bedroom. In the enduring sultry silence while we sip champagne, I watch how his eyes keep drifting toward my titties.

"Sinclair, sweetheart. You made it."

With great reluctance, I pull my gaze away from one temptation to cast it toward another: Spencer Reid. Six-five, broad shouldered, trim waist, Spencer Reid's smooth milk-chocolate complexion looked rich enough to send someone into a diabetic coma. And as I watch him approach, I'm thinking about risking taking a bite of him. He's been Omar's co-producer for the past fifteen years, though he's a decade younger.

"Car trouble," Beverly pops out of nowhere and informs him. Why can't the bitch ease up off me? I cast my gaze over to Spencer, then it's like a lightbulb going off in my head. This heifer has a crush on Spencer. I almost laugh out loud. *Talk about out of her league.*

"Again?" Spencer says. "With that being a new car, maybe you should take it into the dealer so that they can check it out."

"That's probably a good idea." I glance over my shoulder and stare dead into Beverly's face until she gets the hint and flutters off to chat up a group of networking executives.

"Damn," I mutter. "Does she think I need a babysitter or something?"

"Maybe you do." Spencer chuckles and then drains the rest of his champagne.

"What do you mean?"

"Car broke down?" He shakes his head. "Don't you know never to use the same excuse twice?"

Our gazes lock, and I sip my champagne while I deliberate on my response. Finally, I settle on, "I'll keep that in mind."

"Glad that I could help. Too bad you missed your husband's rather touching toast. He went on and on about how you inspired him to take on this new project."

"Really?"

He places a hand over his heart. "It was moving. Really. It almost made me wish that I was married to such a supportive woman myself. Maybe I would be a better man."

Puh-lease. "Who do you think you're fooling? A woman would have to pry your player's card out of your cold, dead hands."

Spencer laughs and tosses in a wink. "You know me so well."

"I just know a die-hard player when I see one."

He eases closer so that my knees threaten to buckle under the seductive scent of his woodsy cologne. "Had a lot of experience with those, have you?"

"More than I care to admit." I hold up my glass and meet his twinkling gaze again. "Congratulations, by the way. I'm sure *Defiance* is going to be another big hit."

"Thanks for the vote of confidence. We're going to need it."

His head nods to the side and I follow its direction to the chatting Hughes brothers, the directing dynamic duo. I vaguely remember talk about the how the brothers were one part genius visionaries and two parts pain in the asses. However, the only thing that matters in this town is the bottom line; and so far, the Hughes brothers have been a ten-year hit machine.

"I'm sure you'll be fine." I lean in closer and lower my voice. "Just invest deeply in Excedrin and you and Omar will come out smelling like roses."

"Fuck the roses and give me a number one movie. You know what I'm saying?" He winks again while flashing his perfect lumineers.

I could fuck this nigga right here on this stage if I gave him any indication I was game. But it will never happen. That's playing with a fire that's entirely too close to home. For right now, he'll just have to be one of the numerous men I think about while Omar fumbles around, trying to get into the right hole.

Excusing myself, I drift over to another group, this one apparently of various agents and publicists. The entire time I'm making small talk, I feel two sets of eyes following. I ignore it for a while, but then finally cast a look around the sound stage to catch both Nelsan and Spencer looking at me like I'm a juicy porterhouse steak.

"I heard you had car trouble," Kent Webber, one of this town's superagents says, approaching. He's a reasonably good-looking dude, fit. But nothing really stands out about him—other than his ability to wheel and deal. "You know I'm sort of a weekend mechanic. Maybe I should take a look under the hood."

"That's not necessary. My battery just needed a jump," I add for good measure. I take a seat in one of the metal chairs and still feel those sets of eyes travel up the length of my body.

Beverly clears her throat and even jams a hand on her hips as if to say: *Negro, please.*

Spencer jumps and flashes her a smile.

I just smile, loving that I've put him in an awkward position: gawking at his co-producer's wife. I lean back in my chair, knowing I still had Nelsan's full attention. Frankly, I love flirting. It's one of those things that make me feel like I still have it.

Kent continues to talk my ear off, asking questions like, *Have you ever considered going into the business?* This is a standard question that all men in this town ask. As the stream of chatter goes in one ear and out the other, I slyly flirt with Nelsan by taking my time crossing my legs à la Sharon Stone in *Basic Instinct.*

Nelsan gets a *good* look at my panty-less crotch. His eyes widen while his pink tongue darts across his lips like he's starving for some good pussy.

I fight like the devil to prevent a smug smile from spreading across my fully glossed lips. I'm being bad and loving it too much. After a minute passes, I chance another sneak peek toward Nelsan, but my eyes drift past his right shoulder. Instantly, my breath freezes in my lungs while my heart drops to the pit of my stomach as Omar's black gaze smote me into a pile of ashes.

Oh shit.

7

Brijetta

"Damn, baby. I said I was sorry," Trey huffs, following me into the large custom-made walk-in closet.

I'm still so mad that I can literally chew lead and spit out nails. For the last four hours I've had to deal with contractors and beg Amaya not to quit, even though I completely understand why she'd want to run from this place screaming and pulling her hair out. Hell, half the time I feel that way. But I can't and won't, and it took me doubling her salary to prevent her from doing it, too.

"Fuck it, then." Trey tosses up his arms. "I don't know what you want me to say."

Popping down into the animal-print chaise lounge, I'm suddenly overwhelmed with having to pick out an outfit for yet another Hollywood party for God knows what this time. I swear people party more than they work in this town—and party hard. For some reason, one's ability to handle gallons of alcohol and snort their weight in cocaine was just as important as being able to land the right agent and score the right film at the right time.

"Are you at least going to say something?" Trey thunders, crossing his arms and staring down at me.

"What do you want me to say? What is there to say?"

"You can at least acknowledge that you hear me!"

"I heard you. You're sorry. Just like you were sorry the last time—and the time before that."

"I can't talk to you." He waves me off and then storms out of the closet. "You want to catch an attitude because I'm not perfect and shit."

"NEWSFLASH: I ALREADY KNEW THAT!" I roll my eyes and then drop my head into the palms of my hands. If I wasn't exhausted, I would've thrown a shoe or something at him. "Asshole," I mumble under my breath.

While I struggle to calm myself down, I realize that I really don't want to go to this party. I'm tired. But I don't trust Trey going to this damn thing alone. God knows what kind of trouble he'd get into if I'm not around. And, yes, it's exactly what it sounds like. I'm Trey's best friend, wife, mother, *and* babysitter.

Somebody has to save him from himself because he's not strong enough. So far we've been able to keep the monkey on his back out of the papers, but that's not to say that we haven't had a few close calls. It'll just take one photo of him with a goddamn needle in his arm to destroy his action-figure, superstar status. He knows this and still . . .

I continue to wrestle with conflicting emotions and even battle off a few more tears. When I lift my head and wipe my face, I catch sight of Trey darkening the closet's doorway. I don't like it when he sneaks up on me like that.

"Why do you put up with me?" His wet eyes match my own and he sounds as defeated as I feel. In a lot of ways, he looks like a lost child.

"You know why," I whisper.

A sincere look of incredulity and love covers his face when he croaks, "I don't deserve you."

"Don't be silly. Of course, you don't." We both crack a smile and then continue to gaze at one another—lovingly.

"Tell you what," he says, walking back over to me on the chaise. "What do you say that we stay in tonight?"

"Really?"

He sits down next to me, loops an arm around my waist, and quotes *Shrek,* "Really. Really."

I feel like crying all over again; this time with relief. "I would love that."

"Good." His head dips low so that he can brush those Hollywood lips against my collarbone. "We can have something catered from Napoletana, pop the cork on some red wine, and maybe even dance cheek to cheek before the fireplace."

"Oooh. This is starting to sound like a hot date."

"Uh, hmm." His lips drift upward so he can nibble on my left earlobe. "And guess what we can do afterward." Trey runs his hand underneath the thick, white towel wrapped around my body.

I slap his hand away. "Not so fast, slick. You haven't earned it yet."

"Ah. You're going to make a brother work for it?"

"I'm going to make you sweat for it." We both chuckle before his soft lips cover my own. After that, I just melt. His touch, his taste—everything about him hypnotizes me. I turn so that he can ease me back against the chaise while he crawls his way on top. He's no longer the little lost boy that I fight like hell to protect, but the dominant man that I've fallen completely in love with.

When he's like this, I forget about the hell he's put me through and the countless tears that soak my pillow. Suddenly, it just doesn't matter. It's just these moments in time, when he looks at me like I'm the most beautiful thing in the world. And he always has; even when I was three hundred plus pounds. A lot of times, I struggle believing that and I keep trying to alter my image so that I look like someone who belongs on a superstar's arm. For every surgery or nip/tuck, Trey's reaction is always, "I love you no matter what."

And he means it.

He loves me. I know he does. It's in his eyes when he looks at me, in his voice when talks to me, and definitely on his lips when he kisses me. No surprise, Trey opens my bath towel and proceeds to rain kisses all over my body. For a few minutes, he gently plays with my new breasts, but it's clear that his mouth and hands have another destination in mind.

"I'm so sorry I fucked up," he whispers as my legs slides open. "I didn't mean to scare you, baby. I'm so sorry."

Fat tears swell from behind my eyes and then leak from the corners when Trey's fingers peel me open like a flower and he plunges his tongue deep into my pink, melting sugar. I can't help but release a low, winding moan as I reach down and lock his head in place so that inner pussy monster can be free. And he doesn't disappoint. He nips and tugs at the base of my clit and then dives back inside to hit all four walls.

"Ah, baby." I thrash my head around and struggle to keep air in my lungs while honey starts to drip, stream, and then pour out of my body. After a series of mini orgasms, I'm finally hit with one so explosive that I'm actually screaming out his name at the top of my voice. Mind blown, I'm left mentally floating.

"Do you forgive me, baby?" Trey asks, his warm breath drifts over my thighs like a second apology. "You know I didn't mean to hurt you." He starts to crawl back up my body, peppering kisses as he goes. "You mean the world to me. I don't know what I'll do if you ever left me."

When his lips reclaim mine, I can taste me on his tongue. I can also taste the truth of his words. *He loves me. He loves me. He loves me.*

"Promise me that you'll never leave me," Trey begs when his lips return to my collarbone. "Promise."

"I . . . promise."

With one swift thrust, Trey smoothly connects our bodies together. Fair to say that all rational thought just vanishes and I'm left with so many wondrous emotions that a different stream of tears starts to flow from my eyes.

"I'm sorry, baby. I'm so sorry," he repeats over and over as he kisses and strokes my pain away. I don't think I can love my husband any more than I do right now.

Hours later, I wake in my king-sized silk sheet haven with an empty space beside me. The room is dark except for a faint sliver of moonlight streaming through the open window.

"Trey?" I jump up, clutching the top sheet and glancing around the master bedroom. When my eyes zoom to the closed bathroom door, I relax a bit. But suspicion creeps up my spine. I quickly climb out of bed and traipse across the room naked. "Trey, are you in there, honey?"

Silence.

I try the door, but it's locked. *Oh shit.* "Trey, honey?" I knock on the door.

"Just a second!"

Placing my ear against the door, I try to hear what's going on. "Baby, why do you have the door locked?"

Suddenly, the door jerks open and Trey is glaring down at me.

"Damn! Can't I take a piss without you hovering over me?" he snaps, then storms past me.

I don't know why his mood swings continue to surprise and hurt me, but they do. I take a deep breath and close my eyes to prevent my tears from dampening my long lashes.

"C'mon. You coming back to bed?" he asks.

"In a minute. I have to use the bathroom."

"Humph! Maybe I should stand outside the door and bang on it while *you* take a piss." While he slips under the sheets, I storm into the bathroom and slam the door behind me. *Why? Why? Why do I keep putting up with his bullshit?*

I march over to the shower and turn it on full blast; but

before I jump in, I need something for the ache in my new titties. With a drug addict in the house, I know better than to
keep my pain pills in the medicine cabinet. I turn toward the
linen closet, reach in the far back, and grab the fourth tissue
box and pull it out. Inside was my bottle of Percocet, but to my
surprise, the damn thing is empty. I clutch the bottle while
Trey's sweet apologies float back into my mind. "Bullshit. Bullshit and more bullshit."

8

Sinclair

I fucked up.

I've seen too many niggas flip the script to mistake the cold black look in Omar's eyes for being anything other than rage. Kent keeps chatting away about how he thinks he can make me a star while I wonder how anyone is missing the murderous look that has blanketed my husband's face. But then Beverly walks up to him and, like a light switch, he puts on a smile and turns up the charm.

Meanwhile, I still have alarm bells going off in my head. *I don't know what he's tripping about, it's not like he just caught me fucking.* That thought is of little comfort.

"Anyway," Kent says, reaching inside his jacket and pulling out a business card. "If you change your mind, I'd love to represent you."

I flash him a smile and accept the card. "Thanks, but I really don't—"

"Hey, just think about it." He winks. "Just look what I was able to do with Zayna."

It takes everything I have not to roll my eyes. Sooner or later, when I come to these damn parties, someone would toss Omar's first wife, Zayna, in my face. Zayna this. Zayna that. Sure the bitch was one of the few superstar R&B singers to

become a superstar actress, but it's more annoying that everyone in this town seems to think that the sun and moon rose
and sat on her ass, too. On top of being mega-successful, end-
less stories of her charities, political activism, and easy way
with children are recited ad nauseam. Honest to goodness, I'm
starting to think the woman was a saint.

And like all saints—she's six feet under.

From the corner of my eye I see Omar finally pull himself
away from Beverly and head straight toward me. At 6'4" and
with skin the color of dark chocolate and wide, mountainous
shoulders, Omar has a way of drawing every eye to his pres-
ence.

"Omar," Kent exclaims, smiling and extending a hand.
"Maybe you can help me talk some sense into your beautiful
wife here."

I refuse to look up. There's no need. I can feel my husband's anger pulse off of him in waves.

"And how's that?" Omar asks.

Ignorant to the palpable tension flowing between us, Kent
continues, "I'm trying to make her the next big thing. With
that face and that body, you know I can do it, man."

"If anyone could, it's you, Kent."

Talk about surprised. I glance up to make sure Omar isn't
drunk or something because he's made it perfectly clear to me
that he didn't want me in the business.

Kent perks up. "So you'll talk with her?"

"Sure. I'll see what I can do."

I pick up on the sarcastic tone and know that he's just bull-
shitting the man. Figures. That's all anyone does at these damn
parties. His gaze shoots back over and entraps my own. "Glad
to see that you could finally make it."

"Car trouble," Kent echoes the lie I'd spread around the
room.

"Beverly told me."

Omar's mouth flatlines, while I read *"Bitch, please"* in his eyes. "I think we should take it back to the dealer. You'd think a quarter-of-a-million-dollar car wouldn't give you so many problems."

I smile benignly, but remain silent as I stand up from my chair. Something tells me that he's just looking for that straw that's going to make him go the fuck off. The first eighteen months of our marriage, he'd been the ideal husband, minus his lack of game in the bedroom. He had been patient, kind and attentive. However, the last *six* months, I'm beginning to suspect that not everything is good in the hood. More and more, he's been exhibiting signs of having control issues. He has an opinion on everything from my hairstyles to my clothes. It's annoying, but a small price to pay for the life he's afforded me.

But when it comes to Omar being the big Hollywood producer, he portrays himself to be patient, kind, and attentive. This split personality is a sign warning me that I have a potentially crazy motherfucker on my hands.

"Well, I gotta head out," Kent says, looking at his watch. "*US Weekly* is throwing a bash tonight. You going, Omar?"

"Nah, I have a lot of work tonight." He loops an arm around my waist and then locks on like he's afraid that I'm going to bolt or something. "Besides, things are wrapping up here and we need to be getting home ourselves," Omar says.

"Cool. Well, congratulations again." He shakes Omar's hand and then tosses me a wink. "You make sure you think my offer over."

"Will do." I watch as he strolls away. In my head, I'm wondering how I should play this now that we're alone. Omar's arm tightens around my waist. "Damn, baby. Easy up," I say, trying to joke and ease myself out of a questionable situation.

He doesn't bulge; in fact, his hold now feels as if it's going to sever me in half "You ready to go, *hon?*" His tone is like honey drizzled over sharp glass.

"What about your guests?" I glance around, but there's now just a handful of people milling about and they look like they're getting ready to head out, too. "Well, I guess I'm ready when-ever you are," I say coolly, while my brain screams, *Unhand me, Negro!*

"You two have a good evening," Beverly calls after us with a friendly wave.

Omar's firm escort feels more like a rough drag when we escape out the studio's back doors. I lose my footing and nearly tumble out of my shoes more than a couple of times.

"Get your ass up," he hisses.

"What is wrong with you?" I ask, determined to play my part to the end.

He doesn't answer; instead, he leads me back to my car and practically crams me into the motherfucker. "You drive your ass straight home. You hear me? Don't even *think* about turn-ing down the wrong street or pulling into a gas station."

I open my mouth to snap back, but Omar slams the door in my face and then marches over to his precious Bugatti sports car. "Oh, this trick has lost his rabbit-assed mind," I hiss under my breath. I glare at my husband as he makes it to his car and slides in behind the wheel. I have half a mind to lock my car door and sit my ass right here. The last thing I expected was for Omar to pull up behind me and tap the back of my car. "What the fuck? Is this motherfucker crazy?"

I glare back at him in the rearview mirror and the asshole taps me again. His engine revs and I get the distinct impression that he's not above completely losing it and ramming my back end. "Oh, you just wait until we home. This man got my ass confused," I growl, shifting my car into gear and peeling out of the studio's parking lot as if someone had dropped a flag in a street drag race.

Reducing the thirty-five-minute drive to our sprawling estate in Holmby Hills to fifteen minutes, I waste no time jumping out of the vehicle and storming into the house. Maybe the best way to handle this is to scare his ass into believing I'm leaving. The first major fight in a marriage is an important one. It sets the standard of what's to come—and what's allowed. I have no intentions of letting Omar get the upper hand. In dramatic flare, I race up the grand staircase and then down the long hallway. By the time I burst into the master bedroom, I'm damn near out of breath.

However, when the front door of the house slams shut, no joke, it sounds like a bolt of thunder has struck the house.

"Just ignore his fucking ass," I coach myself, grabbing a Louis Vuitton luggage bag and then cracking it open on the center of our huge bed.

Omar steps into the room and in one glance jumps to the conclusion I intend. "Put the suitcase away," he orders in a smooth, controlled tone. "You're not going anywhere."

"Just watch me," I challenge, and head back to the closet and grab an armload of designer suits. After I smack them down on the bed, Omar's large hand wraps around my throat and lifts me clear off the floor. Stunned shitless, my eyes bulge while I flail my arms in the air. In the next instant, Omar slams me against the wall and rattles the few remaining marbles I have left around inside my head. *What the fuck?*

"I *said* your ass ain't going no-fucking-where," he growls.

I claw at his stranglehold around my neck; my feet pedal in the air. *This crazy motherfucker is going to kill me!* I work my mouth but can manage only a gasping sputter. This shit can't be happening.

Omar's brown eyes seem to turn to black onyx right before my eyes. My chest starts to hurt, my heart is hammering so bad.

"Where the fuck were you this evening and don't you even think about fixing your mouth to tell me no bullshit like your battery was dead. I swear to God I'll have your body chalked in white if that bullshit comes out of your mouth."

Heart racing, I struggle to control my panic. I'd sensed this motherfucker had a temper bubbling just below the surface, but I never suspected no shit like this.

"B-baby," I sputter as tears seep from the corners of my eyes. "I-I swear."

His grip tightens around my neck. "DON'T. TEST. ME."

Where is all the oxygen? I need oxygen. I claw at his hand as darkness creeps around me. How in the hell am I going to get out of this shit? If I tell this crazy and deranged mother-fucker the truth, I might as well kiss my ass good-bye.

"You think your ass is slick, don't you?" Omar hisses. His eyes drag down my body. "Well, I've met slicker bitches than you. Believe that shit."

He releases me and I drop like a stone against the bedroom's hardwood floor. While I gasp and cough, it feels as if the sudden rush of oxygen is only making me dizzier. "You're . . . crazy," I rasp, pushing myself onto my knees to try and crawl away.

"Crazy, huh?"

He straddles over me and grabs me by the back of my dress. Thinking his ass is about to start choking me again, I start crawling faster, but he drops down on top of me and I crumple beneath him. "Get off!"

"Nah. Nah. I'm crazy. Remember?"

I hear the zipper on the back on my dress and I realize what he's doing. I try to scramble and claw my way from underneath him, but all I'm successful at doing is helping him strip my dress off of me.

"Who are you fucking, Sinclair?"

"OMAR, STOP IT!"

He flips me over and I immediately send my hands sailing across his face. When that doesn't work, I ball them up and start punching away. But nothing deters Omar from getting me out of this damn dress. When he yanks it down over my hips and exposes my naked pussy, I freeze.

In a flash, my mind goes back to this morning when Omar commented how much he liked watching me get dressed in the morning. I had purposely taken my time sliding on my black panties, shaking my ass and teasing him. "Please," I say in a calmness I don't feel. "It's not what you think."

SLAP!

His quick backhand feels as if he's just dislocated my jaw.

"Let's get something straight. You don't know me well enough to know what the *fuck* I'm thinking. If you did, then you would be begging for your damn life right now. You were out riding somebody's dick today, weren't you?"

"NO!"

SLAP!

"LYING BITCH!" *SLAP!* "Then you stroll your hot ass into that party and flash your pussy to Spencer like a twenty-dollar trick? Bitch, have you lost your ever-loving mind?"

I reach out to him. "B-baby—"

He slaps my hand away and hisses, "Don't *baby* me. You got two seconds to tell me who you're fucking. ONE!"

"No, baby. You got it all wrong," I say, struggling again to get up.

Omar shoves me back down. "Did I tell you to get your ass up? You move when *I* say move." He grabs hold of my shoulders, picks me up, and slams me back down. My head hits with a hard *THUMP* and tears instantly splash down my face. "I told you before you married me that I wasn't going to tolerate any bullshit. My name will *not* be dragged through the mud in this town. You hear me?" He grabs me again and my head hits with another, *THUMP.* "I've worked too hard to make something of myself in this town to let you drag it through the mud just because you can't keep your damn legs closed."

"Omar, b-baby."

"WHO—"

THUMP!

"ARE—"

THUMP!

"YOU—"

THUMP!

"FUCKING?"

He releases my shoulders for a half second, and out of survival instinct I try to scramble and crawl away again.

"I told you not to move!"

SLAP!

My hands cover my throbbing jaw as I glare up at him. "Muther-fuck!"

Omar grabs my right hand. "Where in the hell is your ring?" he thunders.

Stunned speechless, I glance down at my bare hand; my heart sinks to the pit of my stomach. *The hotel.* I'd left my ring on the nightstand at the hotel. How in the hell did I forget about my ring? Slowly, I lift my head and watch in horror as Omar unbuckles his leather belt.

My dream. "What are you doing?"

"What—you thought you were going to make a fool out of me?" Omar shouts, sliding his belt free from his waist.

I blink but have no time to react before the first lash strikes me across my ass. *Whap!*

A scream leaps from my throat while a sting of pain races across my skin. I suck in a breath as the belt slaps against my back. I scramble and crawl away, my demented husband is there, flogging me all the way to a corner of the room.

"Where have you been?"

WHAP!

"Who are you fucking?"

"Nobody, baby! I swear!"

"Oh, you swearing now, you lying bitch? I don't know what the fuck you thought, but you got me twisted."

WHAP!

"I upgraded your ass and this is how you repay me?" He rains more blows across my body. "I've bought you the finest clothes, the best cars, and made sure that you didn't have to worry about a damn thing, and you're fucking around? I got news for you, honey, we can do this shit all night until you give me a fucking name."

I try to block the wild blows that are coming from every direction. I still can't wrap my brain around this whole situation.

"Who is it, goddamn it?" he yells. "And don't tell me nobody because I know for a fact that your ass left out of here with panties on."

WHAP!

"STOP, OMAR. PLEASE STOP," I beg. The belt smacks my hand and wraps around my arm. I make the mistake of trying to pull it from his grasp only to be assaulted by a series of faster and quicker blows.

WHAP! WHAP! WHAP!

"Who the fuck is he?" he roars.

I can't think, let alone speak, so I take this ass beating, somehow managing to complete my first real and sincere prayer that soon this crazy shit will all be over soon. Here I am a grown-ass woman getting beaten like an unwanted child. But the lashes continue. My back. *WHAP!* My legs. *WHAP!* My arms. *WHAP!*

No matter how tight a ball I curl into in that corner, I can't avoid the pain.

"What's his name?!" Omar keeps demanding over and over. "Give me his fucking name!"

After what seems like a lifetime, I break. "Clevon!" I shout, sobbing from my soul. "His name is Clevon James. Please . . . stop hitting me."

9

Jaleesa

Every Monday, Tuesday, and Thursday at the crack of dawn, I meet my good friend and publicist Andy Goldman for an advance Pilates class. Despite it being five-thirty in the morning in a town where the average bedtime is an hour earlier, the class is religiously jam-packed with some of the most famous faces. When I first heard about this class, I was stunned to learn that there was a waiting list. I sat on that thing for two years before a spot finally opened up. During my very first class, I met tall, skinny as a rail Andy.

"You told him that you had an audition for *Defiance*?" Andy, a beautiful biracial androgyny, stretches his penciled and waxed brows so high they nearly kiss his hairline. "And what are you going to tell him when this nonexistent audition doesn't happen?"

"I'll cross that bridge when I come to it," I huff, lifting my legs off the floor and pressing my hips and pelvic bone into the mat. "Right now, I just need to concentrate on getting my hands on that script."

Beside me, Andy pops his glossed lips and shakes his head. "Giiirrl, I hope you know what you're doing because you're playing with fire."

"It definitely won't be the first time." Forty-five minutes

later, we pull our sweaty bodies off our mats and pretend that every muscle in our bodies isn't talking smack about what we'd put them through this morning.

"I don't think Maury bought it," Andy says, wiping his face and neck down as we head toward the door.

"Please don't say that."

"Just think about it," Andy goes on. "If Omar Fines *really* wanted you in his film, you wouldn't have to interview at all. He'd just give you the role. I say Maury is just giving you enough rope to hang yourself."

I draw a deep breath. "I know. I just don't want you to say it."

Andy walks me to the door of the ladies' locker room and folds his arms. The thing that's most annoying about Andy is that he's both handsome and beautiful at the same time. His bone-straight black mane is pulled back in a ponytail. His flawless skin glows, his teeth are blindingly white and straight, and his ass is quarter-bouncing firm. "Figured out what you want to me say to all these inquires about your being fired off the Denzel flick, yet? They're killing you in the tabloids, you know."

"I don't know. Just spin it in a way that makes it clear that I *quit*. I wasn't fired."

"I tried that already. Nobody is buying it, especially since the director has already Tweeted, Facebooked, and MySpaced that he kicked your no-acting butt to the curb."

My mouth nearly hit the floor. "He what?"

"C'mon, Jaleesa. You gotta get with the times. He posted that shit before your plane landed back in Los Angeles." He shakes his head at me while I try to wrap my brain around the train wreck that is my life.

"Can't I sue him or something?"

"For what?"

"Slander."

"Girl, what the hell are you smoking?" He eyeballs me

strangely. "There's no such thing anymore. Everybody can say and make up whatever they want about you. You know that."

"Shit. Everybody sues *me* for every wild hair they get up their asses, how come I can't jump on the bandwagon?"

"I'll just continue to tell them 'No comment.' " Shaking his head, he turns toward the men's lockers. "But eventually you're going to have to answer the question."

I roll my eyes at his back and then stomp into the ladies' locker room to grab my gym bag. While I storm my way out of the Sports Center, I'm having a major argument with myself on exactly how I'm going to combat the eventual questions when I get the courage up to face a magazine or log online to see what the blogosphere is saying about the whole incident. I'm very aware that the longer I stay away, the longer I can re-main in denial. I'm so busy calling myself a fuckup of epic por-tions that, at first, I don't even notice Andy leaning against my hybrid Lexus. It's all about Green technology these days.

"Girl, please pick up that long face. I'm two seconds away from feeling sorry for you."

I switch on my Hollywood smile. "That will be the day."

"Hungry?"

"I'm an actress," I remind him. "I'm always hungry." Ten minutes later, I'm ordering stuffed French toast with a side order of turkey sausage at Blu Jam Café. No surprise the place is packed. I keep my sunglasses down and pretend that I don't want anyone to recognize me; then I'm immediately annoyed when no one does.

"You need a backup plan," Andy tells me when our wait-ress delivers our order.

"You got one?" I ask only half joking.

"Yeah, find a new agent, move to New York, and try to get some theater work under your belt."

"Damn."

"What kind of friend would I be if I didn't give it to you straight?"

"One that I would like better," I admit, before angrily taking a huge bite out of my turkey sausage. Of course, it's going to be my only bite, so I make sure I chew for a very long time. So much for my liquid-only diet.

Andy just takes my hostility in stride. He's been in this business too long to ever take anything that falls out of an actor's mouth personally. "Be that as it may, I think that it's time for you to change it up. Lay low for a while, study your craft, and then stage a comeback. If you do it right, you might even be able to pull off an Academy Award win."

I struggle to follow his logic.

"Everyone loves a good comeback story."

I think about that for a full second before shaking my head and dismissing it. "Too risky. Nowadays out of sight means out of mind. No, Sinclair is my best option right now."

Andy sucks in a huge gulp of air as he stabs his California omelet. "Even if she can get you a copy of the script, how does that lead to an audition?"

"C'mon. A woman like Sinclair definitely has pull with her husband."

"Please. The last people Hollywood husbands listen to are their wives." He shakes his head. "It amazes me just how little you know about how this town operates. How long have you been working in this city?"

I roll my eyes.

"Why don't you call Spencer Reid? Y'all had a thing once."

"Puh-lease. Dead end." I roll my eyes again.

Andy's certainty and morning sermon is starting to grate on my nerves—and kill my appetite, even if he is just telling me the cold hard truth. I reach for my borrowed Louis Vuitton bag and whip out my cell phone.

"Who are you calling?" Andy asks, eyeballing me.

"Who do you think? Sinclair. I don't want that heifer flaking out on me. I've got too much at stake." I click on her contact number and jam the phone under my ear while I wait and drum my acrylic nails on the table. On the third ring, I groan because I know I'm about to be transferred to voice mail.

Andy's brows jump up again, but I ignore him and purr out the sweetest voice I can manage. "Sinclair, darling. This is Jaleesa. I'm just calling to check and see if you'd been able to get a hold of that manuscript for me. You know I think you're an absolute doll for pulling this solid for me. Oh, and if you can find out which casting agency Omar is using for this production, that would be wonderful. Call me on my cell as soon as you can. Thanks, girl. I owe you dinner." I make smooching noises over the phone and quickly hang up. "Trick."

Andy sucks his teeth and starts shaking his head.

"What? Too much?"

"Puh-lease, it'll be a miracle if you pull this shit off."

"I don't believe in miracles," I tell him, crossing my arms and plopping back against my chair. "I believe in cold, hard manipulating."

"Look, I ain't the one to be running up in nobody's church, either, but I think, in your case, that it's time for you to start believing in a higher power than your own." He stabs his omelet again. "You know if you don't like the New York Broadway comeback route, you could do what the white B-list actresses do in this situation."

"B list?"

"I'm giving it to you straight. No chasers, remember?"

I'm grinding my expensive lumineers down to dust, glaring at him. "All right. Hit me."

"Land yourself one of these big-balling directors, producers, or executive studio heads flooding around this town. Your girl Sinclair did it. Ain't no shame of being the bitch behind the man as long as you get to play in the same sandbox with the Hollywood elite. Do it now while your titties are still natural and up off the floor and you don't need Botox like a daily multivitamin."

I can't help but shake my head. Me? Being ushered behind

the scenes? I can't see that happening. I was born to be in the spotlight. I knew it and I made sure that everyone who has ever met me knew it, too. I've spent years practicing in the mirror for my close-up and giving my bedroom audience of stuffed animals fake award acceptance speeches. I can't just toss in the towel and try to ride the wave of somebody else's shine.

"Okay. I take it that's a no go?" Andy says after reading my expression for a hot second. "All right. I figured that I'd just toss that out there and see if it'd stick."

"I'm a star, Andy," I remind him. "Not just some extra walking around in the background. I'm just going through a little hiccup, but everything is going to get back on track and I'm going to be back on top before you know it."

"If anybody can do it, you can," he says, but only half-heartedly.

That's all right, though. He is right about one thing. I do need a partner in this game. I know I touched on this yesterday when thinking about Brijetta and her man. I need to be putting as much effort in creating the next black Hollywood power couple as my acting. Hell, Jada Pinkett-Smith did it, and it's not like that heifer has a stellar résumé on her own. Ninety-five percent of her status and shine comes from her man. If his name wasn't attached to their production company, she would just be another struggling black actor hustling heartburn, indigestion, and diarrhea commercials.

Andy's cell starts buzzing and he pops that sucker under his ear like a Wild Wild West gunslinger. I lean back in my chair, sip on some coffee, and deliberate on whether to chance a second bite of this turkey sausage that's calling my name.

"Regina, I don't know where you're getting your information from, but Ms. Love was not fired. She quit over creative differences."

My gaze jumps back up so I can watch my boy work.

"Yes, it's unfortunate that the director would react in such a rash and childish manner, but it just supports why my client found it so difficult to work with him. Uh-huh. You can quote me on that." Andy winks at me. "Yes, yes, Regina. We will absolutely have to do lunch soon. You just have your people call my people. Uh-huh. Smooches." He disconnects the call.

"Perfect," I declare. At least one thing I've managed to do is lock down the perfect publicist.

Andy opens his mouth to say something and his phone immediately starts ringing again. "Hello, Perez." He rolls his eyes and shakes his head. "No, there's no truth to it whatsoever." He levels a look at me.

Clearly, our quiet time is officially over. Andy's work day has officially begun. I reach for my purse, toss a few bills on the table, and then whisper, "I'll catch up with you later."

Andy bobs his head as I scoot out of my chair and drop two kisses on each side of his face. "Later," I say, then perform my Hollywood strut toward the front door. Ten minutes later, my ass is headed out to Holmby Hills to drop in on Sinclair. In this hustle, I'm not about to leave anything up to chance. I need that script and I need it *now.*

10

Omar

"Clevon James!" I spit the name out like the vile thing that it is. I knew that bitch was screwing around. None of these bitches in this fucking town knows how to keep their legs closed. It doesn't matter how much you keep them stacked up, caked up, or even blinged the fuck out, they all feel like they can play muthafuckas. Well, Sinclair, or whatever the fuck her real name is, has rolled up on the wrong playa for that bullshit. Hell, I don't just know how to play the game in this fucking town, I've mastered it.

I told that trick when I put a ring on her ass that I expect and will receive loyalty in this marriage, and I mean that shit. Grabbing my BlackBerry from my hip, I quickly pull up my man Matthew's contact number and then wait for him to pick up. When he doesn't pick up his direct line, I try the main number.

"Morrison Detective Agency, this is Helen. How may I help you?"

"Hello, Helen. This is Omar. Is Matthew in?"

"Ah, you're in luck. He's just walking through the door. Can you hold for a second and I'll transfer you into his office?"

"Not a problem." I pull the Bugatti over to the shoulder of

the 101 Freeway so I can concentrate on the call. A second later, Matthew's deep Barry White-like voice floats over the line.

"Omar! My main man. What's so important you're calling my office at the booty crack of dawn?"

"I got somebody I need for you to check out for me," I tell him, getting straight to the point.

"Well, that's nothing new. You get any more clues on this mysterious woman you married yet?"

I suck in a deep breath and pretend that the slight jab doesn't bother me. I took a major chance in marrying Sinclair when my head told me not to, but just like the marriage before, I was vibing off what I was feeling instead of listening to common sense. When Sinclair enters a room, every man can't help but notice her. She has an infectious laugh, and when she turns on the charm, it has a way of separating a man from his wallet— and his brain.

"Nah," I finally tell Matthew. "But it's this dude she's been creeping around with." There's this palpable silence on the line that just screams, *I told you so!* "Spare me any sermons that you're thinking about preaching and just check this dude out for me. You think that you can handle that?"

Matthew chuckles. "A'ight, man. Whatever you say. Hit me with what you got."

Now, that's what I want to hear. "His name is Clevon James. According to Sinclair, he's some personal trainer over at the Sports Center. He could be just a harmless gigolo getting in where he can fit in with lonely Hollywood wives, but I want to check his shit out first before I pay his ass a visit."

"Yeah. Yeah. I feel where you're coming from. Can't be too sure who's connected to whom these days." Matthew chuckles, but I know he doesn't find none of this funny. These trifling women nowadays never see past a big dick and a smile out to here—not until they try to separate or end shit. The next thing they know, they're being blackmailed to keep all those private sex tapes they didn't know that they were starring in under wraps. I've seen it a thousand times and had to deal with it myself personally a few years back.

The whole marriage fiasco that was Zayna is something that still has the power to wake me from a dead sleep. She had so many players caught up in her web of lies and deceit that I had to the do the only thing a brother in my situation could do: get rid of her. Rock-a-byed her ass to sleep and then made that shit look like an accident. The shit went down a lot better than I expected. There was an international outpouring of sympathy and support directed my way and, in that small window of time, I managed to get several projects that were dead in the water off the ground. My next four films were box-office gold—put my little independent films in the same money realm as Tyler Perry, sans a big 6'4" black dude in a tent dress.

When it comes to making movies and money, I am as sharp as they come; but when it comes to women, I'm like the rest of these knuckleheads out here: a sucker.

"I'll get back with you as soon as I have something," Matthew promises. "It shouldn't take too long."

"Good. Good." My smile stretches back across my face. "Hit me on my cell."

"You got it."

I disconnect the call and then work my way back onto the highway. After another forty minutes dealing with bumper-to-bumper traffic, I finally make my way to my father's church, the Power of Prayer Ministries off Redondo Boulevard. I am the son of a preacher. Back in the day, my father was a well-known traveling tent revival type whose special knack for casting out demons was legendary. Too bad he isn't successful casting out some of his own—which is why he left the back dusty roads of Alabama and started preaching to the hookers and hos of Hollywood.

Me, I'm much more disciplined, charismatic, and *paid*.

I've worked too hard to build myself up as a pillar of the community for my new wife to make a fool out of me. The bitch has pulled more disappearing acts in the last six months than Houdini in his whole career. If she thinks that she can outhustle a hustler, she has another thing coming.

"I should have never married her," I mumble under my breath. I've lost count of how many times I've said that in the last few months—probably as many times as my dick convinced me I'll never find another woman so damn freaky in the bedroom.

In that respect, she put my first wife to shame.

"Good evening, Omar. You looking for the Reverend?" Sister Robin Scott asks the moment I stroll through the church's administration office.

I look up at my father's secretary and long-time lover and muster a thin smile. "Yeah, is he in?"

Shamelessly, the near-350-pound woman flashes her dimples while her eyes drag over my tall frame draped in an immaculate Armani suit. Not a wrinkle or crooked edge in my sharp Caesar haircut. I'm a walking poster board of success and I aim to keep it that way.

"How is Sister Sinclair doing?" Robin inquires, finally lifting her lustful gaze back to my face. "Y'all two lovebirds still enjoying the honeymoon phase?"

I stomp down my irritation for being asked such a personal question.

"Yes, I feel very blessed that the Lord has sent Sinclair into my life when he did."

"Uhmmm-hmmm. He was pretty quick with it, too."

Her insinuation isn't lost on me and I have to resist the urge to slap a few shades of black off her coal complexion. *Just who in the hell does this bitch think she's talking to?*

"The Lord is always on time."

"Humph! I don't know about that. I've been praying for a husband for twenty years and he ain't showed up yet."

Try dropping half your body mass, fat ass. "Well, I'll definitely put in a good word for you." After a flash of my $10,000 veneers, I start back toward my father's office.

"Wait," she says, picking up the phone. "I'll just let him know that you're here."

"Thanks," I say, but don't bother waiting for permission to head toward my father's office, and Sister Robin knows better than to try and stop me. I'd like to say that I'm surprised to see my father tucking his shirt and buckling his pants when I stroll through the door, but that would be a lie. The young girl of the day must be a new member to the church because I never seen her around before. She, at least, had the decency to look embarrassed while she finished wiping the corners of her mouth with my father's embroidered handkerchief that my mother made for him several Christmases ago.

"Omar! Son!" My father strolls over to me with outstretched arms and wraps them around me as some show of fatherly love. "I thought you weren't going to be able to swing by until later this afternoon."

"Obviously." I cut a gaze over to his morning appointment.

"Ah. Sister Tyra here is a new member of our church. Ain't that right?" He turns his brown and slightly jaundiced eyes toward the young girl. She quickly bobs her head like a good girl, but still manages to avoid making eye contact with me.

My father removes his arms from me only to wrap them back around the small-framed lady. "Now, you feel free to stop by my office anytime you feel like you're in need of more prayer," he tells her. "The Lord expects his Christian soldiers to stand and kneel together, especially in their darkest hours of need. I'm always available to deliver a word and a prayer."

Sister Tyra keeps bobbing her head until she's escorted out the door. "Sister Robin, can you see about helping this good sister get her lights back on with the electric company? Thank you." He smiles again and then firmly shuts the door in the girl's face. After that, his smile evaporates and he quickly transforms back into the father I know. "Would it kill you to call before you just pop up?"

"And miss these small treasured moments? Not on your life."

"Smart ass."

"The last I checked, the apple doesn't fall that far from the tree."

My father winks. "True that. Now, whatcha got for me?" He walks over to his desk; I follow and plop down my leather briefcase. Daddy dearest claps his hands together and instructs me to hurry up and open it. Quickly, I enter the combination to the two locks and pull it open. Like always, my father sucks in a long breath and starts picking up stacks of hundred-dollar-bills and fanning through them to make sure that his favorite dead white man Benjamin Franklin is printed on all their faces.

"Have I ever told you that you are my favorite son?" he asks, popping up and turning toward his private safe tucked behind the big framed picture of Jesus.

"It wouldn't happen to have anything to do with me being your *only* son, now would it?"

The good Reverend shakes his head. "Still don't know how to just take a compliment and just roll with it, huh? In that regard, you're just like your mother." He pulls open the safe and starts stacking his embezzled loot into the iron box. He goes through an awful lot of trouble to hide his dabbling in the film industry. Of course, film is being a little too loose with the term, since most porn is just straight DVD productions now.

I've long stopped judging my father and the dirt he likes to play in. A hustle is a hustle is a hustle, right? This money has nothing to do with me. I just agreed to deliver it for him.

"So how is things with the new missus?" he asks out of the blue.

"Why do you ask?"

"That bad, uh?" He shrugs. "One of these days, you'll listen to your old man and learn that you don't marry the beautiful ones. Those are the playthings. You want a woman to do right by you, then marry a woman with a decent set of natural tits, a face that doesn't scare anything out of the dark, and can cook things without the use of a microwave. Do that and you'll have a woman who'll take your shit and ask to wipe your ass afterward. Trust me on this."

I would love to argue with him, but at this point, I'm starting to believe that he may be on to something. "Maybe next time," I tell him after he grabs the last stack of Benjamins.

"Ah. So there may be a next time?" He chuckles and closes up the safe. "Maybe before you do away with this one, you'll let your old man have a go with her. Check out what got you so sprung?" He grins.

I glare.

"Well, it's just an idea." He moves the picture frame back in place as I grab my briefcase and head toward his office door. "But if you change your mind . . . ?"

"You're pushing your luck, Dad," I warn, then slam the door during his robust laughter. *Sick old bastard.*

11

Sinclair

I wake up this morning with every inch of my body aching and stinging. I try to stop the images of last night's ass beating from replaying in my mind, but so far, no dice. That mutha-fucka whipped me like a runaway slave. All that was missing was my feet being cut off. *What the fuck?*

The whole episode has my mind completely blown and my body undecided if I need a coroner or a medic. I lie there in bed for another twenty minutes before managing to pull back the sheets and climb out of bed. The minute my gaze lands on my body, I'm completely horrified by the hundreds of red welts that have completely blanketed my body. I rush to the bathroom—or rather I went as fast as my aching body pos-sibly could—and get a good look at myself in the mirror.

No lie. I look *fucked up.* My hair is a tangled mess. My day-old makeup has aged me ten years. My lips looks like an entire beehive had gone to town on my lips, and my welted-up body looks like a crime scene. I'm so completely stunned about this situation that I don't know what to do. A bitch never thinks getting their ass beat would ever happen to them. Nah. Nah. That shit happens to weak-minded bitches who think it's their job to put up with little boys with daddy issues. That may or may not be the case with Omar, but I gotta keep it real with myself. A bitch just doesn't up and walk out on this kind of lifestyle. You just don't.

And it's not like Omar kicked me out after he found out about Clevon, which he could have. Instead, he made it perfectly clear that he still wanted my ass to stay put. But to stay put so he can possibly beat on me some more? Shit. I don't think I can handle that, either.

I turn toward the large Italian marble tub and run myself a hot bubble bath. This was something that I'm definitely going to need to soak and think about. Somehow I needed to get the upper hand back in this situation or risk everything just spiraling out of control. These situations only end two ways: somebody leaves or somebody dies—which technically dying is just a form of leaving, anyway.

"I knew his ass was potentially crazy," I hiss under my breath. That train of thought quickly leads me to another. "I better warn Clevon." It isn't easy, but I hop up out of the tub and leave a soapy trail of bubbles back into the bedroom where I dig my cell phone out of my purse. Before I can pull up Clevon's contact code name, the phone starts ringing.

"Sinclair, darling. This is Jaleesa."

My eyes roll back so hard that they damn near get stuck at the back of my head.

"I'm just calling to check and see if you'd been able to get hold of that manuscript for me. You know I think you're an absolute doll for pulling this solid for me."

"Not yet. But I did talk to the screenwriter last night and he promised to have a copy delivered today, I think he said."

"Oh, and if you can find out which casting agency Omar is using for this production, that would be wonderful."

This trick here.

"Call me on my cell as soon as you can. Thanks, girl. I owe you dinner." She makes smooching noises over the phone and quickly hangs up.

"Trick," I complain after disconnecting the call. I see right now that I'm going to have to cut this girl off. What the fuck? Am I her damn agent now? I try to shake my irritation off and then punch up Clevon's info. Wouldn't you know it, I'm instantly transferred to his voice mail.

"Hey, Clevon, it's me," I rush to say. "Look, I think we need to cool off for a while. I slipped up and my husband knows about us. I just want to warn you and tell you to keep an eye out. I'm not quite sure if he's going to step to you or what. It's fair to say that I think that he's a little off his rocker and at the moment anything is possible. Just to be safe, don't call me. I'll call you. All right. Bye."

I turn away from the nightstand and squeak aloud when I see Omar darkening our bedroom door.

"Should I even bother to ask who you were talking to?"

Wide-eyed, I step back and bump so hard into the nightstand that it sends the French lamp crashing down to the hardwood floor. "I—I didn't know that you were home."

"That much is obvious." He calmly steps into the room. His dark eyes twinkle in the face of my fear, and in that moment, I realize that he's getting off on it. Yet, at the same time, I can't seem to get a handle on it.

"Do you seriously think that little call is going to help your boyfriend?" he asks.

While I struggle to get my mouth to work, I squeeze into a small space between the nightstand and the bed.

"For that matter, do you think that I should just let some flunky personal trainer just *steal* what rightfully belongs to me?"

Belong? Fuck it. I hop onto the bed and scramble to the other side.

Omar's speech continues while his gaze tracks me with amusement. "I made myself clear when I slipped that ring on your finger that I expect loyalty in this marriage. I *will* not tolerate any embarrassment of *any* sort from you."

"Omar, baby. I made a mistake," I finally plea. "I swear it will never happen again."

"Oh, I *know* that it's never going to happen again." He reaches down and starts unbuckling his belt again. "You want to know how I know?"

I'm afraid that I know the answer.

"I'll kill you," he says, locking gazes with me.

Fuck it. I'm out of here. I race toward the door only to have the damn thing slam in my face and lock. *What in the hell?* I glance over my shoulder to see Omar holding some kind of electric gadget and smiling like the devil.

I turn back toward the door and start pulling and tugging, but the lock refuses to budge. I'm trapped in this hell naked and wet with this crazy sonofabitch. Behind me, the first lash of his leather belt whips across my bare ass and I swear on everything I own that I jump five feet into the air.

"SHIT, OMAR! STOP!" I scramble away from the door and take off toward the bathroom—only to have it slam in my face, too. I race toward the walk-in closet. The same thing happens. *Does this asshole have the whole place wired?*

The second lash catches me on the back of my legs and hits a previous welt that nearly causes me to black out and stumble to my knees.

"I thought your ass would have learned your lesson last night, but I see that you're hardheaded."

Tears pour down my face. Why didn't I leave this morning when I had the chance? "No, baby. I learned my lesson. I swear."

"Is that why I returned to find you talking to that muthafucka on the phone?" His black gaze looks like polished onyx. "That's all right, though. I'm going to have fun breaking your ass." He sends five quick lashes across my body. They sting so bad that I can't even get myself to scream out anymore.

"WHO DOES THAT PUSSY BELONG TO, BITCH?"

Whap! Whap! Whap!

"DON'T MAKE ME KEEP ASKING THIS SHIT! WE CAN BE UP IN THIS BITCH ALL DAY!"

Whap! Whap! Whap!
"WHO DOES IT BELONG TO?"
Whap!
"YOU! YOU, BABY!"
The beating stops and I slowly peek through my eyelashes to see Omar huffing and puffing over me. "Let me guess. You're thinking about leaving me now?"

"No, baby. I would never do anything like that."

He cocks his head, with doubt clearly reflecting in his expression. "You really think I'm a fucking fool, don't you?"

There's just no right answer with this man.

That shit-eating smile returns.

"You still love me, baby?"

Oh shit. "Yes, baby. Of course I do." Despite my best efforts, I can't stop my voice from trembling.

"Prove it. Get on your knees."

I waste no time following his command. At this point, I'd do anything to make sure this muthafucka doesn't hit me again.

"Pull junior out and show him how much you love him." He brushes back the messy pile of hair from my face like the loving husband he used to pretend to be while my gaze falls on the large bulge in his pants. I wasn't imagining things last night. His shit was definitely bigger and harder when he's smacking my ass around.

"Whatcha waiting for, baby?" That hard edge starts creeping back into his voice and I quickly unzip his pants and pull *junior* out from behind his silk briefs and cram him into my mouth.

One thing that I've never had complaints on is my head game, and right now a sister is motivated to deep-throat his ass past my tonsils. Judging by the low hissing I hear above me, I'm guessing I'm getting him off in just the right way.

"That's right, baby. Take that shit to the balls." He keeps stroking my hair back and working his hips in a steady rhythm.

"When you get this muthafucka to spit, I want you to crawl up in that bed and spread your legs wide. You got that, baby?"

"Mumpgh humn," is all I can get around his flesh-covered steel rod.

"That's it, bitch. Get that candy out of there. Whooo." His hips pick up the beat. "I don't want no more conversation, I want you to just do what the fuck you're told. You got that shit?"

"Mumpgh humn." He releases my hair, and reaches down, and pinches my titties until more tears pour down my face. "You're going to be a good bitch from now on, aren't you?"

I nod and choke and slobber on his dick a little bit. When his salty cum finally blasts down my throat, he holds my head still for a few long seconds and only releases me when I'm just a half a second from passing out.

"That shit taste good to you, baby?"

I nod and lick my lips to prove how much I mean it.

"Now, what are you suppose to do?"

I hop up and race over to the bed. A piece of glass slices the bottom of my right foot, but I ignore it and get my legs open lickety-split. Omar takes his time walking over to the bed, stroking his dick the whole way. "Let me see you play with it."

Ding! Dong!

Both of our heads twist toward the bedroom door. "Who the fuck is that?" he asks, his eyes shooting daggers at me. "Is that your boy, trying to make your morning appointment?"

I shake my head. "I don't have any idea who that is."

The look on his face is clearly calling me a liar. He moves away from the bed, sheathing his hard cock back behind his silk boxers. In a blink of an eye, he has his pants back on and is pulling a gun from out of the bedroom safe.

"I hope you're right for your sake," he says, before grabbing the remote and unlocking the door. "And you better not make so much as a sound up here or I'll really give you something to

yell about." With that final warning, he rushes out of the bedroom.

Springing out of the bed, I go over to the door only to
find it locked again. Next, I rush over to the window and
glance down. *Jaleesa! Damn. What the hell does she want now?*

12

Kwame

"I fucking miss my baby." I shake my head and draw a deep breath. Instead of smelling my wife's flowery perfume, I'm stuck smelling the funk of I don't know how many niggas in this pissy hellhole they call a prison. It is pitch-black while I lie back on my cot and stare up into nothingness. I have no problem remembering every detail about my wife, though it's clear that she ain't studdin' my ass. I ain't seen her since they locked my ass up for a couple of kilos of coke and a stolen handgun. My ass was set up by some pig promising me he had a connect to unload the shit.

Tracy tried to warn me. Told me she had one of her funny dreams about the whole shit, but my hard head wouldn't listen. Sometimes her dreams came true and sometimes they didn't. Let her tell it, she was half psychic or some dumb shit. I just remember my palms itching for some quick cash to get us up on our feet.

I was a dumb muthafucker that night.

"You ain't the only nigga fienin' for some pussy," Shawn, my new cellmate of four months, says.

I chuckle under my breath and think about opening my last pack of cigarettes. Maybe some nicotine could take the edge off the painful throb of my cock, but I doubt it.

"You know what I miss most?" I ask.

The cell falls silent, but then Shawn finally takes the bait. "What?"

"I miss the way my baby's full lips would wrap about my cock and how she could suck my soul out without hardly trying. I'm a big nigga, and I swear I was fucking her tonsils on the regular. It was the best shit in the world."

"Nigga, you crazy."

I smile. "Maybe. But I'm telling you, my girl was the shit. Pussy sooo tight I used to break out in a sweat just trying to ease into that shit. And when I got in, that pussy melted like butter."

"Fo real?"

"Uhmm-hmm." I'm thinking about Tracy's ass so hard I can't help but ease my dick out my Hanes, reach over for my plastic jar of petroleum jelly, and remove my left sock. In no time, I have my dick greased down and the sock wrapped so tight around my shit, I'm able to fool myself into believing that I'm deep into Tracy's pussy.

"Tell me what she looks like again," Shawn says almost breathlessly.

I know he's jacking off like I am, and if we were anywhere else but here, I'd beat his ass for even thinking about my chick; but dreams are all we got in this bitch, and I'm just not going to deny him his God-given right to a good nut.

"She's five-nine with golden honey skin, maple brown eyes, full lips, and a set of tits like Bam! And has an onion ass like KA-POW!"

"Aw shit, like Beyoncé?"

"Better," I sigh, fluttering my eyes closed and enjoying this jack with the sock's friction. I vividly describe how honey drips from Tracy's pussy when I'm plunging into her and sucking on those fat titties. Then I recall how sweet her honey tasted when I used to bury half my face inside her to hit the back of that G-spot. All that sugary shit would drip down my chin while her legs would flutter like a black butterfly around my head . . .

"You like that, daddy?" Tracy asks, grinding her pussy against my face.

"Uhmm-hmm," is all I can manage as I cup her ass cheeks determined to lap up every drop until I pass out into a diabetic coma. It's Tracy's eighteenth birthday. I'd dipped into my stash trying to make this a night she'll never forget. We both don't have much, but at least we got each other. We used to say that shit all the time.

"I want you to fuck me, baby!" Tracy grabs my head and hisses through her teeth. "I want that shit in my pussy right now."

Hell, she didn't have to tell me twice. My dick had been hard since we walked into that overpriced suite at the Ritz, but I've been holding back, trying to let her know that tonight is all about her.

"Are you ready for me, baby?" I ask. " 'Cause I'm about to tear this shit up."

"That's what the fuck I'm talking about." Tracy's eyes twinkle in anticipation as her long legs now hug my hips.

I suck in a long stream of air while her tight walls put up a bit of resistance, but I'm still able to sink my ten-inch dick into her. "Aw, yeah. I'm gonna bust this shit wide open." I start pumping: long strokes, short strokes, and a few combinations.

I move her legs from my waist to my shoulders and even at one point fold them over her head. Her slick honey now looks like creamy candy coating my dick while my balls slap her ass into submission.

"Oh Jeeeesus!" Tracy cries out.

I couldn't have said it any better. The way we got down was like a religious experience. In no time at all, our bodies are drenched in sweat and I have three seconds to decide whether to pull out or lace her neck with a string of homemade pearls. Tracy throws her hips back at me one good time and takes the decision from me.

"Oh shit. Oh shit." My toes curl and my calves cramp, but I won't turn loose this good pussy. . . .

★   ★   ★

In my cell, back to reality, my mouth drops open as I feel my nut rise and then burst. The sock catches a lot, but the rest of my shit explodes over my hand and splashes back onto my flat abs.

"Whooo!" Shawn howls from the bottom cot, sounding like a wounded animal.

After a moment, we're both just left panting in the dark—both of us far from satisfied.

"Nigga, I swear you tell the best stories."

I smile in the dark, grateful this brother can't see my heartbreak, just like I can't see his.

"At least your old lady is holding you down on the outside," Shawn says. "Me and my old lady had a little falling out before I got locked down."

I don't bother to correct him about my situation. These brothas don't need to know my business. "Yeah?"

Shawn sucks in his breath. "Shit. She tried to bust a nigga's head in when she caught me fucking another bitch."

I take a guess. "Her girlfriend?"

"Her mother."

I can't help but laugh at that dumb shit.

"Hey, don't knock it until you try it. Just because some pussy is sporting some gray hairs don't mean it ain't good pussy."

This place is crammed with wild-ass stories like this.

"Well, me and Tracy are different," I lie, trying to convince myself more than him. "We're soul mates."

"Nigga, get the fuck outta here with that bullshit." It's his turn to laugh.

I ignore his ass. Niggas just can't understand the bond between me and Tracy. Despite my not seeing her ass for a dime, I know the real reason. Tracy had vowed never to travel down the same dead-end road like her momma. She didn't want shit to do with a nigga locked down.

I can respect that.

I remember the first time I laid eyes on her. She was seventeen, strolling the aisle at Macy's department store, robbing the bitch blind. I stood back, peeping out her game and waging mental bets on whether or not she was gonna get caught.

She was smooth with her shit. I gotta hand her that. She never did get busted. She was a criminal without a record— which made her the best kind. I hung back and pretty much followed her from store to store. She shoplifted shit from clothes to makeup to a couple of cheap gold chains. When I stopped her outside of the mall, she nearly shit a brick, thinking my ass was mall security or some shit. . . .

"Hey, shawty, hold up!" I yell, racing up behind her.

Her stroll doesn't break stride as she walks with her head up toward the bus stop.

"Yo, I said hold up!" My hand clamps down on her shoulder. "Yo, I'm talking to you."

Shawty spins around like a hurricane, ready to rip into me. "Get your muthafucking hands off of me!"

I jump back, hands up like a nigga that just got the drop on his ass. "Yo, calm down, shawty." I smile and take in her beauty. From a distance, I knew that she was fine, but up close the chick is banging. She has a curvy frame, but her onion ass is begging to bust free from the back of her jeans, while her double Ds stretch the hell out of her T-shirt and ask a nigga: GOT MILK?

Damn! Just damn!

"What? Are you in a muthafuckin' staring contest?"

"Naw, shawty, you're just fine as hell."

"My name AIN'T shawty."

I finally remember to lower my hands. "Then what is it?"

Her soft maple-brown eyes rake me over, peeping out my tall frame, broad chest, fade cut, and fat lips like LL Cool J. I know what I am working with, know that all the fine shawties in Detroit are always peeping and tryna get me to holla at them. I didn't see why she would be any different.

"My name is Nonya."

I frown. I've heard some fucked-up ghetto names, but, "Nonya"?

"Yeah, none of your business." She turns on her Lady Jordans and switches that fat ass with a little more humph than she did a few minutes ago. I wait to see if she'll look back, to make sure I am checking her out. She makes it all the way to the end of the sidewalk when I think she's not gonna look, but then, finally, a small glance over her shoulder and a subtle smile widens her glossed lips.

I am in love. . . .

"Well, at least you gonna get up out of here soon," Shawn says. "I hope they don't put one of those faggots from C block up in this bitch when you leave—especially one of those iron-pumping muthafuckers who's convinced himself that ass is just as good as pussy."

I catch the worry in his voice.

"Don't worry. I'll see if Li'l Jimmy can look after you." Niggas have to have the right connect to protect their asses—literally. "You gonna be a'ight."

"And you're finally gonna be knee-deep in some pussy," Shawn playfully reminds me. "I should hate you on principle."

"Yeah, I can't wait to see the look on my wife's face."

"You haven't told her you're getting out."

I smile. "Nah, I want it to be a surprise when I walk through the door. I bet that she's going to shit a brick."

"You're probably right."

13

Trey

I don't know why I do the stupid shit I do. And I don't know why Brijetta loves me like she does and just puts up with my nonsense, but I'm grateful that she does. I'm not one of these men who don't know how good they have it at home. I'm not like these other actors who are constantly looking to upgrade from one aspiring actress to the next. I've had my taste of that limelight, and I'm not interested in ever going back.

To have what little bit of privacy you can manage to carve out splashed across magazines for no other purpose than for the public's enjoyment is a violation that the rare few can ever get used to. Which is why I married someone not in the business in the first place. Most people have no idea how much pressure it takes off you when you don't have to compete for the spotlight in a relationship.

I have to face it. It's a miracle to even be in the position that I'm in right now. I attribute my success in Hollywood to a lot of luck with a dash of hard work. It's just luck that I come from two good-looking parents. Luck that a Hollywood agent had picked me out of crowded mall while I was cruising the place for girls with a couple of friends ten years ago. And it was luck that I landed roles that some A-listed actors had passed on that went on to become great commercial successes—successes that I had never dreamed about in my younger days.

Look. I have no delusions about being some great talent that's going to land himself an Oscar one of these days. If I do, it'll be because whatever studio head I'm working for greases the right palms. My great attribute to the film industry is that I look good while running to save the world and delivering sharp-witted one-liners into the camera.

That's it. It's not rocket science, but it's a job. A job that pays damn well, I may add. I make twenty million a picture upfront, then millions more with points on the back end that encompasses everything from DVD sales to network broad-castings. What can I say? Kent Webber is really a kick-ass agent who looks out for a brother. Bottom line, it's crazy money. I make more off one film than my parents and grandparents made their entire lifetimes combined.

I know that it's kind of crazy to say that I never aspired to be in the industry, especially since I grew up in this town. But it's true. I never gave much thought to what I was going to do or what I was going to become. I just rolled with the punches and did whatever felt right at the time. I was sort of popular in school, though I wasn't what one would call a jock, a theater geek, or even a rebellious cool kid who just partied all the time. I was a little bit of all those people, and in the end they all sort of liked me in return.

When Kent had approached me in the middle of the food court, I thought that he was just pulling my leg about him being able to turn me into a star and all the money I could make. I heard about people like him gassing kids up in the malls and the next thing you know you're being cast in a string of kiddy porn. But it turned out that Kent was the real deal.

Today, I arrive on the movie set a quarter 'til ten. A whole hour early so I can get a quick peek at the dailies before going over my lines with my assistant during hair and makeup. I have a crushing headache and I'm still woozy from that little drug cocktail I had yesterday, but I still have everything under control. It's not like I have a problem or anything. The fact that I can get up and still be on time for work is a testament to that. I've never missed a day of work and when a director yells "Action," you can best believe that I know my lines.

Does that sound like I have a problem?

So, yeah, I technically have OD'd like seven times, but it was usually when I was experimenting with some new shit or shouldn't have trusted somebody I was partying with to shoot me up. They were big mistakes that I won't repeat, so everything is cool.

Trust me.

"Morning, Mr. Hamilton," one of the interns on set gives me a big head nod as I climb out from the back of my limousine. I return the favor, but until I get my hands on some Excedrin and a few cups of coffee, he's going to have to wait on the smile. I breeze past the buffet table, just grabbing one croissant. There are a few more greetings called out to me as I make my way to the small screening room and settle down next to Art Edison, the director on this shoot.

"Right on time," he says, glancing at his watch. "You need to teach a course at the Actors Studio or something," he jokes, before signaling the guy in the projection room. The lights dim and the stock that was filmed yesterday plays up on the big screen. It's not unusual in this town for actors to proclaim that they never watch themselves in their movies and blah, blah, blah. Well, I'm here to tell you that's all bullshit. We all *love* watching ourselves, looking at ourselves—we're all vanity-obsessed people. That's like a cook saying that he doesn't taste his food or a painter painting with blindfolds on. It's an outright lie. We absolutely need to know how to work with light, which is our best side, and where that pesky camera adds that ten pounds.

Do we always like what we see? No, we always think we could have done each and every take better—but we watch.

By the time the last playback scene finishes playing, I'm feeling that this film has about a fifty-fifty chance of being either a blockbuster hit or a major bomb. I guess it'll all depend on what type of magic the CGI department can create.

When I make my way to my trailer, I'm finally coming off what's left of my high and feeling myself start to spiral down. That's not good, especially since the first scheduled scene is a high-energy one that's going to have me doing a lot of running and leaping with hydraulics before a green screen.

"Ah. There's my golden ticket," Kent greets me the moment I walk into my trailer. He closes the morning trade papers and tosses me a wink. "How the hell are you?"

"I can't complain," I say, closing and locking the door behind me.

"Can't or won't?" Kent challenges with a goofy smile.

"Won't," I amend. "Complaining never gets you anywhere in this town."

"Amen to that." Another wink.

I move past Kent and grab an orange juice from my mini-fridge in the small kitchen area of my trailer. "So what do I owe to the pleasure of this visit," I ask.

"What else? I got a job for you."

I instantly shake my head. "No can do. I promised Brijetta that I'd take a break after this picture. We need it. I promised to take her somewhere nice—probably Dubai or something tropical."

"They're offering twenty-five million and two extra points than our boiler plate back-end deal." He laughs like a misfiring tailpipe. "It's not exactly the kind of deal we can just walk away from."

"Says who?"

"Says me," he fires back with a couple of inches shaved off his smile. "Look, I get that you promised the little lady a little R & R, but I think she'll understand that you can't just up and walk away from a deal of a lifetime. These kinds of career moves should be expected when she married into the industry. So you have to put off a vacation for a couple of months. Dubai isn't going anywhere—this job, however, that's another story."

Kent is in his element when he's spinning a deal, but given how much I fucked up with Brijetta yesterday, the last thing I want to do is go back on a promise.

"Do you want *me* to talk to her?" Kent offers.

"Hell no." I laugh.

Kent places a hand over his heart. "Please don't tell me that she's still upset about that little misunderstanding a couple of years ago."

"You mean the one I broke your jaw over?" I remind him.

"Right! If anyone should be still pissed off about that, it should be me." He actually has the nerve to look like he really means that shit.

"You called her fat and told her that she had no realistic chance of hooking a guy like me."

He shrugs. "So I was wrong. It happens from time to time."

"You humiliated her in the middle of a major *Vanity Fair* party."

"More like motivated," he corrects me. "Look, she dropped the weight and invested in some plastic surgery like a real Hollywood wife. Hell, I even hear that she got a new set of plastic tits. How are you enjoying those, by the way?"

"How did you hear about that?"

"C'mon, baby. I hear about everything that goes on in this town, especially when it concerns you."

I shake my head. "You're starting to get a little creepy on me."

"I'm just trying to make sure you're happy. And if Brijetta does that for you, then it's all good in the hood. What's going to make both you guys happy is the amount of money we can bring in off *Defiance*."

Kent has finally said something to catch my attention. "You're shitting me."

"Would I do that without offering to clean it up?" His grin stretches back across his face. "This picture has already generated quite the buzz, and it'll be a different kind of role for you. Who knows, there might be an Academy Award opportunity in this one."

I roll my eyes at that.

"C'mon, don't knock it. Haven't I proven by now that anything is possible in this industry? Besides, you can't always be cast as the super action hero forever. You start laying down the tracks for deeper material now so that we have something to fall back on a decade from now."

I ain't going to lie. I'm tempted.

"C'mon, Trey, baby." Kent delivers a playful jab on my right shoulder. "Have I ever steered you wrong?"

Yes. Yes. A million times, yes!

Clearly reading the hesitation in my eyes, Kent moves in close and lightly brushes his hand under my chin. "C'mon, now, baby. Don't forget who really loves and takes care of you out here. No matter what you think you're getting at home." Our eyes lock and before I can stop myself, I lean in and give my long time agent, friend, and lover a long, passionate kiss.

14

Jalessa

I can't believe my luck when Omar Fines opens his front door. To be honest, I have only met him in passing one time, and Sinclair hasn't exactly invited me over but a handful of times—and then Omar was always excused as being out working on one blockbuster or another. I just assumed that he wouldn't have been home this late in the morning, either. As it is, coming from the gym, I'm hardly dressed to impress.

"Yes, can I help you?" Omar asks.

"Oh my. I can't believe my luck," I say, gushing. "Fancy meeting you here."

His eyes narrow suspiciously. "I live here."

Okay. Now I look like an idiot. "Of course, you do. Silly of me. I so rarely get starstruck." I take a deep breath. "Is Sinclair home? She said that she had a package for me today."

"What sort of package?"

"Well"—I cough to clear my throat. *It's do or die time.* "I, um, sort of asked her if she could get me a copy of the *Defiance* script. I just know that I'll be a wonderful addition to the cast."

His face finally relaxes. "So you're an actress?"

Shit. This asshole doesn't know who I am? "Yes, we met briefly at a *Vanity Fair* party a couple of years back." I quickly wave that comment off. "I'm sure you've met thousands of actresses since then."

"At least."

"Jaleesa Love?" I ask, hoping it would ring a bell with him. "I'm sure Sinclair must've mentioned me a least a few times. We've become really good friends."

"Ah, Ms. Love," he says, nodding his head.

"Great. She has mentioned me."

"Well, not exactly. Weren't you just fired off that Denzel Washington flick?"

"Actually, I regretfully had to terminate my contract due to creative differences with the director."

He gave me a look that said he wasn't buying it.

"Please, Mr. Fines. I know that it's really unconventional of me showing up here and trying to beg for a part, but I have to tell you that I really, *truly* believe that I'm perfect for this movie."

"You haven't even read the script."

"I know that I'll love it." I hold my breath and meet his gaze. "Mr. Fines, I'm not going to lie. I'm desperate. I'll do anything to get a role in your movie."

Suddenly, a small prick of light shines in his black gaze. He glances up to the ceiling and then smiles at me. "Anything?"

I got him. "Yes, sir. Anything."

Omar finally steps back and opens the door. "Won't you come in, Ms. Love?"

"Absolutely." I practically float inside the house. And what a house it is. The few times I've come here, I couldn't help but be overwhelmed by the place's magnificence. Omar Fines spared no expense decorating this place and it showed.

"Ms. Love, I have to tell you, I don't normally conduct business like this, but, uh, seeing how you're a good friend of my wife's—"

"Oh, yeah. I just really adore Sinclair."

"Good. Then maybe you wouldn't mind sort of joining us with a little game?"

"Game? What sort of game?"

"Oh, trust me, it's all in good fun." He reaches up and brushes a strand of hair from my face. "Of course, if we decide to let you play, we expect you to keep the strictest of confidence."

Is this negro talking about what I think he's talking about? "Of course. You can count on me."

He laughs. "I didn't get to where I am today by just taking people at their word. Won't you step into my office?" He sweeps his arm out to the left and I follow the direction he wants me to go until I see a handsome study down the hallway on the main floor. Even in here I'm almost too scared to touch anything in fear that I might break it.

"Please. Have a seat." Omar walks around to his desk and pulls out a couple of sheets from the bottom.

"What's that?"

"A standard confidentially contract," he says flippantly. "I usually have potential staff members sign these, but I think it'll work for this as well."

"All right—but does it say anything about me getting the female lead in *Defiance*?"

He gives me a lopsided grin. "I was thinking more of a supportive role."

"Minimum thirty minutes screen time?"

"Ah. Something tells me that you've done this before."

"Of course. This is Hollywood." We remain in the office for a full twenty minutes hammering out a pretty damn good agreement. One that put a pretty sizable smile on my face. The question now is what exactly I have to do for this career-saving agreement. I sign my name across the dotted line and almost instantly feel like I've just sold my soul to the devil.

Omar signs his name with a flourish and then turns to put the document in a safe hidden behind a picture frame. He also places a gun there from his pocket. *What the fuck?* "I'll make sure a copy is mailed to you before the week is out," he tells me. "Now, won't you follow me upstairs?"

I hesitate for half a second, but then remember what was at stake before climbing the stairs. Once we're on the second level, I feel a sudden change in the energy. He stops before a bedroom door and tells me to wait right there. He pulls something out of his pocket and I hear the door click before he steps inside. I've seen a lot of strange things in this town and I have to say that this is right up there at the top of the list. I think I hear some arguing and press my ear against the door to see whether I can make out what is being said.

No sooner do I press my ear to the door does the damn thing jerk open and Omar gestures for me to come in. My eyes immediately seek and find Sinclair sitting at a vanity chair, brushing out her hair. I smile, but then my eyes fall to what look like welts across her back.

What in the fuck?

"Sinclair and I were just discussing how happy we are that you can join us."

I try to find Sinclair's gaze in the mirror again, but she's not having it. I suddenly suspect that this whole ménage à trois is Omar's idea and not Sinclair's; but given what I have on the line, I'm not about to walk my ass up out of there until I fulfill my end of the deal.

"Is that right, Sinclair?" Omar presses.

Finally, a smile curves Sinclair's face and she meets my eyes for the first time. "We're thrilled."

One thing is clear; I'm not the only actress in the room.

Omar walks over to his wife and presses a kiss on the back of her head. "Why don't you climb back over into the bed so we can pick up where we left off?"

Without a word, she rises to her feet and I have to tell you that the girl is stacked. I mean, I knew she had a nice frame by the clothes she wears, but damn I'm going to have to change up my routine at the gym.

Sinclair situates herself in the center of the bed and her husband leans over and whispers something to her. She spreads her legs and then peels open her pussy. It's a pretty pussy. Now, I haven't had *that* much experience with women. I tried it a couple of times out of curiosity back in my early twenties— so I think I can flub my way through whatever the hell I have to do here.

Omar looks up from his wife to stare at me. "Care to join us, Ms. Love?"

I swallow hard and start unbuttoning my clothes. As I walk toward the bed, I have a sneaky suspicion that Sinclair and I won't be friends after this. But that's all right, I landed a hot acting gig in next year's summer blockbuster. A bitch can't ask for more than that.

15

Brijetta

"You what?" I jump up from the dinner table and throw my hands up in the air. "You promised that you'd take a break after this film." I'm trying to push the tears back down, but it's not working. I seriously need a break from this bat-crazy bullshit in this town. Trey needs it as well, though he will never admit to it.

"Kent says—"

"Kent says! Kent! Kent! Kent! I'm so sick of this man's name I don't know what to do."

Trey drops his fork and plops back in his chair. "Now you're being unreasonable."

"*I'm* being unreasonable? You break a promise to me and I'm the one that's being unreasonable? That's rich." I start pacing around the dining room while my neck starts burning up. "Half the time I feel like you're married to Kent more than you are to me."

"Paranoid much?"

"Don't you mock me! Don't you dare!" I quicken my pace as I feel a sudden migraine coming on. "You know how I feel about that man. I don't understand why you're so loyal to him, anyway. The man is an ass."

"True. But he's also a great agent," Trey defends. "You know that I wouldn't be where I am today if it wasn't for him."

"Oh, here we go." I toss my hands up in the air again. "God knows he's not the only *great* agent in this town. The place is crawling with them."

"You ever heard of a thing called loyalty?"

"Yes! I would love it if you would show a little my way some time," I snap. "That man has been nothing but rude to me since the moment we met, and you continue to stick up and defend him. It would be nice if you would be that way toward me."

"What are you talking about? I broke the man's jaw when he insulted you."

"And then the next day you sent him flowers in the hospital, apologizing." I jab my hands onto my hips and work my neck. "What? You didn't think I'd find out about it? Just because you don't read credit card statement don't mean that I don't."

Trey props his elbows up on the table and sighs loudly. "Please. I don't feel like fighting."

"Too damn bad, because I do."

"Fuck, Brijetta! What do you want me to do? It's a fucking role of a lifetime."

"Is that what Kent said? Because it seems to me that he says that shit about every picture. It's always more money than the last time or more perks than ever before. Next damn thing you know he's going be telling you that you're going to win a damn Oscar by jumping off buildings and shit."

Trey cut his eyes up at me and I know that I've just hit the jackpot. There's nothing to do but just laugh at this bullshit.

"You know—whatever. You're going to do what the fuck you want to do anyway, so go right ahead. Me? I'm out this bitch!" I turn and storm out the dining room.

He jumps out of his chair and storms after me. "Where in the hell do you think that you're going?"

"What the fuck do you care? You have Kent, don't you? I'm sure he'll do a wonderful job taking care of you. Find you all the right parts, get you the right trophy wife, and dig your dirty needles out of your arms. Fuck me, right?" Tears start pouring down my face. In this brief moment in time, I'm doing a hell of a job convincing myself that I'm about to leave.

"I can't believe that you're overreacting like this?"

"That's right! It's all me. It's always my fault. You keep telling yourself that." I storm into our bedroom and attempt to slam the door behind me, but he's right there to throw the muthafucka back open.

"Brijetta, you need to calm down and let's talk about this shit!"

"There's nothing to talk about!" I grab the Louis Vuitton luggage from out the back of the walk-in closet and drag it out over to the bed. "You broke a promise. Another one! You can't give up the alcohol. You can't give up the drugs. You can't give up your work. And it's painfully clear that you can't even give up that slithering serpent of an agent of yours."

"Baby—"

"Don't baby me! I'm sick and tired of this bullshit," I declare as tears splash down my face. "I ask you to keep one promise. ONE!" I'm grabbing shit from the rods and hangers and just stuffing it in the luggage. "It's not like I ask you for much."

"I know, baby. I know." He tries to reach for me, but I push him off. I'm so tired of his lies that I need to get away—just for a little while so I can recharge and reboot. "Just one more picture, Brijetta. I swear after this one—I'll take *six* months off."

My eyes start rolling again. "I must have 'Boo Boo The Fool' stamped on my forehead for you to try and run that bullshit by me."

"Baby, I—"

"You what? You *promise*? Does it look like I'm in the

mood for another one of your promises?" I zip one of the suit-
cases up and shoot toward the bathroom, where I grab an armload of toiletries and cram them into another bag. "I'm out."

"Brijetta!"

I grab my purse and keep my shit moving.

He tries again with a little more bass. "BRIJETTA!"

Shaking my head, I stomp down the staircase. This is about
making a point as much as it is about me needing breathing
room.

"DON'T YOU WALK OUT OF HERE WHEN I'M
TALKING TO YOU!"

"Or what?" I laugh. "What are you going to do?" I jerk
open the front door and struggle to get my shit out. "What
you need to do is decide who is more important to you: me or
Kent."

"BRIJETTA!"

He follows me all the way out to my Mercedes and finally
tries to snatch one of the bags out of my hands. That's when I
just lose my mind. I drop the one bag that I'm holding and I
open a full can of whoop ass.

"I'M SICK OF THIS SHIT! WHY DON'T YOU GET
IT?" I swing at his face, chest, and anywhere else that might
cause damage. I'm feel like I'm fighting not just for him or our
marriage, but for my sanity. There's too many nights where I
lie in bed feeling as if this toxic town is slowly killing us. I know
that it sounds crazy, but damn it, it's how I feel. And I have done
everything in my power to get my husband to hear me, but he
just absolutely refuses to do so.

I go at it for a while before Trey manages to lock his arms
around me. "Settle down, baby. Just settle down. It's going to
be all right."

It takes a while for the fight to drain out of me and when
it does, it leaves me as a pathetic, weepy, hot mess. Trey continues to hold and rock me back and forth. I don't know how

long we remain on the front lawn while I try to collect myself, but I know when I finally pull myself out of his arms that I can't go back into that house.

Not now.

Not yet.

I pick up my bags again and open the back door of the car. Trey's expression twists. "You're still leaving me?"

"We need . . . space."

His voice hardens. "How much space?"

"I don't know." I start shaking my head and shrugging my shoulders again. "I'll call you."

He goes from looking pissed to incredulous, but I can't let that affect me. If I do, I'll never get out of here and get some breathing room. Instead of answering him, I slide in behind the steering wheel and start up the car.

Trey taps on my window and then yells through the glass when I don't roll it down. "AT LEAST TELL ME WHEN YOU'LL BE BACK!"

While tears continue to pour like twin waterfalls, I shift the car into drive and slam my foot on the gas pedal. It's all I can do since I don't have an answer for him. This sudden act of defiance infuses me with both strength and terror. *What have I just done?*

I glance up into the rearview mirror and see Trey just standing there, watching me. I'm grateful that I can't make out the expression on his face, because my heart is already shattering into a million pieces. Its sharp shards stabbing my chest.

Three hours later and a second tank of gas, I'm still driving around Los Angeles with my tears really putting my waterproof mascara to the test with nowhere really to go. I guess I could check in to a hotel, sleep for a little while, and then tomorrow really think about what I've done or what I'm going to do. Then again, I guess I could always—

Ring! Ring!

The sound of the cell phone's classic ringtone shatters the

car's silence and nearly causes me to jump out of my skin. By the time I finish digging it out of my purse, I almost have two accidents.

"Hello, Mom," I greet after seeing her face on my caller ID screen.

"Chile, where are you?" My mother's southern twang has held firm even after thirty years from migrating west. "How come I got this husband of yours blowing up my phone looking for you?"

I should have known. "It's a long story, Momma."

"I ain't got nothing but time," she volleys back. "What's going on, Brijetta? Y'all two have a fight or something?"

"It was . . . definitely an *or something*," I admit. I usually keep my family out of my personal business. I spotted early on that no matter what went down, they usually took Trey's side while the general census was that I should just be tickled pink that I even managed to land such a fine catch. He's rich, he's handsome and a bona fide superstar. He could do no wrong in their eyes and I needed to stop whining and complaining.

"Brijetta Lizbeth Taylor, I know you hear me talking to you!"

"Yes, Momma."

Now, I don't know what's come over you, girl. Trey says that you got all upset because he has to put off taking you two on vacation because he has to do another picture. Is that true?"

Great. Now it sounds like I'm just being a diva.

"Chile, don't make me come through this phone. Answer me when I'm talking to you. Is that why you stormed out the house?"

"It's a little more complicated than that, Momma."

"Little girl, hush up. You think your father ever in his life took my ass on a vacation? Uhm? You want to know what I think?"

Not really.

"I think your *skinny* ass has gone Hollywood. You hanging

around all those rich folks and you done forgot how to be humble. You got a man. A *good* man that's *working*. He doesn't beat you or run a bunch hoochie mommas up in your face. He buys you nice things, you have maids up in your house, and now you're driving around in *his* Mercedes threatening to leave? Have you lost your ever-loving mind? Do you know how many women that would claw your damn eyes out to snatch a little of that?"

Silence.

"You hear me, girl?"

"You told me to hush."

"Don't get smart, girl! Your ass ain't too grown that I won't take a switch to it. Now, I suggest you get off your high horses, turn your ass around, and go see about your husband."

My hands clench on the steering wheel. "Momma, you just don't understand."

"What don't I understand, Brijetta? That loving a man is hard? Hell, every bitch out here know that shit. What—you want to tell me that Trey ain't perfect. Hell, I know that shit, too. But if you're going to be waiting for the perfect man or the perfect situation, you gonna be out here like the rest of these bitter bitches crawling into an empty bed. Make no mistake about it, a woman *needs* a man. Forget about all this modern bullshit you done heard. There are gonna be times when you'll convince yourself that you can do bad by yourself or that you don't need a man to be happy. But every trick that has ever told herself that has found out that being alone is pretty fucked up.

"Now, I ain't saying any piece of man will do, but a *good, working* man with his finances in order ain't what you toss back into the pond, baby. I'm telling it to you straight. Don't learn this shit the hard way. Listen to your momma, you hear?"

"Yes, Momma."

"Good." She pulls in a deep breath. "So you're going home, right?"

Silence.

"Brijetta?"

I pull in one of those long breaths myself. "Yes, Momma. I'm going to turn around and go home."

"You hear that, Trey?" Momma says.

"Yes, Momma Kate. Thank you," Trey says.

My mouth drops open. "You were on the phone this whole time!"

"Now, what difference does that make?" my momma snaps. "I told you the man was on my phone. My God, Brijetta. Stop trying to make a mountain out of a molehill all the time."

My anger renewed, I disconnect the call and toss the phone into the back seat. For the next few hours I just let the sucker ring while I continue to drive around Los Angeles like a night stalker. It isn't until I can barely keep my eyes open that I finally head for home.

The sky is a soft pastel of pinks and blues as dawn slowly arrives. I pull up the long drive of my beautiful palatial home, exhausted. I leave my bags and phone in the back seat of the car and just grab my purse before walking in. It's no surprise that the place is eerily quiet.

Maybe Trey has already left for work and I can get a few hours of sleep in before having to face him later this afternoon. When I reach the bedroom, it's clear that was just wishful thinking.

Trey is sitting on the edge, his hands braided in front of him. On the nightstand is a gun.

"I thought you weren't coming back," he whispers, not looking up.

I'm frozen. "When did you buy a gun?"

"I told you so many times that I didn't know what I'd do if you ever left me." He starts rubbing his hands and shaking his head. "You promised that you'd never leave."

I fold my arms and watch him with weary suspicion.

"You don't think I'll do it, do you?" He finally looks up at me with tear-stained eyes. "You want me to kill myself, don't you? That way you'll finally be free of me. Is that what you want?"

I don't answer.

Trey snatches the gun from off the nightstand. "IS THAT WHAT YOU WANT?"

I gasp as my chest tightens. "No, baby. That's not what I want." I swallow this huge clump of air wedged in my throat. "Please. Put the gun down."

"I don't believe you." He places the barrel against his temple and clicks off the safety.

"Trey. Don't. Do. This." With my hands held up in front of me, I creep into the room. "I—was just upset. Of course, I was coming back, baby."

"I called and called you." He starts rocking back and forth.

"I know. I'm sorry, baby." I creep closer. "I swear that it will never happen again." His expression looks so tortured that I now know just how much I hurt him. "Please forgive me, Trey. I'm sorry. We'll take a vacation after the next movie. It's okay. I'll wait." Closer.

"I'm just trying to make everyone happy," he says.

"I know you are." Closer.

"It's like you don't understand the kind of pressure I'm under."

"I do. I do. I swear." I'm just inches in front of him now. "Give me the gun, baby. It's going to be all right. You'll see."

He shakes his head, his finger twitching on the trigger. "I don't know. Maybe it's just all for the best that—"

I make a grab for the gun just as the damn thing goes off.

PART II

Skeletons never stay in the closet. . . .

16

Sinclair

"It's an iron-clad prenuptial agreement," my attorney Eric Lowe says, pushing the papers back at me. "If the marriage is terminated for any reason in the first seven years, all you'd stand to cash in is fifty thousand dollars for each year you've been married. It's only been two years." He shrugs his shoulders. "I'm sorry."

I suck in a slow, patient breath while trying to ward off another migraine. I knew what he was going to say before he said it, but I wasted another couple of hours of my day to hear it, anyway.

"Can I get you some thing to drink, Mrs. Fines? You don't look so well." His blue eyes indeed reflect a deep concern as he stares down at me.

"Actually, I really could use a drink. The stronger the better." I flash him a weak smile and then reach for my damn prenuptial papers.

"You know I hate saying this, but I did tell you not to sign those," he says, walking over to his office bar.

"Yeah, yeah. Don't remind me." The truth of the matter is I was so in awe of Omar Fines and blown away by his money and lifestyle, that I didn't really understand all the complexity of clauses I was signing. Now I'm in a marriage from hell that it's not completely clear that I can walk away from.

The beatings have tapered off, but Omar keeps finding new and improved ways of keeping me terrified. I'm used to being in control of situations. As for Clevon, I haven't seen hide nor tail of him, and according to a few friends of mine at the Sports Center, he just up and disappeared. *That* put real fear into my heart. Is it possible that this hotshot movie producer has the power to make people just disappear? Is he mobbing that deep?

Of course, on the flip side, if I keep my mouth shut and my legs closed to miscellaneous sex, then I could continue to play with my luxury toys, drive my fancy cars, and rub elbows with the rich and famous. Surprisingly, that's all still very tempting to me. That's fucked up—and what's worse, I know it. Still, when you grow up with nothing and manage to accumulate something, you'll fight like hell not to go back to nothing. That's just a fact.

Pride be damned.

"Here you go, Mrs. Fines. Will a scotch on the rocks do?"

"Absolutely." I accept the offered drink and down half the contents in one gulp.

"Better?"

"Much."

Eric smiles. "I'm sorry that I don't have better news for you, but I've seen this happen plenty of times before. These big Hollywood types plant a big ring on some young, beautiful, and unfortunately naïve woman such as yourself, convince you to spend your youth with them, and then about the time your first wrinkle shows up, they're out the door."

I frown. "What do you mean?"

Eric sits behind his big glass desk and braids his fingers together. "Look, Mrs. Fines, I like you. And I really wish that you had listened to me earlier, but you have to know by now that your husband has no intention of being married to you a full seven years."

I drain the rest of my drink before asking, "What do you mean?"

Eric's neatly groomed and waxed brow lifts. "Do you really need for me to say it?"

"Humor me."

He pulls in a deep breath. "What a lot of powerful men in this industry do with these prenuptial agreements is put in all these strict restrictions that last for a period of time, in your case, seven years. In others, generally with women younger than you, it's ten years. In what generally happens is six months before these contracts expire and you stand to be entitled to half of everything hubby owns, suddenly he's feeling that you two are having irreconcilable differences."

"Shit."

Eric tosses up his hands. "Again, I'm sorry to be the bearer of bad news."

I pop out of my chair. "Shit. Shit. Shit." I start pacing a hole in his carpet. Omar has completely caught me slipping. I got so swept up in this fantasy that I didn't realize just how many steps this muthafucka was ahead of me.

"It's the shining diamond syndrome," Eric supplies, sympathetically.

"Excuse me?"

He nods toward the huge rock on my finger that Omar had retrieved and I finally get it. "Sonofabitch!" While I'm stewing in anger, Eric glances down at his watch. I'm wasting his time. "Well, I guess I better go." I grab my purse and head for the door.

My attorney stands from behind his desk. "Again, I'm sorry, Mrs. Fines. If I were you, I'd start stashing for a rainy day."

I glance over at him. "Trust me, I'm about to get caught up on this game real quick." Then a question that Clevon had asked me a while back floats to the front of my mind. "Um, I have a question. If something was to . . . happen . . . to my husband—God forbid—would I also just be subjected to the allowance to the number of years married or . . . what?"

Both of my attorney's brows stretch. "Hypothetically speaking?"

"Of course."

"No, this prenuptial would be dissolved—but I'm not your husband's attorney and I have no idea what is written in his will. But as *your* attorney, I suggest you find out. Just so that you know where you stand and there are no surprises."

"Yes, I'm starting to hate those."

"Most grown-ups do."

"Thanks again." I slip out of the office with my back just a little straighter while I walk across his posh lobby. During my drive home, my mind starts spinning. I can't believe how I just walked all willy-nilly into some old Hollywood trap. I've been walking around thinking my shit didn't stink and that I had hypnotized this man with my frame and mad sex game. Trust. I feel like a fool right now.

My foot eases off the accelerator when I spot the Sports Center. *I wonder.* I have three seconds to either breeze by or whip my ride into the parking. I, of course, elect to do the lat-ter—mainly because I'm pissed off. What's the point of mind-ing my p's and q's if in the end Omar plans to end our marriage any time before now and the next few years?

Once I'm parked, I don't just jump out of the car. I kind of scan the area to see whether my husband has someone follow-ing me. It may be a tad paranoid, but if he has the power to make folks disappear, then it's probably in my best interest to keep an extra eye out. I sit in the car a full five minutes, watch-ing every car that whips into the parking lot after me. Nothing suspicious. I ease out of the car, pop the trunk, grab my work-out bag, and do a quick run/walk into the gym.

Yes, I feel ridiculous.

"Ah, Mrs. Fines," the front desk clerk greets me cheerily. "Long time no see. You must've been off on some fabulous vacation, I'm sure."

"Well, not exactly." I glance around. "Is . . . um . . . Clevon back?"

A knowing smirk hooks the corners of the receptionist's lips. Suddenly I feel like I'm engaged in some dirty dealing.

"I'm afraid not," she says. "It is kind of weird, but he just up and disappeared, isn't it? I mean, he was really one of the most popular trainers we ever had here at the Sports Center."

I roll my eyes as my shoulders deflate with disappointment.

"But"—the receptionist strikes a finger up in the air—"he did leave something for you should you stop by."

"He did? When?"

The smiling young girl turned around and plucked a thin envelope from a slot on the counter and then handed it over. "When he walked out of the door, he just told me to make sure that we give this to you the next time you came to the club."

I'm suddenly giddy as hell while something starts doing cartwheels in my chest. "Thanks," I say, taking the envelope and then marching right back out of the club with no further pretence of wanting to work out. Outside, I perform another quick run/walk back to my car and then finally rip open the envelope before the driver's door had slammed closed.

My dearest Sinclair,

I received your message regarding your husband finding out about us.

I have to admit that I was, at first, ecstatic about the news. I thought that it meant no more hiding. You would be free to leave him and I could take care of you. I could, you know? Just say the word and I will sweep in like a knight in shining armor.

Humph. I knew Clevon was a bit of a romantic, but this really takes the cake.

> *After I received your call, I guess your husband hired some big goon to try and shake me down. As I've told you before, I've done some things in my past that I'm not too proud of. I've served a bid over something I believed was self-defense. Anyway, your husband's man starts laying all this pressure about exposing me if I didn't roll up out that spot. He even made it clear that your husband was willing to throw two hundred large my way if I just leave the Sports Center.*

"That sonofabitch!" He gets two hundred thousand and I get a lousy fifty a year?

> *As you can imagine, I was quite impressed with the offer. With that kind of cash, it could help me start my spot where I can be my own boss. I'm sure you understand. However, I view Mr. Fines's investment into my own gym as a stipulation to leave the Sports Center—not to quit seeing my favorite client. So if you're still looking for a brother who can hit some of the spots your pencil-dick husband can't reach, use the number at the bottom of this letter and let's see about putting a few more dents in my bed's headboard.*
> *Forever yours,*
> *Clevon James*

Beneath his name was his new contact number and I damn near broke a nail trying to punch that shit into my BlackBerry. Adrenaline has my heart racing and is giving me a natural high. There's just something about engaging in activities that you ain't got no business doing that's makes life exciting. I just need to tighten up my game a bit more and remember my old adage in not getting caught.

"Hello."

A smile blankets my face at the sound of Clevon's voice drifting over the line. "Hello yourself, C-man."

Clevon's warm chuckle has a way of making my nipples tingle.

"It's about time you called," he says. "Six months causes a brother to wonder if he put the mack down as hard as he thought."

"Oh, you did the damn thing, playa. I just had to make sure that home fires had cooled down. You know how it is."

"Sheeeiit. You ain't filed papers on this smug bastard yet?"

I suck in a deep breath. "Man, things are complicated. Things are more fucked up than I thought."

"Yeah? Then why don't you come on over here and let me see if we could put our heads together and see what we come up with together," Clevon offers.

"Just our heads?"

"Anything you want."

I start up the car. "You don't have to ask me twice. What's the address?" Grabbing a pen from my purse, I write down instructions that'll take me out to West Hollywood. Just thinking about Clevon's monster dick gets me squirming in my seat. Two seconds after I disconnect the call from Clevon, Omar starts ringing my phone. Knowing now that it's better to answer than to ignore it, I pick up before the second ring.

"Hello, baby. What's up?"

"The usual, doing a lot of press junkets. Where you at?"

I roll my eyes, because every question is a test. "Just leaving the gym."

Pause. "What—you looking for your boy?"

"C'mon now. We have award season coming up and I got to start getting right and tight if I have to start squeezing into those small designer gowns."

Silence.

"You can either trust me or don't. It's your choice." As I ease onto the main highway, I'm surprised by his laughter.

"Let's get one thing clear, Sinclair. I'll never trust you again. You just better hope that I never catch you." With that puzzling response, Omar disconnects the call.

Now I'm spooked and I ease my foot off the accelerator. The timing of the call couldn't be a coincidence, could it? *Fuck!* I fly right past the exit to Clevon's crib, cursing and slapping the steering wheel like the damn thing owed me money. I can't believe that I'm about to pass up riding some good dick that's just waiting for me.

"Shit! Shit! Shit!"

It takes me a full hour to calm down. When I do, I'm sitting in my own marbled tub, chockful of lavender bubbles and sipping on a strong Pinot Grigio. "Stop being emotional," I keep telling myself. "Work smarter, not harder." I desperately need to get ahead in this game. Quick, fast, and in a hurry. When I'm completely relaxed, I start to doze off. A surprising image floats to the front of my mind: Kwame.

"Hello, Tracy. Miss me?"

17

Kwame

Two months later . . .

Freedom.

It's a nice word. No one really knows how much they love it until it's taken away from them. That includes my ass. After serving a little over a dime in Detroit's finest prison, I'm ready to live life. I can't say that I'm a completely changed man, but I'm definitely a more precautious muthafucka. No more banging and stealing first and then thinking about the shit second. NawhatImean? It's time to be smart.

First thing's first, though. I need to find my wife and let her know daddy is home. I can't wait to see her face when I knock on her door. One thing for sure, whatever sideline brother she's dealing with is going to have to fall back or fall six feet under. Whoa. Whoa. There I go again. I'm already talking about capping brothers I don't even know exist yet. Change ain't going to be easy. I can see that shit right now.

"Yo, man! You looking for a ride?"

I slow my pimp walk to look up at a familiar smiling face. Familiar because it looks just like mine. People been talking how much we look alike, and now that he's standing in front of me, I see that shit is true.

"Yo, Mike. What up?" The smile that splits across my face is genuine. I hustle over to the nice shining black SUV and can't help but let out a long whistle at the spinners my cousin is floating on.

"You like that?" Mike asks, poking his chest out.

"You know it, man. You must be balling out of control, son."

He adjusts his shades and then pops his collar. "Well, I don't want to brag or nothing—especially out here in front of Federal PIG's, but your boy is handling business. Now that you got your freedom papers, hop your ass on in here so we can roll out."

My cousin doesn't have to tell me twice. I leap into the passenger side in a single bound, slam the door, and let my ass just melt into the leather interior. "Nice." I can't stop rocking my head.

As Mike peels out of Mound Correctional Facility, I give the old brown brick building a one-finger salute. "If I never see that muthafuckin' place again, it will be too soon."

"I hear what you saying. They're holding some good soldiers. You feel me? When the white man be about his paper nobody got shit to say, when niggas try to come up, it's all blue lights and cold steal locking you down. This shit out here ain't nothing but supply and demand. So what's the problem?"

I'm shaking my head because Mike has always been a militant brother when it came to street paper. For twenty-five, he has an old mind. It's like he was born in the wrong time. He would've fit right into the whole 60s vibe. The devil has blue eyes, by any means necessary, black power—you name it.

I let Mike go on about street politics and whatnot while we roll through my beloved hometown. When we hit the Mt. Elliott/Palmer area, my jaw starts sagging. I can't believe what my eyes are seeing.

"It's a damn shame, ain't it?" he asks after watching my face. "Damn near looks like a Third World country, don't it?"

"You ain't lying." My gaze drifts over one dilapidated building after another. There's trash blowing in the streets, as well as random garbage piles here and there. Grass is growing in between the cracks of the sidewalks, and anything that's standing still is tagged with gangster signs—some I ain't even heard of.

"This is what it looks like when folks just don't give a fuck no more," Mike says.

"You going to blame this on the man, too?"

"Nah, this is some self-inflected bullshit," Mikes says straight up. "Ain't no reason to lie about that shit." He quirks up a smile. "I can't wait 'til Momma sees you, man. You being her sister's only child, you know she kind of looks after you like you are one of her own, don't you?"

I nod. "I know. And I appreciate the love. For real—but I need to find this crackhead Felicia first. That's *if* her ass is still around."

"A crackhead from back in the day? Good luck. You know those got expiration dates, right?"

"Yeah, but she is probably my only lead in finding Tracy. Since you didn't keep your eyes on her like I asked you."

Mike's head drops back against the headrest as he howls with laughter. "Tracy? Man, is you for real? That chick got ghost right after they locked your ass up. I ain't never seen nobody make skid marks that fucking fast. You didn't warn me that I was supposed to be watching the Road Runner, man."

I wave his nonsense off. "You just fell off your job. That's all that is."

"Whatever, man. Beep. Beep."

He wins a smile from me with that. "Goofy-ass muthafucka."

"So where this crackhead is supposed to be at?"

"Somewhere around here. She used to get out of the elements in this one industrial building by the Packard plant."

Mike shakes his head. "I'll roll you by there, but I wouldn't hold my breath, man."

"Appreciate it." I continue to take in the depressing scenery until I see the building Tracy would drop by like twice a year to check on her momma. Tracy used to hate rolling through here, and I never blamed her for it. In their relationship, Tracy was more like the mom than the other way around. Tracy doesn't know this, but I swung by here and asked Felicia if I could marry her daughter a couple of nights before I dropped on one knee. It turned out to be one of those rare nights where Felicia wasn't quite as high as she wanted to be.

She appreciated the respect I showed her and I like to think that there was a nice future in-law bonding going on. That's not to say that she didn't hit me up for twenty dollars before I left, but whose family is perfect these days?

Mike pulls up to the curb to what used to be some kind of manufacturing plant and I hop out, realizing for the first time just how long a shot this really is. Nearly every window is broken and it looks as if sections of the place have been broiled out by a couple of fires.

"Yo, man," Mike calls out from behind the wheel. "I gotta piece for you if you need it."

"Nah, that's all right. Wait. You got some money on you? Information doesn't usually come free."

Mike's face twists, but he un-asses a few Benjamins.

"Thanks, man. I'll get this back to you."

Mike eases back in his seat and just watches me push open a door that hasn't had a lock on it in decades.

"Hello?" I call out. "HELLO? IS ANYBODY IN HERE?"

I hear some scuffling and rustling. At the moment I can't tell whether it's from humans or rats. Neither one of them scares me much. I'm here so I might as well keep it moving. "Yo! I'm just looking for a chick named Felicia," I call out.

Silence.

I move in deeper. "I just got out of the joint and I'm looking to find my family."

Silence.

Deeper. "I'm not a PIG. You have my word on that."

"Your words don't mean shit. Man, we don't know you," a harsh, gravelly voice snaps out of the darkness.

"True that. True that. But if Felicia is up in here, she can vouch that I'm her son-in-law."

"Felicia who?"

"Smith. She's an older lady—probably mid-fifties."

"Never heard of her. Now git!"

"Yes, we have," a female voice argues.

"Shhh, Mable. Damn!"

"Mable?" I call out, feeling a little audacity of hope myself. I just wish I could see these folks in the dark. I don't know if I have a gun trained at my head or not. "Do you know where I can find Felicia Smith?"

Silence.

"Please, Mable. I swear I am who I say I am."

The man and woman exchange harsh whispers back and forth. Just when I think I'm nearing the end of my rope, Mable comes to my rescue.

"Felicia cleaned herself a couple of years ago. Claims she found God over off East Grand. She cleaned up real nice. I saw her in one of those nice church hats I used to collect back in the day. You remember those, George?"

"Yes, Mable," George hisses, sounding bored with this conversation. "Will you just say your piece so this man can get out of here and we can smoke this last rock?"

"Don't be rude." I hear a smack. "Just 'cause we live like animals doesn't mean that we have to behave like them."

I chuckle softly to myself at their banter.

"Anyway. Where was I?"

"She goes to church off East Grand," I remind her.

"Who?"

"Felicia Smith."

"Oh yeah. Her. Now, let me think. I believe she also has an apartment duplex off Henry—not too far from Harper Woods.

She got one of those big ole oak trees smack dab in the center of the front yard. Can't miss it."

My face explodes with a new smile as I peel them off a Benjamin. Any more than that I'm afraid they'll smoke their way to the grave tonight. "Appreciate the help." I hold out the money and one of the two nearly takes my finger off with it.

"How much is it?" I hear Mable ask as I turn away.

"Ah, shit. We're going to party tonight!"

When I hop back into Mike's ride, I give him the thumbs-up and our new destination. Mable, the crackhead, gave me excellent directions. We find the apartment duplex with the large oak tree off Henry with no problem. And as luck would have it, Felicia is just walking through the front door with an armload of groceries when we pull up.

"Looks like you need a little help with that," I say, strolling up to the door.

She looks up with a frown on her face and clearly is just seconds from asking me what the hell I want when recognition sets in. "Kwame?"

"You remember me," I say, grinning and taking the groceries out of her arms. I have to admit, she looks pretty good herself. For the first time, I can see her and Tracy's strong resemblance. "I'm glad to see that you're taking good care of yourself."

"Humph. That didn't have nothing to do with me. That's been all the Lord's doing."

I just nod, smile, and hope that I don't have to stand here for a long testimony that usually comes when folks try to get into heaven after a lifetime of raising hell.

"So you must be here looking for Tracy," she says, surprising me.

"As a matter of fact, I am. Just got out of the joint today."

"Uh-huh. For dealing out the devil's drugs."

"How about we strike a deal? I won't judge you for your past and you give me the same courtesy?"

A silence floats between us before she finally says, "Deal."

"Good." I set her groceries down on the table. "So, where's Tracy?"

Felicia shrugs her shoulders. "No clue. I haven't seen her since about the time you got locked up."

"Felicia, c'mon. You being a new child of the Lord, I suspect that you know that He doesn't take too kindly about false prophets. I haven't read the good book myself, but I've been told that it's filled with passages of stuff like that."

Felicia's lips twitch.

I hit the bull's-eye. Tracy may not have liked the way she was brought up, but she never could sever her tie completely from her mother; therefore, it's only logical that she told her where she's moved to.

"Why don't you just forget about her?" Felicia says. "She's moved on—and happier now."

"Now, that doesn't sound like you don't know where she is, does it?"

She clamps her mouth shut again, her lips still twitching.

"C'mon, Felicia. Tell me where my *wife* is at."

18

Jaleesa

"CUT! CUT!" Marcus Hughes tosses up his hands. "What the fuck?!"

I wince as the entire production crew groans and mumbles under their breaths as I once again flub my lines. "Sorry. I'm so sorry," I say, even though I've been saying it now for the past half an hour. I don't know why I just can't find my groove or my mojo on this picture. It's like I'm just this one big giant ball of nerves every time the director yells, "Action."

"Take five, everybody!" Marcus slaps his clipboard down and then gives me this look that he either wants to shoot, strangle, or stab me to death. Or maybe he wants to do all three. I can't blame him on that. "Matter of fact, let's just call lunch."

"YOU HEARD THAT, EVERYONE: LUNCHTIME," the assistant director yells and a long bell rings.

"Cheer up," Trey Hamilton says, giving me a light elbow to the side. "It's not like it's the end of the world."

"No, it's worse than that. I'm costing the production a ton of money."

Trey bobs his head, not bothering to sugarcoat anything. "Well, it seems to me that you just need to relax. Loosen up."

He gives me the most mellowed, serene look that I instantly try to copy—and fail.

"I just don't get it. I never used to get like this. Now everytime that damn red light comes on, I feel like a deer caught in headlights."

"Ah, I know what your problem is," he says as he starts to lead me off set.

"You do? Well, clue me in, Einstein. I'll take whatever insight you can give me."

"It's simple: You can't shut your brain off. You're critiquing your performance inside your head before you even act. The results: You freeze up—unable to make a decision on how to perform the scene." He waves it off and flashes me his big Hollywood money-making smile. "Every actor goes through it at some point. We have the whole world judging everything you do. That buzzing gets inside your head and starts to drive you insane."

"Yeah. Yeah." A lot of what he's saying is making perfect sense. "So what do you do to turn your brain off?"

Trey glances around a full 360 degrees before whispering, "Come to my trailer."

The idea of sneaking off alone with Trey Hamilton to his trailer definitely gets my hackles up. Sure, he's Brijetta's man and all, but like I said before, none of this shit is personal. And is it my fault that this muthafucka is so damn fine? Shit. She needs to have his ass on a leash.

There's no mistaking who's the star on these types of film. They're the ones with trailers suited to shelter a family of five and complete with such amenities like a kitchen, bedroom, and bathroom. The rest of us get shit that a homeless person would look sideways at.

"Oooh. This is really nice," I purr, looking around.

"Lock the door behind you."

My lips start twitching. *All right. This is where the magic is going to start happening. Time to see what Mr. Superstar is working with.* I lock the door and strut my way behind Trey to this small table. I remain standing for a moment, wondering if he just wants me to just start stripping or put on a little dance for him. I'm down for whatever. Who knows what other favors I can get out of this?

"Now, do you trust me?" Trey asks.

Hell. I don't even trust my damn momma. "Sure, baby. I trust you." I reach down, then pull the hem of my top over my head, and then strike a pose.

"What are you doing?" he asks, frowning.

Embarrassment inflames my face. "I-I thought . . ." I quickly shove my shirt back on. "I'm sorry. I must've misunderstood." I turn to scramble for the door.

"Where are you going?" he asks. "I thought you wanted my help?"

Now I'm completely confused. That is, until he reaches under his seat and pulls out this very old-looking cigar box.

"Now, this shit here that I'm about to introduce you to is guaranteed to get your mind in just the right frame where you can quiet that critic buzzing inside of your head and keep you focused on what you're supposed to be doing."

I inch back over to the table. "Yeah?"

"The shit works for me," he endorses with a simple shrug. "Why don't you just try it and see if you like it. If you do, then I can get you hooked up with my connect. You feel me?"

Drugs? Squeaky-clean, all-American superstar Trey Hamilton dabbles in drugs? I blink at him. This information is just blowing my mind. Never in a million years would I think this clean-cut black actor had crossed over to the dark side. What about all the *stay away from drugs* campaigning he does for the little kiddies?

"What? You don't party?" he asks.

"Uh, oh. No, that's not it." I sit down at the table. Partying is the one thing that I know how to do—and do well.

A large, child-like grin spreads across Trey's face as he claps his hands together and then acts like a mad scientist as he starts mixing and cooking his shit up. "Now, I'm just going to hook you up with just a little taste—you fly for a few minutes and then you'll land softly in time for the next marker. I promise you, you're going to nail your next take."

"All right," I say, rolling up my sleeve. "Let me see what you're working with."

"Nah, give me your foot. That'll be better. You don't want those nosy fucks in wardrobe seeing any fresh marks. All these muthafuckas around here have a direct connection to the tabloids and bloggers. The last thing you want is them blasting your business across the rags, saying you got a problem or some bullshit."

Does Brijetta know her man gets down like this? Shit. I bet her ass would have a shit fit if she knew her golden ticket loved sugar smacks. I almost bust out laughing, thinking how Brijetta flaunts her shit around and acts like her and her man were perfect.

Trey pulls the plunger back and fills up the hypodermic needle while I kick off my right pump and then prop my foot up on the table. I'm hoping this shit is as good as he says it is. I ain't had any good smack in a hot minute. I suck in a small breath when the small needle punctures in between my toes. A second after that, something warm rushes through my blood that absolutely feels euphoric.

"Oh sheeeeit," I just barely make out, with Trey smiling at me.

"Yeah, I thought you might like that. Ride that wave, baby."

I smile and start rubbing my hands all down my body. Once I start, I can't stop. Every inch of my skin feels like a giant G-spot. Next thing I know I'm moaning and coming and I'm still fully dressed.

"Damn, you done made me want to have a little taste of this shit, too," Trey says. From the corner of my eye, I see him cooking himself up some of this shit, too. A couple of seconds later, I literally don't give a fuck what he's doing. I'm lost in my own world where people love and adore me. . . .

Everywhere I turn there's flashing lights and reporters asking which designer I'm wearing down the red carpet.

Draped on my right arm is Trey Hamilton, looking superstar fine with a golden hypodermic needle on a chain around his neck. We share knowing smiles and then a tender kiss just for the camera.

"You just remember who made you a star, baby." To my left, Kent Webber cocks a half smile at me and winks.

"Don't worry, baby," I slur. "I know I owe it all to you." I blow him a tiny kiss just when my ears pick up someone crying. I look around, wondering who could be crying on such a fabulous night like this.

Brijetta. Wouldn't you know it? I finally pick her out at the end of the velvet rope with her fat hands covering her fat face. Clearly, since Trey had come to his senses, she decided to drown her misery in a few tons of fried chicken. She's so completely round that I'm convinced I can just push her over and roll her away from ruining my event.

"Just ignore her," Trey advices. "She'll get hungry soon and wobble away like she always does."

I laugh and then thrust my chin up for more snapping pictures for the paparazzi. Then there's this knocking from somewhere. It's low at first, but it soon grows louder and more persistent.

"Will someone please get that?" I ask, while keeping a smile on my face.

The knocking grows even louder until I finally stomp my foot and growl, "GET THE DAMN DOOR!"

I jerk upright, still a little dazed and confused. Across from me, Trey's head is rocked back with this little goofy smile on his face.

Knock! Knock! Knock!

There's someone at Trey's trailer door. I quickly grab the drug paraphernalia, cram everything back into his old cigar box, and shove it back under Trey's seat. "Trey, wake up." I slap him a few times and he moans lightly. When he peels open those pretty brown eyes of his, I can't help but smile. "You got company."

Knock! Knock! Knock!

"Mr. Hamilton, you're needed on the set in five!" someone shouts.

"I'LL BE RIGHT THERE," he yells back, blasting open my eardrum. We take another look at each other and start giggling.

"How you doing?" he asks, sitting up.

"High as fuck," I answer honestly.

"High—but relaxed?" he asks.

I think about it for a moment. "Yeah. Yeah. I mean that initial trip was like—whoa. You know? But right now, I am feeling pretty cool."

He bobs his head and wipes the drool off his mouth. "Cool enough to do this next take?"

"There's only one way to find out." We both straighten ourselves out and then head out of the trailer. No sooner do we make two steps toward the set does Brijetta just appear out of nowhere.

"I don't believe this shit!"

Before I can react or say shit in my defense, this ex–Hungry, Hungry Hippo delivers a right hook across my jaw. Knocking me the fuck out.

19

Brijetta

"Nasty trick!" I shake my shit out because it feels like I just broke my hand, and then turn on Trey. "Is that the bitch you want now?"

Trey's eyes are as big as saucers as he drops down next to Jaleesa. "Get away from that ho! That's the last bitch you need to be worried about right now. What the fuck was she doing up in your trailer with the door locked?"

A crew of people finally get over their initial shock and scramble to help one of their supporting stars. I hear Jaleesa moan, and I rear my foot back and kick that bitch square into her gut. "Bitch, if you even think about taking my man, you better wake the fuck up and apologize!" For good measure, I kick the bitch again.

"Brijetta, stop!" Trey springs up and tackles me back a few feet—which is probably a good thing because I ain't above stomping a bitch to death. "What in the hell has gotten into you?"

"Don't play me sideway, Trey! I ain't stupid. I just saw that bitch walk out the trailer with you, after I'd been banging on the muthafucka for twenty minutes!"

Everyone is crowding around and listening, I frankly don't give a flying fuck. I've been through too much—including nearly being shot when his high ass was fucking around with that damn gun a few months ago. The way I'm feeling, I'll do him a solid and take him and his bitch out, if that's what it has to come down to.

"It's not what you think," he hisses, grabbing me by the arm and dragging me toward his trailer.

"You're a goddamn liar. Let go of me!"

"I can't believe that you came down here and made a scene like this! You know all this shit is going to make the tabloids!"

"I DON'T GIVE A . . . AHH!" He shoves me into his trailer and I stumble up the stairs.

"Get your ass in here!" He steps over me and starts tugging me up.

I get up and kick the door shut. If he thinks my ass is scared, he got another thing coming. "You were fucking that bitch up in here, weren't you?"

"NO!"

"BULLSHIT!" I pop him in his face. "Now, go ahead. Tell another muthafuckin' lie!"

Trey holds his hands up and steps back. "Brijetta, I'm going to warn you one time, keep your hands to yourself."

"OR WHAT?" I snake my head and get all close and personal in his face. "WHAT THE FUCK YOU GONNA DO NOW? HUH?"

He tries to step back again as if he's trying to be above the petty bullshit. But fuck that. If I'm in the mud, I'm going to drag his ass into it, too.

"I'll tell you what you're going to do, you're going sit up here in my face and start crying and whining about how you'll just die if I left and, Brijetta, please. I'm sorry. Well, FUCK YOU, muthafucka!"

Finally, this nigga snaps and grabs me by my throat. Even as he bangs my head up against one of the small kitchen cabinets, I dare his ass to do something.

"WHAT, MUTHAFUCKA? WHATCHA GONNA DO?"

"Brijetta," he warns again.

"WHAT? DO SOMETHING! HIT ME! I DARE YOU TO!"

Trey cocks his hands, but the shit just hangs in the air.

"YEAH! THAT'S WHAT I THOUGHT! YOU AIN'T GONNA DO SHIT!"

The trailer door bangs open and Kent storms up in here. "What in the hell is going on in here?" he hisses. His hard glare takes in the scene. "Everybody can hear you two up in here."

"Like I give a fuck!" I yell back when Trey releases his hold on my throat.

"Ah, I see that Miss Gutter Mouth finally reconnected with her true roots. I knew you couldn't keep that shit covered for long." He smirks, closing the trailer door behind him. "What did I tell you, Trey? You can dust them off and dress them up, but a project ho ain't never gonna have no home training."

"FUCK YOU, ASSHOLE!" I leap toward him, but Trey quickly jumps in between us.

"Brijetta, shit. Chill your ass out," he says, finally putting some bass into his voice.

"I should have known that you'd find your balls in time to stick up for this greasy muthafucka. Did you just hear what he said to me? You ain't got shit to say about that?"

"What do you want me to say? Right now you are acting like a project chick with no home training. You're screaming and yelling about shit that didn't fucking happen. Now you've interrupted production, and that's going to cost a lot of important people a lot of money."

"Then you should have thought about that shit before you thought to fuck that girl all up in here."

"DAMN IT! I DIDN'T FUCK THAT GIRL!"

"Then why was the muthafucking door locked, huh?" I pop him on the head again.

"Brijetta," he warns again.

"What, nigga, what?"

He steps back again. "For the last time, I told you that I didn't *fuck* that girl."

"BULLSHIT!"

"Fine. You want to smell my dick?" He starts unbuttoning and unzipping his pants. "Will that make you fell better?"

I fold my arms until he drops chow. Dick swinging, he pushes me down onto my knees and then shoves his crotch all up in my face.

"You smell any muthafuckin' pussy on that? Huh?"

I sniff all around, desperate for any musty twang left by that bitch.

"And before you say shit about me taking a shower, do smell any fresh soap?"

I do, but it's very light, clearly from this morning and not within the last hour.

"Uh-huh," he says, stepping back. "I bet your ass feels real stupid right about now." He drags his boxers and pants up over his hips while I climb back up onto my feet. From the corner of my eyes, I see Kent standing, arms crossed and looking very amused.

"Well, I'm still dying to hear the verdict," he says dully.

"FUCK YOU!"

"No," he starts off calmly. "FUCK YOU, YOU CRAZY PSYCHO BITCH!"

"Oh, I got your bitch!" I launch toward him again, but again Trey is right there.

"Brijetta!"

"What? You just going to let that man call me out my Christian name right in front of you? What kind of punk-ass shit is that?"

"I'm just calling it like I see it," Kent says, tossing his hands up. But there's just something in his eyes that's just begging me to bring it on. I've never liked this man and I'm more than willing to bring it to him.

"What's your problem with me, Kent? How come every

time I turn around your ass is right there? Huh? And you always got something to say?"

"This is a movie set. I'm just here doing my job, *Mrs.* Hamilton. The better question is, what are *you* doing here? You shouldn't you be nipping and tucking something?"

"This muthafucka here!" I launch yet again. This time my arms are swinging to take his ass out. Instead, I clip Trey on his right eye and in response he pops me dead in my mouth. I immediately feel my bottom lip burst open and blood gush into my mouth. Stunned, I slap a hand across it and blink stupidly at Trey.

His eyes spring wide as he realizes what he's just done. "Oh shit, Brijetta! I'm sorry."

Kent cracks up as if it's the funniest shit he's ever seen—completing my humiliation.

I rush around Trey, needing to get away from this place as fast as I can. He reaches for me but just grabs air as I sprint away. Kent leaps out of the way to avoid me shoving him into a wall; then I break free from the trailer, still pretending that I don't care that the entire set is watching me run with blood oozing from in between my fingers or that outside the set cameras click away.

20

Trey

"Why do you always have to antagonize her?!" I shout to Kent as I grab my jacket and car keys so I can go chase after my wife.

"Me? She started the shit—or did you miss where she just laid out your co-star out there?"

I don't even want to get into this shit with him. He knows exactly what I'm talking about, but he wants to stand there and play innocent. "You know what?" I say, heading toward the door. "We need to end this. Things are getting far too complicated—more than it needs to be."

"What?" He grabs me by my left shoulder and restrains me. "What do you mean 'end this'? You're choosing *her* over me?"

I turn, looking at him incredulously. "I've been telling you for years now that I love her. She's my wife. A fact that either you chose to overlook or ignore."

"Whoa. Don't blame me. I'm just following your lead. You seem to forget about the little missus, too, when I got your dick boxing my tonsil a couple of times a week."

I glance back at the trailer's door to make sure the damn thing had closed when Brijetta stormed out. It had. "I promise you we won't have that problem anymore. It's over. Done. Brijetta is the one I love. She's the one I want to spend the rest of my life with. If you'd been paying any attention, you would've known that I've been trying to end things with you for a while."

Kent rolls his eyes. "Spare me the gay guilt, Trey. I know what this is all about. I've dealt with men like you my entire life. You want the world to believe that you're something you're not, so you run out there and marry the first fish you can find in hopes that no one ever notices that extra sugar in your tank. Well, you ain't fooling me, superstar Trey Hamilton. I see you. I see who you really are. You'd be better off if you'd stop dodging mirrors and shoving that crap in your arm and just face the truth. YOU'RE GAY!"

I shove my fist so hard into Kent's face I can just feel and hear bone crack. It might've been fine if I stop the one time, but I keep on punching him until a team of people run into the rocking trailer and save his life. "YOU STAY AWAY FROM ME! YOU'RE FIRED!"

Kent tries to talk, but there's so much blood pouring out of his face, it is clearly impossible.

Remembering Brijetta, I turn and hightail it out of there. In the back of my head, I know if I leave the set that I'll effectively shut down production for the day, but I definitely need to fix this shit with my wife. The knots in my stomach start to sink like stones when I recall how I hit her without thinking. There's no way that she's going to forgive me for this.

"Why didn't I stand up for her?" I chastise. "Why can't you be what she needs you to be?" I shake my head at my reflection in the rearview mirror. *You want the world to believe that you're something you're not.* I cringe at the sound of Kent's voice echoing in my head.

How can I explain me and Kent? I can't. And believe me, I've tried. No matter what he says, I'm not gay. I'm not. At least not in the sense that I go out cruising for guys or finding myself attracted to them. Kent is the only man that I've ever . . . look, it's nothing that I'm particularly proud of. And for a long time I think I just felt that I owed Kent so much. I mean, I wouldn't have the superstar career or the house or the money if it wasn't for him.

Lord knows that he never misses an opportunity to remind me of that fact. And don't think that I'm not terrified right now that he doesn't just run to the first Hollywood reporter or blogger and get a serious case of diarrhea of the mouth. Who cares if he jumps out of the closet, I'll be the one who's crucified. I'm halfway to my house and I'm already regretting smashing Kent's face in. If he talks, what will I do? What will Brijetta do?

"Shit!" I slam my hand down on the steering wheel. I'm damned if I do and damned if I don't. But right now I got to make this shit up with Brijetta. If that's even possible. Of course, all of this would happen in the middle of rush hour and I end up spending damn near two hours to make it to the house.

She's not home.

Instead of stopping and jumping out of the car, I just loop around the driveway and head back out. An hour later, I pull up to Momma Kate's house with Brijetta's Mercedes parked in the driveway.

I shut off the engine and just stare up at the house. I really don't have the energy for this shit. And dealing with this is definitely going to be a big ole pile. The front door opens and Momma Kate's robust frame steps out onto the porch. She shields her eyes to squint out at me just as the screen door snaps shut behind her.

"Ain't no sense in just sitting out there all by your lonesome. Get on in here and see about your wife! You got a lot of apologizing to do!"

One thing about Momma Kate, she sure in the hell didn't think twice about broadcasting her business, and everyone else's for that matter. I plaster on a smile and climb out of my car.

"Waste of time flashing those big ole puppy dog eyes at

me. Save it for Brijetta." She turns and then disappears behind
the screen door. I look to the two houses nestled on each side
of Momma Kate's to see her neighbors and good friends, Ginny
and Nanette, leaning over from their porches, trying to get a
good look at the drama.

"Afternoon, ladies," I say, smiling and giving them a small
nod.

"AFTERNOON, TREY," they singsong back at me.
Nanette, the self-professed cougar, even tosses in a wink.

I leap up onto the porch and take a deep breath before
pulling open the front screen. The living room is about the size
of a matchbox and I don't think that it ever occurs to Momma
Kate to shut off the heat. It's a modern miracle the plastic hasn't
just melted right off her precious furniture.

"I was just about to take Brijetta something to eat," she
tells me, holding up a tray of food. "She's back there in her old
room."

"I can take that to her," I tell her, then retrieve the tray
from her hands. But before I can turn toward the hallway, she
stops me.

"Do you love her?"

The question surprises me and I think it shows on my face
because she folds her arms and just stares me down.

"I like you," she offers. "I don't think that I've been shy in
saying that. Now, I know from experience that marriage is hard.
When the preacher says that you go through trials and tribula-
tions, he ain't lying. For the most part, I think it's a woman's duty
to always be there for her man, especially one that knows his
duty in taking care of and providing for the woman."

This is the first time that I've seen Momma Kate struggle
to get to her point.

"Now, what's with this hitting business?" She pulls in a deep
breath and shakes her head. "That's one thing I don't abide by.
A man should never raise his hand toward a woman. Not ever."

"Yes, ma'am. I fully agree with you. Everything happened so fast . . . I need you to know that it was not intentional."

She nods. "I just need to hear that you'll never do it again."

"I'll never do it again."

"And I need for you to mean it—because if my baby shows back up here with her mouth all busted up again, there's not a rock on this God's green earth that you can hide under that I won't find you and send you on home to glory. You understand me?"

Momma Kate holds my gaze and I have no doubts that she means exactly what she says. "Yes, ma'am. I mean it. It won't happen again."

"All right, then. Go on."

I stroll down the hall and stop outside my wife's old room. "Brijetta?" I knock. "Baby, it's me."

Silence.

I glance back down the hallway to see Momma Kate, folding her arms and leaning against the wall. Shit. She's going to stand there and watch me beg.

"Go on," she whispers.

I take another deep breath and return my attention to the closed door. "You were right and I was wrong," I start off. "I should have stood up for you."

Silence.

"I fired Kent."

I hear the bed squeak, the shuffling of feet, and then, at last, the doorknob turning. She opens the door just a crack; wide enough for me to see her bloodshot eyes, tear-stained face, and swollen lip. "Ooh, baby. I'm so sorry. I didn't mean—"

"You mean it? You fired him?"

"Yeah, right after I broke his face."

She gasps, but then pulls the door wider. "You broke his face for me?"

Not technically. "I shouldn't have allowed him to talk to you the way that he did. Clearly, you two don't get along . . . and if he can't respect you as my wife . . . then he doesn't need to be representing me. We're a couple."

Just like that a light just beams out of her eyes while her smile stretches from ear to ear. She wants to throw her hands around me, but I'm still holding this tray.

"Here, give me that," Momma Kate says, reclaiming the food.

Brijetta instantly flies into my arms and as I swing her around, I'm confident everything is right with the world again. That is, until an hour later, when the big fights on the *Defiance* set is *Entertainment Tonight*'s main headline.

Brijetta and I just moan.

21

Sinclair

Kwame has put on a little weight since the last time I saw him. All of it muscles from pumping iron in prison. His once innocent-looking baby face has filled out with more mature lines—especially along his jaw. He's most certainly thuggishly fine with a trim goatee, prison tats, and a slight bowlegged walk. He still likes to give his thick rubber-band lips a lick before he starts to talk, giving them a nice natural gloss and coincidentally drawing women's eyes right where he wants them.

It's been so long since I've seen him that even in my dreams a deep ache stirs around my heart and everything else starts to tingle.

"You're a hard woman to find, Tracy," he says, staring into my eyes.

"You should've stayed away," I whisper over the knot in my throat.

One side of his lips kicks up as he erases the small distance between us. "C'mon, now. You know better than that. We belong together. We always have." He stops less than an inch in front of me so that his minty breath wafts across my face. "It doesn't matter where you go, I'll always find you." He leans in to kiss me and my eyes drift closed expectantly . . .

"Sinclair!"

Omar's morning bark jolts me wide awake. "Wha—what's going on?"

"It's time to get your lazy butt up. We're going to miss Sunday service if you don't get a move on."

After my vision adjusts and accepts where I am, I groan and plop back against the bed. There's no point in my asking if we have to go, because attending Power of Prayer services seems to be sacrosanct in this household. And the way my head is spinning right now, the last thing I am in the mood for is for Omar to preach about how little he asks of me. With one long, exasperated huff, I peel back the silk sheets and climb out of bed. This morning, my usual two-hour preparation job is completed in forty-five minutes. Despite that miracle, Omar is staring a hole in the side of my head when I slip into the passenger side of his midlife crisis Bugatti.

"Will it kill you to be on time for one damn thing?" he hisses.

"Sorry, baby. I'll do better next time," I answer in a bored voice. Every since my last talk with my attorney, I can hardly put in the effort to really give a good damn about this marriage. It's going to end, anyway, and according to everyone, it's going to leave me broke as a joke. Sure, I've managed to start siphoning off a few thousand here and there. Eric helped me open an offshore account, but let's face it, it's chump change compared to what I have to put up with.

"I got too much shit on my plate for you to just be taking your sweet-ass time, that's all I'm saying. *Defiance* is already over budget, Trey Hamilton's wife going psycho and then Trey himself beating up his agent—nobody seems to give a fuck that they're costing me money!"

"Calm down, baby. It's going to be all right," I say in the same bored voice. If I still believed that his money was our money, then maybe I could manage to conjure up some real concern, but seeing how I'm just a 50K bitch on payroll, this is the best he is going to get.

"Calm down," he mimics me and rolls his eyes. "Ain't that about a bitch?"

Now that I seem docile and tame, there hasn't been much for him to rage about in the bedroom. I texted Clevon why I stood him up and then ended all communication.

Omar blazes through the streets of L.A. and then parks in our usual spot, next to Ashton Curtis, the brother who heads the film acquisitions with Paramount. Church, like everything in this town, is just another avenue for the rich and powerful to network, schmooze, and show off. Every suit is tailored to an inch of its life, and every dress comes from some designer in Paris or Milan.

Frankly, once I'm out of bed, I don't mind it so much. The choir is always entertaining because most of the singers seem to believe they're auditioning for the Hollywood elite, so solos seem to go on forever with acrobatic scales that would make Mariah Carey and Patti LaBelle proud. Next up: the sermon. Reverend Fines, an old cat player if ever I saw one, climbs up to the podium and gets his gruff, yelling praise on while constantly swatting his neck with a bleach-white handkerchief. Sweat pours off this man's head like a faucet, but he has the congregation in the palm of his hand.

This whole thing is nothing new to me. Growing up in Detroit, pimping God is just a way of life for a large section of people. Nine times out of ten, you can find those same people telling you that you're going to hell cussing, drinking, and fucking anything that'll stand still long enough. So don't get mad at me if I'm not so impressed when the Holy Ghost causes old ladies to fall out in the aisle in an unsecured wig and no panties. I have little patience when visiting pastors preach the evils of homosexuality while eyeballing the boys' choir or even the Saturday night player sleeping off a hangover in the front pew.

This place is just another Liars' Club and we're all card-carrying members.

One good thing Reverend Fines knows how to do is keep his performance short, sweet, and to the point. Before I know it, he's asking for new and visiting guests to stand up and introduce themselves to the congregation. That's probably about the time the hairs on the back of my neck start to rise and the energy in the church shifts.

A few people shift and stand up.

Reverend Fines gestures to someone in the back of the church. "Yes, young man. What brings you to the Power of Prayer Ministries?"

"God, Reverend!"

My heart drops while the church chuckles at the man's answer. *It can't be!* I jump and swivel around in my seat, and sure enough, there's Kwame, standing up at the back in a deep royal blue suit, looking both GQ and thuggish fine at the same time. Our eyes lock and the bastard winks at me.

Right there in God's house, I hiss, "Oh shit."

22

Kwame

I'd say that judging by the color that's draining out my baby's face that she's a little surprised to see me. As I recall, she hates surprises, but I'm sure she'll forgive me this one time. My gaze shifts to the dude sitting next to her, her so-called husband, who looks like he should be down at the gym, getting ready to box Rocky or something. Surely, she must have married this old cat for the money, because he's old enough to be her real daddy—if not her young granddaddy.

"What's your name and where do you come from, son?" The Reverend continues to interrogate me.

"Kwame Franklin. I'm from Detroit—south side." I smile at everyone. "I guess you can say that I've come to a certain crossroad in my life, fell on my knees and the good Lord brought me straight here."

"Well, AMEN, Brother Franklin," Reverend chuckles. "On behalf of the church, I want to welcome you to the Power of Prayer Ministries."

I toss everyone another smile and sit back down; however, my gaze quickly focuses back to my beautiful wife. Time has definitely been good to her. She has managed to transform herself from the ride-or-die shawty with the fat ass to one of those rich, sophisticated women who lounge in spas, stores, and expensive restaurants all day. It hurts to say, but I gotta give lil ma her props. She has come waaay the fuck up. No point in lying about that.

After the collection plate floats by two or three more times, the Reverend leads everyone in a closing prayer, but I keep my eye on my prize and then slip out of the place before she and her husband un-ass their pew seats.

I did what I needed to do: let her know that *hers truly* is back on the streets. When Felicia first told me that Tracy headed out to Hollywood, I thought her ass was still gaming me. I just couldn't picture my baby girl chasing the bright lights, but then Felicia laid on me that Tracy landed herself a fancy Hollywood producer—that I could see. Let me be clear, I ain't all that happy about my girl lying down with another man—not by a long shot. I still consider that pussy being legally mine—*BUT* given the financial upgrade of the situation, I am starting to see a certain upside to all of this. And why not? The last thing I want to do is get back out in these streets and start slanging again. Shit, I'm edging closer to thirty, and dope dealing while pig dodging is a young man's game. The longer I'm out here in this sunny California weather, the more I want a piece of some of this long, legal hustle the brothers got running out here. And Tracy is the perfect person to pinch me off a little sumpthin' sumpthin' to get me started.

I roll up the 101 toward Holmby Hills in a Mercedes Coup that I'm renting from Luxury Car Rental just so my ass would look like I belong up in this muthafucka. I have to be careful not to fuck up this $3,000 suit I'm wearing because it's the only one I have. That's okay. With Tracy's help I know that my situation is going to be turned around in a hot second. Hell, my palms are already itching for a little bit of that long green. Who knows? Maybe I'll even be able to get to afford one of these bougie-ass cribs with a few of my own illegals gardening and maintaining the yard out here.

Bobbing my head and taking in the scene, I don't think

that I've ever seen grass this green up close and personal. What the hell are they putting in the soil? And the sky—even with the smog it still looks like paradise out here.

Yeah, I see why Tracy moved out here, changed her name, and started soaking up the fantasy life. Now it's my turn.

A few minutes later, I pull up into a very spacious mansion myself. The joint is nice. It sort of puts me in mind of that crib on the *Fresh Prince of Bel-Air*. It's a little old school compared to the other sprawling mansions, but it beats the hell out laying my head down at the YMCA—and despite a few sparse furnishings, the place is empty with a "For Sale" sign nestled in the right corner lot.

The main reason I chose this spot is because it's just a couple houses down from Mr. and Mrs. Omar Fines' estate. For the past two weeks, I've been able to scope out their crib and do a little spying on the missus. It takes me less than a day to discover that I wasn't the only one checking her out. It took another day for me to peep out that it's Tracy's own husband—the second one—that's paying a private dick to follow her around.

Can it be that Tracy's golden goose doesn't trust her?

Surprisingly, the man gets a couple points of respect from me on that. Like the prophets BBD once crooned, "never trust a big butt and a smile." Now, all this paranoia means that it's going to make it a little more difficult for me to break into Tracy's golden cage, but I've never been the kind to shrink from a challenge.

But as luck would have it, three days later, Mr. Fines's private dick disappears. At first that shit threw me, making me think I'd been picked off. After I calmed down and investigated, apparently the private dick's services just came to an end—which left the field wide open for me to get my creep on.

Lucky me.

Inside my private mansion, I change out of my Armani suit and into a pair jeans and a long T-shirt. I've been planning Tracy and my reunion for a week now. I just hope that Tracy will forgive me for one more surprise.

23

Omar

Sinclair is acting strange. While we stand out on the church's front steps, smiling and greeting some of the church's regulars, she's twisting around and craning her neck as if she's expecting a police ambush or something. After twenty minutes of this, I clamp a hand on her arm and pull her aside. "Who in the hell are you looking for?"

"Huh? What? No one."

Now, this bitch should know better than to play me crazy, and I give her a look that suggests that she try again.

"I just thought I saw an old girlfriend in the crowd and now I don't see her. That's all."

I hold her stare, trying to catch her bluffing—but as far as I can tell Sinclair is a pretty damn good poker player. The truth only comes when you're beating it out of her.

"Sinclair!"

We both whip our head around to see Jaleesa Love, waving and threading her way through the crowd. When I get a clear view of her face, I can't help but wince at her swollen black-and-blue bottom lip. Trey's wife must have hit her with a lead pipe or something because none of that half a pound of makeup she has on is doing a damn thing for her.

I plaster a smile on because her attack took place on my

set, leaving my company liable for a possible lawsuit—which is the last thing we need.

A stiff Sinclair turns. "Jaleesa."

Jaleesa touches the side of her face for dramatic effect. "Hey, girl. Figured I'd come for a little holy water and prayer."

Sinclair folds her arms and makes no mention of the obvious. I watch, resisting the urge to roll my eyes to the back of my head because of the number of gazes directed in Jaleesa's direction. Something tells me to turn around and when I do, I see a phalanx of paparazzi across the street.

That's new. Usually the vultures respect the church grounds and allow the celebrities at least this bit of privacy. But ever since the Trey Hamilton love triangle story broke, all bets were off and cameras were popping up everywhere. Everyone wants publicity for their picture; this just wasn't what I had in mind.

I lean forward and recapture Sinclair's arm. "We have to go, dear," I inform her, and then pass Jaleesa a sympathetic smile. "It's good to see you again, Ms. Love."

"Thank you. And don't worry. I'll be on the set bright and early tomorrow."

My brows jump to the center of my forehead. How on earth does she think that she can get jump in front of a camera with her bottom lip the size of a basketball?

"Don't worry about that right now. You just take care of yourself and get better." As I try to lead Sinclair away, Jaleesa moves with us.

"You don't have to worry about that, Omar. I completely intend to live up to my obligations despite the production's lack of security."

"Excuse me?"

"Well, Brijetta did attack me on the set—a closed set."

"Mrs. Love, my company has nothing to do with whatever sideline activities that you engage in with your costar."

"What activities are those?"

Now she's going to play stupid.

"Mr. Fines, I hope that you don't believe the petty gossip that's being reported. I assure you that I've never slept with Trey Hamilton. Brijetta unjustly attacked me on the job, and if you think you're going to use that as a basis to fire me, then I'll have no choice but to—"

"I suggest that you think *really* hard about completing that sentence, Ms. Love. I'm not the kind of man you want to *fuck* with in this town, and I don't take idle threats lightly."

"And I don't make them lightly." She smiles. "We wouldn't want the details of our lovely time together"—she looks at me and then Sinclair—"to be the lead story on *People* magazine, would we?"

It takes everything I have not to beat this bitch down, talking to me. "Have a nice day." I direct Sinclair away from the fame whore and back toward my car. I'm beyond pissed off that the bitch had the nerve to level a veiled threat toward me.

24

Sinclair

First of all, I think Jaleesa has a lot of balls slithering up and wrapping her arms around me like a boa constrictor. We ain't cool no more, and I know I don't have to text her ass a memo for her to know that shit. I don't buy her innocent act. I know that heifer would fuck a Mexican donkey if it meant an acting gig. I know the shit doesn't involve me, but I just can't see Brijetta flipping her lid and laying home girl out for no reason. If I have to choose a side, then I'm Team Brijetta all the way.

Still, I do like how this soap opera drama has Omar munching down on antacids like Skittles. In no time he's dumping me back off at the house and mumbling something about seeing Spencer. I barely get the passenger door shut before he peels off again with a plume of smoke jetting out the tailpipe.

Whatever. I head on into the house, needing a drink. I don't waste any time, either. Climbing the stairs with a dry martini in one hand, I finally push the bullshit with Omar to the back of my mind and focus on my real problem: Kwame. As much as I want to believe it, he was not a figment of my imagination.

How did he find me? Actually, there's a number of ways he could have found me, any number of Hollywood magazines could've ran a picture of me with Omar. Not that many of them care to report on all the behind-the-scene CEOs and studio heads, but Omar and Spencer were tallying up quite a catalog of moneymaking hits—and success always got people's attention.

Still, I can't picture Kwame or any of his people paying that kind of attention to shit that goes on in La La Land. No. He would've had to do some digging.

Felicia.

I freeze at the top of the stairs. Would he have been able to track down my mother? That question only floats in my head for half a second before I have my answer. *Yes.* Kwame was like a hound dog when it came to sniffing out information. *Damn. I should have kept my mouth shut.*

The strange thing about my relationship with my mother is that as much as I hate her, I still love her. No matter how many times I ran away or how many times she fucked up or put me in fucked-up situations, I always boomerang back to her. I'd always drop off food at whatever crack house she was huddled up in or slip her some money or shoes when need be. Every time I'd tell myself that it would be the last time, only for me to show up the next week to do it all over again.

And since I've been in California, I've sent money through the church she claims to have saved her. Since she hasn't killed herself off that shit she's been smoking yet, I'm inclined to believe her. *But why can't she keep her big mouth shut?*

I push in the door to the master bedroom while my thoughts are still submerged on my mother when a voice floats over to me from the bed.

"Hello, Tracy."

I glance up.

"Miss me?"

My martini slips from my hands and shatters on the hardwood floor. "Kwame."

A broad smile stretches across his face. "At least you haven't forgotten my name."

I blink once, twice—three times and he's still lying across my bed with his shit pulled off.

"I'm still here," he laughs. "Sorry to surprise you—your little psychic thingy must not be working these days."

"You can't—be here." I turn and quickly close and lock the bedroom door. "You have no idea what my husband will do if he catches you here!"

"The big old dude you were at church with?" He shrugs. "I got a pretty good idea—since he goes out of his way to hire some private dick to follow you around."

"What?"

"You probably didn't know that, but don't worry, I haven't seen the guy around for a while." Kwame cocks his head. "Mind if I ask what you did to cause Apollo Creed not to trust you?"

My face burns with embarrassment.

"Ah. Another dude," Kwame concludes, stretching farther back among the thick pillows. "Sounds like you've been quite busy with the fellows. I'm feeling a little hurt. Why don't you just come on over here and try to make me feel better?" He pats the empty space next to him.

"What?"

He shrugs. "I'm hurt, but I'm still horny."

Honest to goodness, there's so much shit flowing through my head right now, it's amazing that I'm still standing. After the room is silent for a while, he sits up and cocks his head at me. "Don't tell me that you don't want to. I know you do. We used to be good together. I still remember all your favorite hot spots. Come over here and let me show you."

This must be what it felt like when the devil slithered up to Eve in the Garden of Eden. Kwame is nothing but a big, chocolate body of temptation, and I've never been the type of person who's been able to tell myself no. Never. Ever. If I want something, I go for it and think about the consequences later. I have a feeling that I'm about to do that shit again.

I step past the glass on the floor with my eyes locked on my husband. In some strange way this still feels like a dream. Kwame is not supposed to be in my house, let alone in the bed I share with my other husband. But the semantics aren't important right now. Our bodies are calling out to each other and it's just too powerful to resist.

Kwame's thick lips slope sexily as I sit down on the edge of the bed. "See. That wasn't so hard, was it?"

"Kwame, about my husband—"

"Shhh . . . I don't want to talk about him—especially since he ain't here."

He reaches out to me, rakes his hands through the back of my hair to hold me still. "You haven't told me that you missed me yet." He licks his lips and my eyes fall to his glistening mouth. "You miss me, baby?"

"You know I did. But—"

"Shhh." He smiles knowingly. "Then show me."

With that, he lets me take the lead in fusing our mouths together. No lie. He tastes just the same as he always had: sweet, intoxicating—and dangerous. Any woman will tell you that is the perfect combination.

The clothes come off in a flash and before I know it, I'm being pressed into the bed's red silk sheets with my legs pointing east and west. Kwame unrolls his long tongue underneath my pink clit and starts slopping up my thick juices like it's the nectar of life. Hissing and thrashing around, I make sure to keep a firm hold on the back of his head. I don't want him to miss a spot or drop.

Kwame rolls his hands underneath my ass and then locks them over the curve of my hips. Everything he is doing is feeling so good that I start rubbing and pinching my nipples. Now this is what I've been missing. My boo needs to give Omar and Clevon lessons in this shit here.

"Right there, baby. Right there." I sigh and melt even deeper into the sheets. Lord, I remember what it used to feel like getting serviced like this every morning before being slapped on the ass to go make him breakfast. At first I could never walk straight, but I'd hum and sing the entire time I was over that hot stove. The memory plus an eclipsing orgasm makes me smile and gasp at the same time. When it intensifies I hold his head dead center and then straight hose his mug shot down from his hairline to his chin. Even then he smacks his lips and looks as if he's ready for more.

He'll have to wait for a second course because I'm ready to move past the appetizer and head on in for the main dish. Kwame climbs up my body; his black polish dick is for some reason two shades darker than the rest of him. I've always found that to be erotic and a complete turn-on.

"Kiss him hello," Kwame instructs, straddling my breasts and smacking his dick against my face.

I try, but he makes it a game by moving his dick from one side of my face to the other. I feel like Wile E. Coyote chasing after the Road Runner. After a few seconds I just give up and he finally plops his heavy cock on the center of my lips for a sweet kiss. Of course, it doesn't stop there. One big peck leads to a few smaller pecks—a long lick—followed by a few shorter ones.

"That's right, baby. Open wide."

Still following his instructs, the next thing I know I'm slurping and spitting while he's deep-stroking to the back of my tonsils.

"Ooooh, damn," Kwame mumbles and groans. "I can't tell you how much I've missed this sweet mouth." He reaches behind him and slips a finger in the center of my creamed pussy. "Are you ready for daddy, baby?"

I squirm and nod my head.

"Is this still my pussy?" he asks with a sudden note of seriousness.

Still lost in the moment, I nod again.

"Let me hear you say it." When he pulls his cock out of

mouth, there's an audible *pop*. "Say it. Tell me that's still my pussy."

"It's your pussy."

He slips in a second finger and stirs so much juice around that I can hear it smacking. "How many niggas you done let play in this pussy while I've been gone?"

"Kwame," I moan. His interrogation is causing me to come out of the moment.

"What? I'm just curious. You don't know?"

I'm not answering this question. No matter what number I give him, it's going to be too many.

"Well, I know you're giving it to this brother that you're pretending to be married to—since the last time I checked we're still married and your name ain't no damn Sinclair—so you might as well go ahead and tell me. Hmm?"

"Kwame."

"What? Just give me a number. "

"Kwame."

"Any number."

"Five." *Which is really lowballing.*

His finger stops stirring. "Five?! Damn. It's like that now? What—you turned into a ho while I was locked down?"

I glare up at him. "See. I knew I shouldn't have told you shit. Get off me."

"Tracy—"

"I said get off me!"

"Damn, baby. I was just fucking around with you." His fingers start stirring again and my anger ebbs away. "I understand a sister like you can't put this good pussy on ice while a brother is serving a bid. I can respect that, especially seeing how it's done upgraded your situation." He eases back down my body, his beautiful black cock springing back and forth, hitting my chin, my breasts, my belly, and then the soft V of curls between my legs.

"You love that, nigga?" he asks, spanking my clit with the head of his dick. "Hmm?" *Smack. Smack.*

I shiver and squirm; this shit feels sooo good.

"It's a simple question, Tracy. You love fucking that crusty, dried-up nigga you fuck in this bed? Hmm?"

I shake my head even though I'm fighting not to get sucked into Kwame's mind games. Make no mistake about it. That's exactly what this is.

"No? Why did you marry him, then?" Kwame dips just the fat head of his cock into my sticky, pink candy, but then pulls out.

Groaning, I throw my hips at him to try and get him to put it back in.

"What? What do you want? You want some more of this good dick?"

"Yes. Shit. Stop playing."

"Then answer my questions. Why did you marry this fool?"

"You know why."

"I don't know shit. I get out the clink, looking for my wife, and I find out through your ex-crackhead momma that you done changed your name to some bullshit Sinclair and married some other brother. You know how disrespectful that shit is?"

To keep me from flipping the script, he dips his dick back in, gives me one good, long stroke, and pulls out again.

"I mean. I don't even know that I should even give you any of this dick. You threw the shit away, didn't you?"

Deep stroke.

"N-no."

"No? So you *do* want me to fuck you in your new man's bed, is that it?"

"Y-yes. Please."

Deep stroke.

"So I'm just your goddamn dildo now? Huh?"

"N-no."

"No? Sure looks that way to me."

Deep stroke.

"Tell me why you married him."

Deep stroke.

"F-for the . . . money."

"For his paper? Now, that's fucked up." He lifts my hips high into the air, then slams that black dick so far into me, I'm sure he can see that bitch's one eye in the back of my throat while I scream out of his name.

"That's right. Say that shit," Kwame demands, pumping and grinding like he just clocked in for work. "Out here giving brothers my pussy without asking my ass first. Baby, you must've been out here in the sun too damn long. This is my shit and it's always going to be my shit."

Smack. Pop. Squish.

"You hear my baby talking to me?" he boasts. "My pussy knows when daddy's home."

Ahh. Damn. Kwame's dick game is so damn fierce I don't know how I was thinking that Clevon came close. Every cell in my body is humming and coming at the same time. No lie. I'm struggling to keep oxygen in my lungs and after he flips me over, I don't even care about that anymore. This is heaven.

I must have passed out because when I came to Kwame was peeling open my sore legs again and telling me that break time was over. I never thought it was possible to OD on good dick, but today I'm coming dangerously close. As the hour grows late, I know that I'm going to have to get him out of here so I can clean and defunkify this bedroom. There's no way to mistake what the hell I've been doing in this bitch today.

Right now, I'm satisfied to be curled up under him and peppering his chest with small kisses. I feel so at peace right now. But then the shoe always drops.

"Yo, baby. I really do like this situation that you got out

here. Matter of fact, I can see myself making some big moves, too."

My eyes flutter open as reality finally arrives. "I'm thinking you can help me out and get things started out here. Start up my own gangster paradise, nawhatImean?"

I try to pull out of his arms, but he holds me close.

"I'm thinking about 100K is enough to get me set up. I'm sure you and Mr. Hollywood can manage that."

I choke. "W-what?" I finally manage to sit up.

Kwame calmly stares me dead in my eyes. "I can ask him if you'd like. Seeing how we're married to the same woman, it sort of makes us family."

"Are you blackmailing me?"

He actually has the nerve to look insulted. "What? No, I'm just looking to cash in on a good thing you got going. After all, *I'm* your real husband, and last I checked what's yours in mine. Well, at least half of it is, anyway."

I feel sick.

"Oh," he says, pulling me close again. "And I'm going to need that cheese by Friday."

25

Jaleesa

The paparazzi definitely knows my name now. Ever since Brijetta lost her damn mind and wailed on me like she did for no damn reason, cameras have been clicking in my face nonstop. Some of the shit I've seen splashed everywhere is just downright ridiculous. I've been labeled a femme fatale, home wrecker, tramp, whore, slut—you name it. But more importantly, my face and name are everywhere.

Look, the way I see it is if this shit is good enough for Angelina Jolie, then it's good enough for me. I just wish that I had at least slept with the dude—then at least I'd have something to tease the tabloids with. Maybe I should lie.

"Well, Ms. Thing, you're definitely back on top," Andy says, stretching back down for our weekly massage. "Those that say you can't sleep your way to the top of the heap don't know what the hell they're talking about."

I smile down at the floor while my masseuse rubs the small knot out just below my shoulder blades. "I've told you. Nothing happened."

"Uh-huh," he says, dubiously.

"C'mon, now. You're my boy. You know I would've told you if something went down. Brijetta just flipped her lid for no reason."

"No reason? Half the crew on that set has been bragging all up and down the blogosphere that you two were walled up in Mr. Superstar's trailer with the door locked. If y'all weren't bumping uglies, then what the hell were y'all doing?"

I shrug. "Chilling."

"Oh. Now I look like a silly bitch?"

I laugh. What else can I do? It is what it is. I could tell Andy what really went on, but I'm not ready to play the truth card just yet. I need to hold that shit in my pocket in case the directors or the producers try to squeeze me out of the picture because my face got busted up. I'm going to need their superstar golden boy, Trey Hamilton, to make sure that I don't lose my job—if he fails to do that, *then* I'll let the world know what the "say no to drugs" star does in his trailer during downtime.

My ass dabbling in drugs is not headline news. I've been a fierce advocate for the passage of marijuana in California ever since I got the right to vote. Kent Webber has crafted such a squeaky clean image for his number one client that the only damage control shocker his team had to manage was Trey marrying an ex-fatty nobody.

Now, I know that I should be more busted up over the fact that Brijetta got the wrong understanding about me and her man, but that shit can be rectified on another day. Right here, right now, I'm milking the publicity that she delivered on my lap. Besides, it's not like we're friends—friends. I know that bitch can't stand the ground I walk on. I ain't nowhere near stuck on stupid.

Plus, I went into that trailer fully expecting to fuck her man. I'm definitely a bitch who believes in sharing. And if Brijetta is going to survive being a superstar's wife, she needs to get with the program. I've said it before and I'll say it again: *None* of this shit is personal.

"All I got to say is be careful," Andy says, pulling me out of my internal rant. "Tabloid fame is tricky. If you play it right, it can serve a purpose; but if you get caught up, you'll look like

Robin Givens on the side of the road, wondering what the hell happened to your career. Remember: She had her claws in Brad Pitt waaay back in the day before she foolishly took that left turn down Mike Tyson Boulevard."

"Robin who?"

Andy sucks his teeth. "Y'all young Hollywood bitches need to study up."

After my much-needed spa treatment, I had a limousine service pick me up among another hoard of paparazzi and deliver me back to my West Hollywood condo. The only real surprise is Spencer Reid standing outside my door.

"Damn. I really need to talk to the superintendent about security in this building," I say, laughing and slipping my key into the lock.

"I figure that it would be better if I drop by and deliver the news instead of letting you get it at the security post tomorrow."

My heart drops just as my cell phone starts to ring.

"Or let you hear it from your agent," he adds.

I scoop my phone out from my pocket and, sure enough, Maury's name is on the caller ID. "You're shitting me," I say, glancing back up. "You're firing me because Trey Hamilton has a psycho wife?"

Spencer holds up his hands. "Please understand. This whole incident has us way behind schedule and over budget."

"And that's my fault?"

He cocks his head at me. "C'mon, Jaleesa. Seventy-six takes on a simple three-line scene. It's not like you were doing such a bang-up job before Trey's wife laid you out."

"It was a *lucky* punch. This bitch rolled up from out of nowhere."

He actually has the nerve to chuckle. "Regardless of how that shit went down, the Hughes brothers were already on my phone begging to pull you from the picture."

Doors up and down the hall start cracking open and other tenants start poking their heads out.

"Can we go inside your apartment and finish this conversation?" Spencer asks.

Steaming, I push open my door and allow him to follow me inside. "This shit won't stand," I tell him.

"Well, you didn't exactly do yourself any favors by showing up at my coproducer's church Sunday and issuing him veiled threats." Spencer closes the door behind him.

"I did no such thing."

He removes his jacket and cocks his head.

"It wasn't exactly a threat," I amend.

"Look. Omar is old school. He doesn't appreciate anybody talking to him sideways. You know what I mean? He wants everyone to know he's the head nigga in charge. He's been taking my head off for the last couple of days. Between him and the directors, I'm afraid that you're turning out to be a little more trouble than you're worth."

"So *you're* firing me?"

"I've been overruled," he says, seemingly still making himself comfortable.

"And what if I sue? What if I blab about how I got the part in the first place? Did he tell you about that shit?"

"Not saying yes. Not saying no. But can you prove it? We'll roll the outtakes." He shrugs. "I'm sorry. I really wanted to help you out." He reaches for me, but I step back.

"What? You think you're about to get some pussy now?" He blinks at me. "Man, if you don't get the fuck out of here with that nonsense, I'll bite that muthafucka off right now, so if you want a nub down there, go ahead and pull out your dick. Watch what happens."

"Oookay." Spencer retrieves his jacket from the back of the chair and starts backpedaling to the door. "You're upset."

"You think?"

"All right. I'm really sorry I couldn't do more for you."

"Just get the fuck out." I toss up my hands and roll my eyes. No matter what the hell goes down, a brother always thinks it's the perfect time for him to get his dick sucked.

Five minutes after he left, I stopped pacing around like a caged animal and decided I had no other choice but to play my last—and only—card: Trey Hamilton.

26

Brijetta

"Jaleesa's ass may or may not have been sleeping with Trey, but her ass has definitely been thinking about it," I tell Sinclair, sitting across from me at The Ivy. It feels so good to be finally talking to someone about this wild circus soap opera. I know talking to most of the Hollywood wives in this town would be talking directly to the gossip grapevine. From what I've been able to observe from Sinclair in the short time that I've known her, she seems to know how to keep her mouth shut.

"Do you believe that nothing happened?" she asks.

"He said nothing happened," I say carefully, with a half-hearted shrug. "I guess I believe him."

"That sounds like a full-throated endorsement." Sinclair reaches for her chilled margarita. "Look, maybe I'm not the one to discuss this with. I think it's unnatural for men and women to really be faithful—especially nowadays. There's way too much temptation out here, and sex doesn't always equal love."

I blink while I absorb that for a few minutes. "Does that mean . . . that you and Omar have an open relationship?"

The strangest grin slopes her mouth. "I'd be hard-pressed to tell you what Omar and I have; I'm just tossing my two cents out there. You can take it for what it's worth."

I'm suddenly not sure that Sinclair knows how this whole comforting thing works. "I guess." I reach for my own drink and proceed to sulk for a minute.

"I hurt your feelings," Sinclair says, leaning forward. "I'm sorry."

I wave her off. "No. No. You're just speaking your mind. I can respect that. I happen to have a more conservative view. I believe and expect my husband to keep his vows. If I can keep my pants zipped up, why can't he?"

"Because he has something else with a head down there. And I don't give a fuck what all these glossy advice columns tell you, that extra appendage has more than a fifty-fifty say on how men act or react. Human beings are animals. Our natural instincts are to attract and conquer—at least while we're in our prime. That's the physical part. It doesn't mean that *emotionally* you can't operate on a different level. But when we force a person to choose one or the other, that's when chaos begins— and a whole lot of lying. Not everything needs to be on the same scale as good versus evil. Heaven or hell. Sex or love. It's crazy all the unnecessary pressure we put on ourselves just so we can say we're civilized."

Oookay.

"Sorry," Sinclair says, then takes another gulp of her drink. "I didn't mean to get on a soapbox."

"It's okay." I allow a temporary silence to float between us. I'm stuck wanting to whine about my own problem and weighing whether to ask Sinclair if there was something wrong at her own crib. I realize that it's a bit selfish not to ask, but really, my plate is full. Plus, who am I to dish out advice when I'm the one who's made a big mess of my own shit? Pushing up my sunglasses, I turn my head and see the snapping photographers across the street.

"Don't they ever take a day off?" I complain.

"Doesn't seem like it." Sinclair glances back across the street. "They really are like vultures."

Another silence ripples between us, so I decide to change the subject from Jaleesa. "Well, one good thing has result from this whole mess," I tell her. "Trey finally fired Kent Webber."

Sinclair looks up. "His agent? Hell, I was surprised that he continued to represent him after Trey broke his jaw the last time. Now I hear the brother has so many stitches, he looks like Frankenstein."

"Now, that's a picture I'd like to see splashed all over the rags. Kent Webber is an asshole to the nth degree, but don't quote me on it. Every time I turn around, he was just always right there—with his shitty attitude and snide comments. I know what he said to me at that *Vanity Fair* party once. You were right there while I cried my eyes out in the ladies' restroom."

"I think being an asshole is a prerequisite in order to be anything in this town. Nice guys don't bother finishing in this town. From what I understand, Kent Webber is the best of the best. A lot people think he's the man who made Trey who he is today."

"And he's been paid handsomely for his services. Now it is time for us to move the fuck on. If I never see that man again, it'll be too soon."

Sinclair plops back in her chair and stares at me with a little annoying smirk.

"What?!"

"Nothing." She shrugs. "I've just never seen you like this before. I think Kent Webber gets under your skin more than Jaleesa."

"You can't possibly understand. There's just something about him that just . . . I don't know." I shudder when his face floats across my mind. "What killed me was how Trey always acts like he doesn't understand what I am talking about. It's not normal for his agent to *always* be around. The muthafucka even popped up on our honeymoon, wanting to talk about some bullshit movie. I mean, really. Our *honeymoon?*"

"Okay. I'd say that qualifies as someone with some bound-ary issues," Sinclair laughs.

"THANK YOU." I toss up my hand. "You want to know what Trey said? 'Aww, honey. You're just making a big deal out of nothing.' No shit. I was halfway expecting to wake up and find Kent's ass in bed with us."

Sinclair busts out laughing.

"The shit ain't funny, but good riddance to his ass. For real." I hold up my glass. "A toast."

Sinclair grabs her drink.

"To me, kicking ass and taking names. Don't fuck with me and my man."

"Amen." Sinclair continues laughing.

We downed our drinks and then placed our credit cards on the table in time for our waitress's next sprint by. Leaving The Ivy is a different matter; the moment I'm within thirty feet of my car, rogue members of the paparazzi jog up to me and start hammering me with questions that are none of their damn business.

"Mrs. Hamilton, will you and your husband be getting a divorce?"

"No!"

"Mrs. Hamilton, is it true that Trey and Jaleesa Love have been having an affair behind your back during the filming of his latest picture?"

"No!" I start jogging the rest of the way to my car.

"Mrs. Hamilton! Mrs. Hamilton, is it true that Jaleesa Love is carrying Trey's love child?"

"W-what? Where the hell do you people get this stuff?" I cram my key into the door of my Mercedes and try to open it. By that time, the rest of the paparazzi decided that they aren't about to let the rebels get a possible scoop and they charge to-ward me as well. "That's enough! Back away from the car," I shout, trying to close the driver's door.

One bold photographer grabs it and refuses to let go. "Mrs. Hamilton, how do you feel about your husband and Ms. Love continuing their affair now that they've been exposed?"

"Don't be ridiculous. There's no affair! Let go of my door, asshole!"

"Then what do you say to the reports that she's over at your estate right now?"

"What? That's a lie!"

"No, ma'am. We have a team of colleagues outside your place right now. She's there alone with your husband right now!"

I blink up at them and, as a result, every one of those bastards gets a perfect shot of my mouth dropping open. Suddenly blinded by the phalanx of bright flashes, I give the door one hard yank, not caring how many fingers I break. I start up the car, rev the engine once as a warning, and then peel out the parking lot with these sons of bitches jumping out of the way.

It's a miracle that I arrive home without the entire Los Angeles Police Department with their sirens blaring behind me, because I floated home in little less than fifteen minutes. My blood pressure shoots straight up when I see a limousine pull out of the gate and hang a right.

"No this bitch didn't!" I'm stunned—and torn between chasing after the limousine or whipping up into the estate and yanking a knot in Trey's ass. Also outside the gate is another team of photographers, snapping away. At the last second, I turn onto the property, punch in my security code, and jet on up to the house. When I jump out of the car, I don't bother with grabbing my purse or shutting off the engine.

"WHAT THE FUCK WAS THAT BITCH DOING HERE?"

Amaya takes one look at my face and scrambles out of the foyer. Trey turns to me with his hands up, ready to try and pacify me.

"AND DON'T GIVE ME ANY OF YOUR BULLSHIT. COME STRAIGHT WITH IT. ARE YOU FUCKING HER?"

"Brijetta, calm down."

"I DONE TOLD YOUR ASS ABOUT TELLING ME TO CALM DOWN. ARE YOU FUCKING HER?"

"NO!" he thunders back. "Think about it. What fucking sense does it make for us to be doing something right in front of an army of paparazzi *and* Amaya? Huh?"

That gives me a little pause. Trey isn't the smartest thing in the world, but he's far from being stupid.

"Then what the fuck was she doing here? I've never invited that heifer to this house, and she damn sure ain't welcome when my ass ain't here."

"She came to talk to me," he says, still urging me to lower my voice.

"What—the bitch ain't never heard of the telephone?"

"You wouldn't have been bitching about her calling?" he challenges.

"It's still better than her rolling her ass over here unannounced."

"Brijetta, give it up. It's bad enough that you laid the chick out for no damn reason and got her fired. She came here to ask me to help her get her job back."

"Fuck naw!"

"Why not?" He frowns. "It's not her fault that she got fired. It's not her fault that every tabloid in America is chasing us down and making up stories, either. This is all you flying off the handle for no other reason than you're paranoid."

"Paranoid?" I grab my hips and rock my neck at him. "If I'm paranoid, then whose damn fault is it? Who's always lying every time I turn around? Who's always flying high and manic-depressive in the next damn minute? If I'm paranoid, it's your damn fault. And I say the bitch can sit on the unemployment line. I don't give a rat's ass."

"Brijetta—"

"Nah, fuck that."

"Brijetta—"

"I don't want to hear it." I turn away. "You're not helping her, and that shit is final."

"She'll go to the press if I don't."

That stops me dead in my tracks. "Go to the press about what?"

He sighs and drops his head.

"Trey?" I turn back toward him. "What the fuck does she have to go to the press with?"

At his next wave of silence, I ball my hands at my sides.

He finally draws a deep breath. "She'll tell them what we were really doing in my trailer."

I brace myself as his gaze slowly travels up my face to meet my eyes.

"We were shooting up."

Without thinking, I just coldcock him dead in the mouth.

27

Trey

It'll never be said that my baby doesn't have a strong right hook. If I didn't know any better, I'd think she was related to either Ali or Tyson. I take the hit and restrain myself from lashing back because . . . well, I deserved it and I didn't want Momma Kate chasing after me. When I straighten my face and glance back at her again, I feel like a complete ass watching her eyes fill with tears. In the next second, she takes off running up the staircase and I'm stuck in the foyer, wondering why I can't ever seem to do anything right.

The bedroom door slams, causing a few windows to vibrate despite them being double paneled. I debate for a long time whether to go after Brijetta, but I think this time I should give her a couple hours to calm down. I need a hit, but settle on a drink at the bar in the living room. I down two shots and notice Amaya shuffling around the place, trying to look busy.

"Take the rest of the day off, Amaya," I say. "You've earned it." Really I just want her to stop watching me like a goddamn hawk. I don't know how many times I've told Brijetta to fire the woman, to no avail.

"Okay. I'm just going to go check on—"

"I *said* LEAVE!" The bitch finally scrambles out the living room and a few seconds later, I hear the front door slam. "Good riddance." I pour another shot and stew for a little while. After I get the right buzz going, I feel the stress of the day slowly flow out of me. Still, I pour one more drink and pull out my iPhone to place a call to Spencer Reid.

"Yo, Trey baby, talk to me!" Spencer answers like a true caricature of the exact type of dude that works in Hollywood.

"We got a problem," I tell him.

"Talk to me."

"I hear y'all took Jaleesa off the picture," I say, jumping to the point. "I can't see me finishing this without her, man."

"What? Whoa. Let's slow this thing down, Trey. Our decision to remove Ms. Love has nothing to do with whatever situation you guys got going on. This is a business decision. Nothing more, nothing less."

I down what's left in my glass. "Well, then consider I'm making a business decision of my own. No Jaleesa—no Trey."

"What? Are you listening to yourself? You're talking about walking off the set of a major picture for some supporting actress role. Is that really the fight that you want to pick?"

"Is that the one that you want to pick?"

"Trey . . . if you walk, we will sue your ass—"

"Not before you lose a big chunk of money yourself. You'd either have to shelf this picture or start from scratch with another lead actor. I'm thinking you won't have the financial backing to do that."

A long, lengthy silence hangs over the phone.

"Just hire her back, man. Make it easier on both of us."

Spencer expels a long breath. "Omar ain't going to like this shit, man. He hates ultimatums more than I do."

"That's all right. Give him my number. He can holler at me."

"Trust me, I will." Spencer laughs. "See you on the set?"

"Ms. Love has her job back?" I ask.

"As far as I'm concerned she never lost it."

"Thanks, man. I appreciate it."

"Uh-huh. Seems like a lot a trouble for a woman you supposedly ain't fucking."

"That sounds like a question." I pour another drink. "I don't like answering questions about my personal life."

"Smart man. See you on the set." Spencer disconnects the call and I follow suit.

At least I got that shit out of the way. I pull the number Jaleesa gave me out of my back pocket and dial. She answers on the first ring. "It's done," I tell her. "You got your job back."

"Oh. Thank God, Trey. Thank you sooo much."

"Yeah—well. I trust that, uh, what all went down that day will remain between us?"

"Absolutely. You got to know that I hate even having to bring it up, but it seemed like I was the only one getting unjustly crucified on the stake here. It wasn't fair. You understand?"

I guess she has a point, but I still didn't like the threat of being blackmailed either way. "All right, then. I guess I'll just see you on the set."

"Great. Um . . ."

"What is it?"

"Oh, nothing," she lies easily enough. "I was just wondering if you told Brijetta . . ."

"Let's just leave my wife out of this."

"Of course. Of course. I apologize. The last thing I want to do is bring any unnecessary pain to Brijetta. I thought before this that we were friends and I guess I'm hoping that we will be again."

"That's something you're going to have discuss with her. I do know better than to get in the middle of two women." I start to say my good-byes when she asks, "What about you? How are you doing?"

Finally. Someone is asking me how I feel about something for a change. Next thing I know I'm talking to Jaleesa for two hours.

TREY HAMILTON THREATS TO WALK
IF LOVER IS FIRED

Brijetta plops *Hollywood Gawker* right on top of my bacon and eggs the next morning. "I hope your ass is happy now!"

"Do you mind?" I remove the paper and its offensive headline from off my breakfast and continue to munch. "I don't know why you bother reading that trash, anyway. None of the shit in this stuff is true, anyway."

"It doesn't have to be true for people to believe it, Trey. You ought to know that by now."

"So what do you want me to do?" I say, exasperated. "Tell me and I'll be more than happy to do it."

"How about you spare me the sarcasm? Just recognize that I'm mad and I have the right to be mad."

"All right. You have the right to be mad." I toss up my hands. "I have to go."

"What? You're in a hurry to see your girlfriend? Are y'all going to kick back and shoot up a little before makeup and wardrobe?"

"No, Mommy. But maybe you'd like to come to the set and babysit me today."

"You need a damn babysitter." She cuts her eyes away and folds her arms.

"I'm going to pretend you didn't say that and take my butt into work. You do remember what going to work is like, don't you?"

I hear her gasp as I walk away.

"And what the hell is that supposed to mean?"

"It's pretty self-explanatory. Maybe you wouldn't be so wound up if you had something to do instead of just waiting for me to screw up." I grab my jacket and head toward the door.

"Is that supposed to be a joke?"

"I don't want to fight."

"Let you tell it, you never want to fight. But every time I turn around you're starting shit."

"Bye, Jaleesa." *Fuck!*

"WHAT? WHO THE FUCK DID YOU JUST CALL ME?"

I close my eyes and exhale. "Sorry. I didn't mean anything by it. Don't get the wrong idea. You put the article in front of me and her name was just on my mind."

She bobs her head and starts pacing back and forth. Any sudden moves and my ass is going to get decked again. Finally, she starts backing up. "Fine. Take your ass on. Do you."

"Brijetta—"

"Gone. Get out of my face since you don't want to fight."

I exhale and turn toward the door. I'll call and have some flowers sent later. Maybe that will chill her out. I hop in my car and roll out of the estate. I have to be careful not to take out any of the paparazzi that have lined up bright and early this morning. Once on set, I make it over for the dailies with the directors. Everyone is all smiles, but I know that they hate the type of publicity the picture is getting right now.

After the dailies, I head straight over to my trailer to review the day's shooting scenes only to find the bitch isn't empty.

"Kent."

He stands with his hands up. It's my first time seeing him since the fight, and I'm a little stunned by the damage I'd done to his face. On the right side of his face it's a deep purple with crude stitches running up the side. "Look. Just hear me out."

I shake my head and step back. "Man, this is not a good time."

"When is it a good time? You're not taking any of my calls, and when I try the house that bit—I'm sorry, your *wife* just hangs up on me."

"There isn't a good time. We're through, remember?"

Kent's eyes glisten while he holds my gaze. "How can you

say that?" he croaks. "After all we've been through together—how can you just cut me off like this? Huh?" He cocks his head. "You want me to apologize to Brijetta? Is that it? Fine. I'll apologize. I've been a dick to her, I'm sorry. I'll even send her over some chocolates and flowers, if that's what it takes. What does she like, Godiva? Everybody loves Godiva, right?"

I'm uncomfortable with his pleading tone. "Kent. That's not going to help, man."

"Don't say that."

"It's the truth, man. I don't know what you want me to say."

"I want you to accept my apology and let things go back to normal." His voice cracks, but he quickly coughs to try and cover that up. "We're a good team, Trey—in and out of the bed. You know this."

I glance around, relieved that I'd remembered to close the door. "I can't do this here."

"Then where? You tell me when and where we can talk and I'll meet you."

"No. No." I toss my hands up and shake my head. I can't backtrack. I can't. I've wanted to end this with Kent for so long and thought that I couldn't. Now that I have, I'm more than okay with using Brijetta as an excuse.

"Just think about it," Kent pleads. "I can step back. I can give you two more room if that's what you want. I'll do whatever. Just don't cut me out of your life."

I cradle my head in one of my hands.

"Please," he croaks again. "I'm begging." He steps closer to me. "You know how I feel about you. How I've always felt about you."

Before I know it, he's right up on me, stroking the side of my face. Feelings that I've been fighting, doping, and pleading with start rising to the surface again, confusing me. How? How on earth can I be in love with two people? And worse yet, how can one be a woman and the other a man?

Kent starts pulling my head from behind my hands and forcing me to look at him. "I love you, Trey. I will *always* love you."

"I love you, too." I nod, finally welcoming his lips.

PART III

What's done in the dark will come to the light. . . .

28

Sinclair

"Here's your damn money!" I toss yet another manila envelope onto the bed and then stand back and fold my arms. This shit has been going on for two months, and other than the sex, I'm getting tired of it.

Kwame ignores me and my attitude while he reaches across my bed to check if his bundles of cash are indeed all there. "Damn, girl. You're like my own private little Santa Claus."

"Well, Christmas is over. I'm not going to be able to get you any more cash—not without raising Omar's suspicions."

"Now, let's distinguish what is my problem and what is yours. Keeping that Hollywood brother in check definitely falls into the category of being *your* problem." He tosses the envelope onto the nightstand and then pats the empty spot on the bed next to him. "Now get your fine ass over here and show daddy just how much you missed him."

I stand there pretending I'm not about to give him what he wants for about two seconds before my legs start moving on their own.

"That's right. Stop fronting. You know nobody knows how to give it to you like daddy." When I'm close, Kwame reaches for my hand and then pulls me down onto the bed. He starts peppering kisses all on the back of my ear and down my neck, and I instantly wet my panties with my own creamy, colorless honey.

Our sweet, tender petting ends abruptly for a few seconds when Kwame grips the back of my head and our eyes connect.

"Don't you *ever* tell me what you're not going to do again," his hisses. "If I want to take all that nigga's shit, your job is to say, 'Yes, sir. How can I help you?' You understand?"

I struggle to nod my head.

Kwame's grip loosens, while his gaze starts to drink in my profile again. "I'm going be honest with you. I ain't feeling all this sharing shit. The money is nice, but something is going to have change after a while. You know this shit, right?"

I absolutely know this. The question is what. What chess pieces do I need to move around in order for my ass to be set and happy? Omar has the cash, but Kwame has my heart.

"Tell you what. I'll give you all your money back if you just walk away with me today."

Silence.

"Uh-huh. I thought so." He shakes his head.

I already know that I can't get my hands on any real cash by just walking away from the marriage. The only obvious answer is to get rid of Omar—but that depends on the settlement in the will. Even if that lines up in my favor, every fiber in my body tells me that getting rid of Omar is not going to be as simple as it sounds. He's a high-profile man, not some brother who's just holding down a curb in Detroit that no one gives a damn about. Anything shady has the potential to be splashed across the news and tabloids for forever.

Too risky.

"Just think about it, Tracy. We could take old dude out and have all this shit for ourselves," Kwame says, peeling me out of my clothes. "No more creeping. We can make love every morning and every night. Would you like that, baby?"

How could I say no to that with his lips skimming across

my puckered nipples and his fingers swishing just below my clit?

"You and I are soul mates, baby. We've both known that from the beginning." He takes my hand and wraps it around his growing cock. "You know every inch of this is yours, right?"

I like the idea of me owning the best real estate on his body, but is his dick a fair exchange for Omar's money? That's as far as I get thinking about this dilemma because when Kwame enters me and starts doing what he does best, all I'm concerned about is how many orgasms I can squeeze in during our short time together.

Kwame has always been a great lover, but I can tell his hammering hips and his nasty talk had more to do with competing with Omar than trying to satisfy me—which he did, anyway. I could've told him that he didn't have to try so hard, he easily put Omar's dick game to sleep, but I went on letting Kwame deep-stroke me into a near coma because I'm a greedy bitch. But then something registers in my brain despite the lofty clouds floating in my head.

Did I just hear the door? My eyes fly open while Kwame's face continues to twist and distort as he fights off coming too soon. "What was that noise?" I ask.

"The bottom of your pussy falling out," he chuckles. His hips slap the bottom of my ass.

"No. No," I pant. "I think someone is in the house."

"Ahh. Sheeiit, baby. Squeeze those muscles for me," he says, ignoring me.

I try to push him away. "Omar may be home." Suddenly I pick up the sound of low voices, as well as a set of keys jingling.

Mindless, Kwame keeps ramming. "Then you better hurry up and get this nut before your boy walks in here," he warns, grinning devilishly.

"Stop, Kwame. Get off me," I hiss.

"I'm not stopping until I get what I came for." Clearly, he means it, because instead of hurrying, his thrusts slow and he starts grinning like we still had all the time in the world for this shit.

"Stop playing." I try to pull my legs down from over my head, but he's having none of that. If anything, his grip on my calves tightens while the juices smacking in between us grow louder. "You're crazy. We're going to get caught."

"Fuck him," Kwame spats. "He can sit his ass down over there in the corner for all I care. Now squeeze your muscles the way I like it."

Oh my God! He's serious. I push, squirm, and wiggle, trying to get out of this taco position, while all Kwame does is hiss and moan softly.

"Yeah, baby. That's it. Make daddy come."

I don't believe this! This is the same kind of hardheaded bullshit that got Kwame busted the last time. His ass is always trying to prove a point. Now I hear laughter in the house. Omar is not alone.

"Sinclair! Are you up there, sweetheart?" he calls up the staircase.

Oh shit. Think. Think.

Kwame smiles down at my panic. "Your man is calling. You better answer him."

"Y-yes, honey! I'll be down in a minute."

"In a minute, huh?" Kwame finally picks up the tempo. My head rams the headboard.

"Kwame, stop," I hiss again. "This shit ain't funny." He's not trying to hear me; he's having too much fun torturing me. Unbelievably, I feel my own nut start to rise just when I'm convinced I hear Omar's expensive leather shoes slap the marble staircase.

"You better come, baby. You better come. Your boy is going to catch you fucking your real husband if you don't crack this nut."

I beg and pant at the same time. "Ahh. Kwame—please."

"There you go. There you go. Squeeze, baby."

Bodies slapping, headboard banging, Kwame and I finally explode. But there's no time to languish in my usual euphoric high. I renew my efforts to push him off of me, and this time he falls over to the other side of the bed with a sigh.

"Get into the closet," I bark, jumping up and gathering our clothes.

Kwame stretches back against the pillows. Scared that he's just going to sit there and wait for Omar to come into the room, I quickly grab him by the wrist and tug.

"I swear if you fuck this up, I'll never forgive you."

"Well, I guess we can't have that," he says, finally sitting up.

I take the sheets off the bed while Kwame snatches up his manila envelope of cash.

"In the closet. In the closet." I push and shove. What in the hell is wrong with this man?

"Wait. Wait," Kwame laughs. "Don't you think that it's time for your two husbands to finally meet?"

"You're not funny." I give him one final shove into the closet and then slam shut the door. I then turn, race to the window so I can get some air up in here, run to the adjoining bathroom to grab a robe, and then park my ass on the bench in front of the vanity just as Omar opens our bedroom door.

"There you are," Omar says. "Didn't you hear me? We have guests downstairs."

"I didn't know you were bringing people over," I say calmly, though my heart is beating a mile a minute.

"It's sort of a spontaneous thing. Shake a leg and come play hostess. They are important people from Lion's Gate."

I smile. "Give me five minutes and I'll be right down."

Omar nods, but then takes a quick glance around the room. I'm almost sure that he wants to ask about the sheet-less bed, but mercifully he just slips out the room without another word.

I wait a few seconds after the door clicks closed before jumping out of my seat and rushing back over to the closet. "You have to get out of here."

Kwame grins. "And *you* have to come up with some more money. Two hundred thousand . . . by Friday or I'll introduce myself to Mr. Producer."

"What?"

"Or you can leave with me right now."

"Kwame!"

"Friday it is, then."

Now ain't this about a bitch?

29

Omar

I know that bitch is up to something. I don't know what it is, but I sense that it's something. Here I'm thinking that I had established who rules this house and what is expected, only to see betrayal has reared it ugly head. When will I learn that women only know how to use and deceive men? I should go ahead and kick her ass to the curb, leave her busted and disgusted while I pick up the next trophy wife. It's not like there would be a problem. This town is crawling with beautiful airheads—but there's a strong part of me that wants to conquer Sinclair's strong will. She's fascinating. During our brief marriage, I find her to be a complicated puzzle that I can't put down until I snap together all the small pieces. One day, she's sweet and lovable, and then the next strong and independent, and then there are days when she can pretend to be humble and obedient. We have a wonderful game between us that I want to win for no other reason than to stroke my ego.

She's cheating. I suck in a deep breath, uncomfortable with the idea of disloyalty. *She's cheating.* I grind my back teeth together because I've sensed this for the past couple of months but have been unable to prove it. Sometimes I'm convinced that I smell another man's cologne on her skin or even our sheets. Next thing I know she's buying me the same cologne as a way to cover her tracks. She claims to love it so much that she started wearing it, too. Clever girl. But I know what I know.

I tried beating it out of her again, but I've learned that a technique never works twice with her. Getting that Clevon character's name out of her only came because I had the element of surprise. So I put Matthew back on the case, and in three weeks he's come up with nothing. He's convinced that she's not on the creep and that the whole thing is just my imagination. I'm not buying it. A man's intuition is every bit as strong as a woman's. Trust and believe. She's cheating. I just have to catch her at it. When I do, heaven help her.

I join my guests back downstairs and I smile benignly at them. With *Defiance* wrapping filming in the coming weeks, Spencer and I are back in fund-raising mode for our next project. Our main nuisance at the moment is the whole tabloid fiasco our current star has been generating. These sorts of overhyped soap operas tend to have severe blowback on a film.

"Trust me," Spencer is telling the small crowd, "all this nonsense will soon blow over. We have a hit on our hands. It might do for us to even start thinking about a sequel. I've been talking to the screenwriter, Nelsan Reynolds; he has a lot of interesting ideas that can turn this puppy into a franchise."

Everyone's heads start bobbing along at the same time.

I hook on my usual Cheshire smile, clap my hands one time together, and ask, "Anyone care for a drink? I'll play bartender while we wait for the hostess to join us." I get a few orders of whiskey sours and dry martinis as I head over to the bar. Lining up the glasses, I'm still amazed that the six-week bartending course I took while in college still comes in handy.

Quinn Starr, a silver-haired cat who has been in the game since the days of such greats like Hitchcock, saddles up to the bar. "So tell me, Omar. All bullshit aside, is there any truth to what's being reported in the rags about Trey Hamilton?"

I laugh. "Don't tell me that you pay attention to that stuff."

"Only when it's interesting," he volleys. "There's a kernel

of truth in every lie. Besides, I have a project with another production company and they've been tossing the idea of approaching Trey Hamilton for the lead. I just want to know whether the man is worth the money and the hassle."

"Judging by the dailies, I'd say that he is. I just suggest that you bar his psycho wife from the set." I wink and hand him his drink.

He and the few others who had crowded around the bar laugh.

"Sounds like you all are having a good time in here," Sinclair says as she sweeps into the room.

All eyes turn toward my wife, who in five minutes managed to turn into a knockout. My suspicions aside, I give props where props are due. Sinclair is very good at playing hostess. She has mastered who needs to be charmed, who needs to be listened to, and who needs their ego stroked. These sorts of attributes are instinctual and it reminds me of why I'd married her in the first place—other than the fact that she's quite convincing when she's faking an orgasm.

Watching her work, I pour myself a drink. In no time at all, she has our guests in the palm of her hand.

"Well, it looks as though you married yourself another winner," Quinn says from across the bar.

"You think so?"

He shrugs. "I like her. Ever thought about getting her into the business? Lord knows that she has the face and body for it."

I look over at Sinclair and drink in her profile. This isn't the first time someone suggested that she needed to be in front of the camera. "I don't know. Maybe," I say noncommittally.

"Maybe?" Quinn shakes his head. "You're sitting on top of a goldmine. I know I could make a mint off of her. Your problem is that you just don't like sharing."

Talk about hitting the nail on the head.

"You never have. I could tell when you were married to Zayna."

Just the mention of my ex-wife causes a vein to twitch along my temple. "I'm not going to lie," I tell him. "It took a while to get used to that sort of celebrity."

"You mean the kind when the attention isn't focused on you?"

A smile hitches up one side of my mouth.

Quinn throws his head back and laughs. "You know that your problem is the same as every alpha male: ego. We don't like the word *Mister* in front of a woman's name. Mr. Halle Berry. Mr. Oprah Winfrey. Mr. Zayna Eliot."

I tip my head toward him.

"We want the spotlight for ourselves," he continues. "*That* I can't blame you for. I can't see myself married to a self-made woman, either. It's unnatural. There's only room for one set of balls in a marriage."

The comment catches me off guard so much that I throw my head back with a hearty laugh. In doing so, out the corner of my eye I catch sight of something outside the window. On closer inspection, it turns out to be *someone*. More specifically— a man. Black, about 6'3", and looking dead at me. Our gazes lock for a few long seconds and then the bastard smiles at me.

Smiles!

I set my drink down and watch as this asshole turns and jogs off. *What the fuck?*

"Omar? Is there something wrong?" Quinn asks, and tries to follow my gaze just when the man disappears from sight.

I swivel my head back to Sinclair, who's still busy, laughing and holding court in the center of the room. At this moment, I realize that she has to be the boldest bitch I've ever met.

She turns and looks at me, smiling, that deceiving whore she is. Our gazes meet and I reach and then hold up my glass and try to telepath, *Your ass is grass.*

30

Kwame

Yeah, I know you see me. I stare dead into this uppity brother's face and give him a smile before I turn and take my sweet time jogging off his property with another 100K of his money tucked under my arm. Real talk? I'm not down with all this pussyfooting around. Just like I'm getting tired of all this damn creeping I've been doing—with my own damn wife. I don't know how much longer Tracy thinks I'm going to allow her to play this cat's wife, but I'm here to tell you that it ain't going to be much longer.

In the past two months I've whispered, hinted, and even plotted on ways we could get rid of this cat, but it's like she ain't hearing me. Then I start wondering if I'm the one she wants to get rid of; but every time I work her body over, I know that shit ain't the case. Clearly Mr. Producer ain't handling business in the bedroom, because when she's up under me her body is telling me things she don't want me to hear. Just like I'm seeing some shit she doesn't want me to see. A couple of weeks back I came over to see a few welts on her back and legs, but she claimed she'd walked into a wasp's nest. I didn't buy it, but I also can't see Tracy just letting some man beat on her, either. So I'm keeping my eye out on the situation, and if I find out that old dude is putting his hands on her like that, then I'm just going to have to go back in and serve another bid.

So it must be the paper that she can't walk away from. A part of me can respect that. After all, we're both two former hood rats trying to stay out of the gutter. Only those who grew up hungry can judge us.

Again, that doesn't mean that I'm going to bide by this bullshit much longer. In two months I done siphoned off a little less than a million on sugar daddy, which tells me there's millions more to play with. We can really come up if we play our cards right. Then again, maybe I should take care of this on my own. Put in a call back home and see if I can get a little help putting a plan together.

I'm warming up to that idea as I complete the jog back to my empty mansion I'm borrowing just two houses down. I don't expect that it will be too easy to get back onto the Fines' estate after that little stunt I pulled. Now that I've exposed myself to him, I'm willing to bet every dollar I've taken from him that at this time tomorrow surveillance cameras will be installed on the property. Getting back into between Tracy's legs is going to require some Tom Cruise *Mission Impossible* stunts.

That's all right. I don't regret a damn thing. Like I said, I don't need Tracy's permission to get rid of that Apollo Creed wannabe muthafucka.

"Excuse me, sir, but who in the hell are you?" a woman's voice whips out at me.

I instantly freeze while the front door swings closed behind me. Across the foyer a pair of familiar powder blue eyes. Then it hits me, she's the chick on the "For Sale" sign out in the yard.

"Are you the one that's been living here, sir?" She folds her arms. "I received a call from the neighbors saying they've seen someone of your description. Did the Monroes give you permission to be here?"

"Yeah—um. I'm friends with Mr. Monroe. He said that I could kick here at his crib while he was out of town."

Her brows hiked up. "Interesting. I talked to Mr. Monroe this afternoon and he said that no one should be here."

"Huh. Are you sure? Damn, I left a message on his answering machine and just figured everything was cool when I didn't hear back from him."

Her frosty gaze tells me that she's not buying my story. "Would you like for me to call him again and let you talk to him?" She starts to dig through her purse.

"Nah. Nah. That's all right. I was leaving today, anyway."

"Great. That sounds like that would be for the best. I'd hate to have to call the police and have you removed."

"Whoa. Whoa. That won't be necessary. I'll just go grab my things now."

Still staring at me, she calmly folds her arms and taps her foot. I guess that means that she'll wait. With no choice, I turn and run on up the stairs so I can grab my things. I remain smiley and cordial as I load up my bag into my rental. Even as I start the car, she right there still giving me the stink eye. But just for shits and giggles, I ask, "Hey, uh, you got a brochure I can look at? You know I'm in the market for a place."

For a brief moment, her frown turns upside down at the prospect of a buyer, but then I watch as her gaze hits the tats running up my arm and her thin lips curl downward again. "I don't think that this property is in your price range."

It was my turn to stare at her. I calmly reach over to my black duffle bag, unzip it, and let her get a small peek at Omar's cash. "That's too bad."

Her mouth drops open as I shift the car into Drive and leave her ass with her mouth open. I float out of the neighborhood and hang a right. Feeling like I need to treat myself, I drop over 30K for a Verdana suite room at the Beverly Wilshire for the next month. The place is completely off the chain. I swear to God, Beverly Hills is a place I can really get used to. I can do anything out here, become anybody—just like Tracy.

For the first time, I entertain the thought of letting her go. Like her momma said, she's doing fine without me. I think I finally understand that song "If You Love Somebody Set Them Free." But Tracy is in my system. If I haven't been able to shake her in the past ten years, what hope do I ever have? Nah. Tracy and I belong together. I'll give her a little more time to come to her senses; then I'm going to have to make my move—with or without her permission. Standing outside on the veranda, I reach into my pocket and dig out my cell phone.

"Yo, Mike. What up?"

31

Jaleesa

"C'mon now, Trey. You know you can talk to me about anything," I purr as I snuggle down in my bed, preparing to give him my full attention. "We're friends, right? Aren't friends supposed to talk and listen to one another?" I listen as he pulls in a long breath. For weeks now, I've been at this. Hanging around, showering him with attention even though he professes that we should cut it out because of all the media attention. My constant answer to that: Why should we concern ourselves with the lies they print? We know we're just friends.

For now that's true, but I have plans. Big plans. And frankly, Brijetta's nagging ass is going to help me achieve them. Sure, it's clear to me now that her little golden ticket has a bit of a drug problem; but hell, in this industry it would be breaking news if an actor didn't. I don't mind dabbling from time to time, but I know when to cut that shit out. I've seen waaay too many actresses cracked out in the ladies' rooms in many a nightclub to know all the shit floating out here has a way of sneaking up on you when you least expect it.

Despite that, I still go to Trey's trailer in between takes, but I hit his weed stash more than that harder stuff he be fucking with.

I'm a little put off that Trey has yet to make any move toward me sexually so far, even when he's high as hell, but I'm working on changing that right now. Also, I can't complain about the perks of being Trey's new *friend*. Upon his recommendation, Kent Webber offered to represent me last week. Trust and believe I accepted that offer and then tossed Maury's flaky ass to the curb. It's well known that Kent Webber is about his business. He can turn waitresses and garbage collectors into superstars overnight. Just hours after signing the paperwork, his office called me with three projects—two of which I don't even have to screen-test for. Talk about jackpot. I can't remember the last time I took a call from Maury's office. It was usually my ass begging for him to call me.

"Fine, then," I tell him after a long silence. "If you don't want to talk about it, you don't have to. There's no pressure. I was just noticing that you seem more . . . distracted lately. Is everything good at home?"

He pulls another sigh. "Well, you know, me and Brijetta have been going at it again. She thinks I don't know that piece of shit maid is spying on me. Every time I turn around the bitch is standing right there. Shit. Go clean something. Right?"

I laugh. "Then why don't you fire her?"

"Man, if I had a nickel for every time I did that shit, I could wipe out world hunger. I fire her and Brijetta hires her right back."

"Damn. That's foul. Aren't you the one making the money?"

"That's what I said!"

"And what? She's not letting you be the man of the house?"

Silence, but I can picture him shaking his head. "It's cool, though, I guess," he says, backpedaling like he always does. "B puts up with a lot of my shit. You just don't know."

"So *she* wears the pants in the marriage?"

"Now, I didn't say all of that."

"Then what you saying, then?" I challenge. "She has the right to overrule you because what—you're not perfect? Is she perfect?"

"Hell naw!"

"Because if she is let a bitch know. I've never met a saint before."

He laughs. "Get out of here. Stop playing."

I snuggle closer to the phone. "Nah, I'm just saying that I've known Brijetta a long time and, no offense, she needs to thank her lucky stars that she even has a man like you. I know for a fact that she went all through high school *and* college without a single boyfriend. Now she's married to the hottest actor in the business? C'mon now."

"Yeah, well. I don't know nothing about all of that, I just know that . . . she's perfect for me."

I pull the phone away from my face and frown at the mutha-fucka. *I think this brother is serious.*

"I can't explain it," he's saying when I put the phone back to my ear. "I can't explain a lot of shit."

Silence, but this time I'm shaking my head. Then finally, he asks, "Have you ever been in love, Jaleesa?"

Love?

"I'm going to take that as a 'no,'" he chuckles.

"I've been in a number of relationships."

"That's not what I asked."

During the next silence, my mind drifts back to high school. I so clearly picture Darrin Savoy's young face smiling and laughing and then eventually begging. . . .

"I know what love is," I admit. "Even though at the time I didn't recognize it."

"Ah," he says softly. "I've been there before, too." Pause. "But I think the worst is being in love with two people at the same time."

Hope springs into my heart. "Two?"

"WHO IS THIS?" Brijetta's voice cracks like a whip over the line. "TREY—WHO THE FUCK ARE YOU TALK-ING TO?"

"I think I better let you go," I say.

"Baby, it's not what you think," Trey starts.

"JALESSA? IS THAT YOU?"

"I'll talk to you tomorrow, Trey."

"AWW, HELL NAWW!" She slams the phone down, but I can still hear her on the other line. "TREY!"

"Shit," Trey mutters before disconnecting the line without a good-bye.

Laughing, I finally hang up. *Serves that bitch right.* If you ask me, driving that bitch crazy is the perfect revenge for that sucker punch she laid on me on the set. It's not my fault that she doesn't recognize a good man when she sees one—but I can sure as hell scoop him up when she foolishly tosses him away.

I peel back the sheets and climb out of bed, but by the time I make it to the kitchen for a bottle of water, my phone is ringing off the hook. Given the late hour, I know *exactly* who it is.

"Hello?"

"WHAT THE FUCK ARE YOU DOING CALLING MY MAN?"

Calmly, I open the refrigerator. "I didn't call him. *He* called me."

Brijetta's voice drifts away from the headset. "SHE SAID YOUR ASS CALLED HER. IS THAT TRUE?" There's a loud smack. "ANSWER ME, DAMN IT!"

Now I can't help but laugh at her silly ass.

"Go on now, Brijetta. Stop playing."

"DOES IT LOOK LIKE I'M PLAYING WITH YOU?" *Smack!* "I CAN'T BELIEVE THAT YOU HAVE THE NERVE TO BE CALLING THIS BITCH!"

"Whoa. Whoa. Who are you calling a bitch?" I shout.

"YOU'RE RIGHT. YOU'RE A TRICK-ASS HO. BETTER?"

"And you're Coo-Coo for Cocoa Puffs, B. Don't be calling

me out of my Christian name just because you can't control your man."

"CHRISTIAN? TRICK, DON'T ACT LIKE THE LORD KNOWS YOUR NAME!"

"Whatever."

"AND I DON'T TRY TO CONTROL TREY. I TRY TO PROTECT HIM!"

"Uh-huh." I roll my eyes and take a long swig of water.

"He doesn't know you like I do," she growls. "I know your ass is foul. It's always been foul. You don't care about nothing and no one as long as you get what you want. Well, I got something for your ass. Come around my man again and watch what happens."

Bored, I huff. "Yeah. Yeah. What are you going to do?"

Click.

I glance down and then hang up the phone. "Whatever, bitch."

32

Brijetta

"Baby, calm down," Trey insists, trying to grab hold of me. "Where you think you're going?"

"Where the fuck you think?" I yell, pushing him away. "What the hell do you think you're doing all up on the phone with her late at night?"

"Nothing, baby. We were just talking. Damn!"

"TALKING?" My hands ball up at my sides as I start pacing back and forth like a heavyweight champ. "Say that shit again and watch what happens."

Trey holds his hands up and takes a step back. "I know you don't believe me, but it's the truth."

"You wouldn't know the truth if it bit you on your ass," I snap back. "Have you ever told me the truth about anything?"

"C'mon on now, B. Stop being so damn dramatic. There's nothing going on."

"Puh-lease. Stop playing me stupid. You're fucking the girl. You gotta be. Because everywhere I turn, there she is—cheesing and grinning in my face—talking to *my* husband in the middle of the night. And what's your excuse? 'Oh, baby. We're just friends.' Let me tell you something since you're stuck on stupid: You're married. You can't have muthafuckin' female friends. You got that? You can have coworkers and colleagues. That's it."

"Okay. Now, you're tripping."

"No, you're tripping," I say, mushing him in the head. "I know women. I especially know that low-down trifling ho. I've known her since junior high. Have you ever seen me invite her over here? Have you ever wondered why? Let me spell it out for you: She's. Not. Welcome. The heifer even tried to make a play for my own damn daddy!"

Trey rolls his eyes. "Tsk. Get out of here."

"Call my momma." I cross my arms. "Hear what she tells you." For the first time I think I'm finally getting through to his ass. "Damn, Trey. It wasn't too long ago that she was threatening you to go to the press if you didn't save her job. Now you two are buddy-buddy? C'mon now." I mush his head again. "Think."

Trey sighs and then slowly bobs his head. "All right. Fine. I'll stay away from her."

"Well, hallelujah!" I storm around him and head toward the door.

"Where are you going?" he asks me again.

"Where do you think?"

"B, let it go!" He keeps saying that shit all the way out to my car, but I ignore him. This situation between Jaleesa and I has been a long time coming, and it's just time for us to clear the air.

Dressed in my silk nightgown and houses shoes, I arrive at Jaleesa's West Hollywood condominium and slip right on through the door with a posse of drunken actresses coming through the door at the same time. In the elevator, they all snicker and ask which floor my booty call is on. I give them a look and they leave me the hell alone. Arriving on Jaleesa's floor, I shoot out the small box and jet down the hallway.

Bam! Bam! Bam!

"C'mon, bitch. Open this goddamn door," I mutter under my breath and start pacing like a boxer again. "C'mon. C'mon."

Bam! Bam! Bam!

Finally, I think I hear footsteps on the other side of the door. I don't even bother hiding from the peephole. I ain't scared of this bitch, and it's time to see whether her ass can talk all that shit about controlling my man in my face.

"Brijetta, what the hell are you doing here?" Jalessa asks through the door.

"What the fuck you think, bitch? Open the door!"

She sighs loudly. "B, go home. You're making a fool out of yourself."

"And you're acting like the punk bitch I always knew you were. You talk all kinds of shit on the phone. Put on your big-girl panties and open the door now." Behind me, I hear locks disengage and doors crack open. "I have no problem standing out here and telling your neighbors about your skanky ass. Let them know how you chase around after other women's husbands!"

"Girl, puh-lease. Take your ass home before I call the cops. Nobody gives a damn about you and your damn man. You're so concerned about him, keep him off my damn phone before I break him off something and he forgets how to go home."

Bam! Bam!

"TRICK!"

"Wah . . . wah. Cry your ass home. Enjoy your man while you can, because the next time you kiss that muthafucka it's going to be my pussy you'll be tasting."

My ass just snaps. I start wailing on her door. "GET YOUR ASS OUT HERE, BITCH!" To enrage me further, I can actually hear her laughing on the other side. "That's all right. That's all right." I kick the door. "You can't stay in that sonofabitch forever. Believe me, bitch. I'm going to catch your ass slipping."

I don't know who called security, but they are suddenly there, grabbing my arms and dragging me away. Still, I continue to shout to get my point across. "THIS IS NOT OVER, JALEESA. I PROMISE YOU!"

Now that I've been dragged halfway down the hallway, Jaleesa finally gets the guts to open her door and stick her head out. I immediately break free from the security guards and charge, but that scary-ass bitch quickly dips back inside and slams the door.

"YOU BETTER RUN!" I kick the door, but then security grabs me again. This time they are more successful in dragging me out of the building. And of course, the instamatic paparazzi pop up just as they're handing me over to L.A.P.D. for trespassing and disturbing the peace.

Just great. Another headliner.

33

Trey

I need a hit. I love Brijetta, but all this fighting is stressing me out. I know I'm not perfect, but Jalessa is right—neither is my wife. I have a lot of shit on my plate and I could do with a little more understanding and a lot less yelling. I don't feel guilty for talking with Jaleesa—there's nothing going on with us. This is just a bunch of paranoid shit. Shaking my head as I watch the taillights of the Mercedes disappear off the property, I turn and head back inside and pick up the phone.

"WHAT THE FUCK IS IT NOW, BITCH?"

"Nah. Nah, it's me," I tell Jaleesa. "I just wanted to warn you that B is headed over to your place right now."

"Oh my God," Jaleesa chuckles. "Are you for real?"

"I'm afraid so." I rake my hand through my head as I climb the stairs to the bedroom. "Look, just don't answer the door. I'm sure it'll be fine. She'll just blow off some steam and it'll all be over with."

"Humph. I don't know how you deal with it," she says compassionately. "Her erratic behavior would have driven me crazy by now." Pause. "You know this is exactly what happens when actors marry quote, regular people, unquote. I've heard it time and time again."

I nod along as I enter the master bedroom and head toward the walk-in closet.

"Only actors *get* other actors, you know what I mean? In fact, I think that's why we've been able to get along as well as we have. Don't you?"

"Yeah, I guess so." I go to my section of the huge space and kneel down to the secret compartment behind the second shelf from the bottom. I pull the small board down and reach into the wall for an old cigar box. But feeling it's light causes me to start frowning.

"Good," Jaleesa says. "I'm glad I'm not the only one that feels that way.

I'm hardly paying any attention to her as I open the box and find the damn thing empty. "What the fuck?"

"Hmm? Is something wrong?"

I lower the phone from my ear so I can drop my head down and look into the dark hole. Not seeing anything, I jam my hand inside. *Nothing.* "Shit!" I jump up. "Yo, Jaleesa. I gotta go."

"Why? What's wrong?"

Bam! Bam! Bam!

"Ah, shit. I think your wife just showed up."

"Yeah, all right. Whatever. Bye." I disconnect the call and then start tearing up the closet, looking for my shit. "Where the fuck is it?" I pull everything from the shelf. Maybe I'd stashed it somewhere else last time—but I can't imagine doing that. I've keep my stuff hidden in the same spot for years. Jeans, shirts, shoes—it all came crashing down onto the floor while I tore through there like the Tasmanian devil.

Nothing.

Huffing and puffing, my gaze then drifts to Brijetta's side of the closet and all her neat rolls of designer clothes and shoes. Was her ass trying to be funny? Did she find my drugs and stash it somewhere else? The thought of her and that damn maid sticking their noses in shit that doesn't belong to them, I quickly tear through her stuff, too. "Where is it? Where is it?"

Dresses, blouses, shoes, and purse all land in a heap until the entire closet is blanketed. *Nothing.*

Turning, I storm out of the closet and rush to the bathroom. Towels, linens, over-the-counter medicines all hit the floor. "It's got to be around here somewhere!"

To the bedroom. I overturn tables, nightstands, mattresses, and box springs. *Nothing.* "Goddamn it!" I clench and unclench my fists. *She had no right!* I pull in several deep breaths and try to think—but I need my shit. And I need it now.

Do I have anything anywhere else in the house? I immediate shake my head. My only other safe spot is in my trailer on the set, and that place is shut down right now. There's no getting on there without raising a whole lot of questions. Questions I don't feel like answering right now.

"Fuck it." I race back down the stairs, grab my jacket and car keys, and storm out of the house. Unbelievably, there are one or two photographers at the gate, but I hardly spare them any attention as I peel off. "I can't believe that she would mess with my stuff. What the hell gives her the right?" I hiss, shaking my head and nailing the accelerator to the floor. "Who does she think she is—my mother?" I've talked to Brijetta about my drug use several times and I told her I didn't have a problem. But because I love her, I told her I'd cut back, but it's on me to do that shit. Not her!

I make the usually fifty-minute drive out to Malibu in just under twenty-five. It's a little past midnight and the two-story architectural home that sat directly over the Pacific is dark, with even the security light turned off. Still, I stroll up to the front door and hammer on it like I'm the police. I pace a few seconds and try it again.

Bam! Bam! Bam!

The lights come on. I wait some more.

Bam! Bam! Bam!

"DAMN IT! I'M COMING!"

I step back, fold my hands, but I keep pacing. Finally, I hear footsteps and a shadow behind the frosted glass.

"Trey? Is that you?" Kent asks, opening the door.

I smile. "Heeey. You sleep?"

"I was." Kent pokes his head out and glances around while pulling his robe tight. "You alone?"

"Yeah. Mind if I come in?"

Kent's face lights up even though one side of it is still black and blue. "Sure, come on in." He steps back and I cross the threshold with a craving that's growing by the second.

"So what bring you out here to my neck of the ocean this time of night?"

I walk all the way into the living room before I turn and admit, "I need to get a package from you. I know it's, um, kind of late and all, but I really—really could use it tonight, you know?"

Kent's gaze rolls over me with concern. "Is everything all right?"

I start pacing again. "Can you help me out or not?"

He pulls in a deep a breath and then glances around to the mirror-clock behind the white sofa. "C'mon, now." He walks over to me and drapes an arm around my shoulders. "You know I always take care of you—even when you don't appreciate it. But it is kind of late, how much are we talking about?"

"Look, you got just a little taste for me now, I'll grab like a couple eight balls in the morning."

"Sure. Sure." He squeezes my shoulders. "I think I can manage that for you."

My shoulders slump with relief. I have to admit that Kent is right. He does always look after me.

"Why don't you just come on back here to the bedroom? I can give you a little of my private stash, and then I can see about getting you those eight balls delivered."

"Thanks, Kent."

"Don't mention it." He winks and starts to lead me toward

the bedroom. "This is why we're a good team. Don't you forget that."

I continue to bob my head even though I know that Brijetta will have another cow when she finds out that I hired Kent back on as my agent. For now, we're keeping that shit between us while he agrees not to call the house or come around her for a while. He and my wife may be oil and water, but we're like gin and juice when it comes to business. And in Hollywood, if it ain't broke, you never should try to fix it.

Kent's bedroom is completely white. The walls, linens, and carpet just look like one big-ass cloud. Usually when the sun hits the panoramic glass walls a person can be in danger of going blind.

"Let's see. Have a seat." He gestures to the bed while he waltzes over to a glass globe sitting on his desk, opens it, and pulls out a small baggie.

I smile and lick my lips.

"Let's get you hooked up," Kent says, turning back to me. In no time I'm tied off and popping up a good vein in my arm while he's cooking the shit up. Just when I'm about to feel the pinch of the needle, the phone rings.

"Who in the hell?"

"Let it go to voice mail," I say impatiently. "C'mon now."

Kent smiles. "All right. I got you."

The feel of that cold needle piercing my skin is like a mini orgasm and when he presses down on the plunger, I immediately sigh and shudder with relief.

"There you go, baby. There you go."

I'm vaguely aware of the needle being removed from my arm while the room starts to tilt like a carnival funhouse. Then there's the ringing again.

"Goddamn," Kent complains, standing up and going to answer the phone. "Hello." Pause. "Jaleesa, do you know what time it is?"

I start to get up, but instead fall back against the bed and become fascinated with the patterns on the ceiling.

"Who's been arrested?" Pause. "I see. Nah. Nah. I appreciate you calling and telling me. That way I won't be surprised when I get all the calls at the office. All right. All right. Good night." He hangs up and slowly returns to the bed. "How are you feeling?"

"Goo-Good. Man, I can't tell you how muc-much I appreciate you hooking me up like this. B is . . ." Sigh. "She's just tripping, man."

"Well, don't you worry about her right now. You're at my crib. And when you're here, I just want you to relax." He sits down on the bed next to me and starts walking his fingers up my chest. It sort of tickles and I can't help but smile at him. There's a comfortable silence that settles between us when his fingers unsnap the button on my pants. "You are a beautiful man, Trey Hamilton. Yes, indeed."

Suddenly there's another ringing in the room and I recognize it as my cell phone. "Oh, I better get tha-that. It could be Brijetta." I'm aware that I'm slurring my words a bit. I fumble to get the phone out of my pocket and then drop it.

"I'll get it." Kent picks up the phone and looks at the screen. "Who is it?"

He pauses just as the call stops ringing. "It's just uh . . . unknown caller." He hits a button. "Probably a wrong number or something."

I nod and continue to ride my wave.

"Now, where were we?" Kent tosses the cell phone aside and reaches for my zipper and pulls out my dick. "I'm really glad that you came over here tonight. It beats dreaming about you."

His gentle stroke invokes a moan from me.

"How does that feel, baby?"

I nod and moan some more.

"Good. Now let me really take care of you tonight." Smiling, he leans down and sinks his mouth over my hard cock.

34

Sinclair

"Have you lost your mind? Surveillance cameras?" I snap, strolling into our private gym in the basement of the property. Omar lays back on his bench, pumping his body weights with his personal trainer standing over him, waiting to spot him. "What the hell do we need those for?"

"So I can watch my shit," he spats, still pumping. Sweat pours off of him like a waterfall.

His trainer shouts. "You can do it! You can do it! Keep it going!"

I roll my eyes while this golden cage is starting to feel smaller.

"Is there a problem with me putting in cameras?" Omar asks between huffs.

"Would it make a difference if I told you 'yes'?"

"No," he manages to chuckle.

"Then don't ask and I won't tell." I fold my arms and glare at him as if by doing so he would just poof in a pile of smoke and ashes. I would love nothing more than to swing something at his arms and make him drop the bar on his head. Then, of course, my attention swings back to Kwame. I hope that he's still surveying the place himself and won't do anything foolish like pop up and get his mug shot on Omar's camera. The last thing I need is for him to flip again.

There's a fifty-fifty chance of Kwame doing something stupid. Lately, getting caught seems to be exactly what Kwame intends to do.

"Afraid I'm going to see something that you don't want me to see?" Omar asks, smirking.

"I don't know what you're talking about." I turn away from him and march out before he has the chance to call me a liar.

"SURE YOU DON'T! YOU'RE LITTLE MISS IN-NOCENT, AREN'T YOU?"

I ignore him and keep it moving. My anger continues to mount as I walk by workers from the private surveillance company Omar hired. There's wires and tools lying every-where. This type of invasion of privacy is just going too far. I don't know if I can stay in this cage much longer.

After a long, hot shower I'm still on edge. I dress quickly, grab my purse, and start to head down the staircase. Omar is climbing up with that same evil smirk on his face. "Going somewhere?"

"Yeah, out." I try to pass by him, but his hand snakes out and grabs me by my wrist.

"Out where?"

I try to wrench my arm back, but his grip refuses to let go. "Shopping. Is that a crime now?"

"It might be, considering how much money you've been spending lately."

My heart drops as I stop struggling. "What are you talking about?"

"I got a call from my accountant this morning and he's telling me that there is a sizable uptick in your spending in the last few months."

"Oh? I guess I haven't been paying attention." I'm careful to keep my face neutral.

"Something told me that you'd say that. So guess what—you're now on an allowance."

"What?"

"He who makes the money makes the rules," he says evenly. "Until further notice, you'll get ten thousand a month."

"Ten!"

"Is that a problem?"

"Hell yeah, there's a problem. In this town, I spend that just at the hair salon."

"Then I suggest that you take your ass down to Crenshaw and get your weave whipped because that's all you're getting."

"I don't fucking believe this!" I finally succeed in snatching my arm free.

Omar snickers and starts marching up the stairs. "Believe it, *darling.* There's going to be a whole lot of changes around here from now on!" He laughs the rest of the way up the staircase while I'm stuck on stupid staring at the back of his head.

What the fuck? Ten thousand?

It's not until I hear the master bedroom door slam shut that I finally turn and march my way back down the stairs, grinding my molars into a thin powder as I go. I can't take this shit no more. I'm going to have to make some kind of move.

Ten thousand dollars. That shit keeps floating in my mind. With that little taste of money, I don't think there's a point of even showing up on Rodeo Drive. All I can do with that cash is window-shop. In the back of my mind, I know that I'm acting like a spoiled child, but I can't help myself. Going from nothing to something is one thing. But going from something back down to nothing is a horse of another color. Once you have the taste of the good life, nothing else will do.

If I divorce him, I get nothing. But if he dies, I'll get millions.

I try to shake the thought out of my head. I'm no murderer. I need to think of something else. But what? I damn near drive myself crazy with that thought, so I turn on the radio to try and distract myself.

The Hollywood grapevine is buzzing with news reports that Bri-jetta Hamilton tried to stomp home wrecker Jaleesa Love into the ground last night when she showed up at her West Hollywood condo in . . . get this . . . her pajamas! The DJ and his costar crack up.

"What on earth?" I reach down and turn that mess off. "Drama. Drama. Drama." I shake my head. But I'm not surprised. I now know firsthand that Jaleesa will do anything to advance her career. Brijetta needs to face the truth that Trey and Jaleesa are fucking and just accept it or move on. Just like I need to either accept my situation or move on. Piss or get off the pot, my grandma used to say.

I do end up doing a little window-shopping on Rodeo, but then end up driving around Beverly Hills with no true destination. I know that I don't want to go back to that house. Driving keeps me thinking—weighing my options.

About an hour later, I notice a car that I swear I've seen behind me since I left Rodeo Drive. My hackles immediately jump to attention and I take a few sudden turns down a residential area and wait. Sure enough, the black BMW takes the same turns but hangs back as if he's hoping I won't notice.

"That sonofabitch!" This must be the detective that Kwame had eluded to that one time. I know that I shouldn't be surprised given that there's to be cameras in the house now. But still. I think I have steam rolling out of my ears.

I return to the main road, my gaze split between watching the road and the rearview mirror. The black BMW continues to follow me two cars back.

Piss or get off the pot.

I reach over to my purse, scoop out my cell phone, and find Kwame's code contact number. He picks up on the first ring.

"Kwame, this is Tracy. It's time we make our move and get Omar out of the picture."

"Abso-fucking-lutely!"

35

Omar

BRIJETTA HAMILTON ARRESTED
AT HUSBAND'S MISTRESS'S CONDO

I drop the *Hollywood Gawker* on my office desk and moan. "Just great. This damn shoot is turning into a damn circus!" I pick up the phone and dial Spencer. "Have you heard the news?"

"Heard it?" he barks back. "I've been trying to call you!"

"I told you to fire that bitch! She's turned this whole production into a joke. This sort of publicity always sinks a film."

"Actually, I did fire her, remember. Trey threatened to walk if we didn't hire her back."

I jump up from my chair and start pacing the room. "I swear these goddamn actors! Who the fuck does this cat think he is?"

"Calm down. The shoot is almost over. This whole thing can still blow over by next summer. Besides, there have been one or two incidents when this kind of scandal benefitted the movie."

"Trey and Jaleesa are no Brad and Angelina."

"Look, it's my job to find the silver lining in this scenario."

"There's a silver lining?"

Spencer chuckles. "I sure in the hell hope so. Just ignore this. There's nothing we can do about it now, anyway—other than to keep Trey's wife off the set and let our movie speak for itself."

I bob my head, but my blood pressure refuses to lower. "I'll catch up with you later. Lunch tomorrow?"

"Sure. Have your people call mine," he laughs before hanging up.

I still don't know how Spencer and I manage to be in business as long as we have. We're nothing alike. . . . Then again, maybe I just answered my own question. I pick up the phone again to put in a call to Quinn Starr's office when the doorbell rings. Shit. What's the point in working from home if I got to get up every few minutes?

Exiting out of my home office, I traipse over the dozen or so workers installing the surveillance cameras. When I open the door, I'm surprised to see Matthew Morrison standing on the other side of the door.

"Hey, what are you doing here?"

He holds up a digital recorder. "I have something that you need to hear."

"All right." I step aside and allow him to enter. In my office I gesture for him to take a seat.

"I'll stand," he tells me. "But maybe you should sit down."

"This seems serious. What? Is Sinclair having an orgy or something?"

"Worse."

"Worse?" I sit down, not quite sure how to take that answer.

"She placed a call about two hours ago that I think you'll find interesting." He places the recorder on the center of the desk and hits Play.

"Kwame, this is Tracy. It's time we make our move and get Omar out of the picture."

"Abso-fucking-lutely!"

Stunned, I stare down at the digital recorder while trying to make sense of what I heard. "Play that shit again."

Matthew reaches over and hits Rewind and then Play.

"Kwame, this is Tracy. It's time we make our move and get Omar out of the picture."

"Abso-fucking-lutely!"

"I bet you Kwame is that sneaking sonofabitch I saw standing outside my damn house like I was trespassing on his shit." I slam my fist on my desk and then recall the other name of the tape. "Tracy? Did she call herself Tracy?"

Matthew nods. "You want me to play it again?"

"Nah. Nah." I lean back in my office chair and rub my hands along my chin. "Tracy." I think on it. "She doesn't look like a Tracy."

"Think she looks more like a Sinclair?" Matthew asks.

"More like a Jezebel." I shrug like it really matters or some shit. "So she thinks that she's going to do me in, huh?"

"Sounds like it. You want to call the police?" Matthew asks, sitting down in the chair across from my desk. "I think we have enough evidence there for them to set up a sting or something."

I laugh. "The police? Don't be ridiculous. We can handle this on our own."

The room plunges into silence while I contemplate my next move.

"Kwame. Kwame. I know I heard that name recently." Then it hits me. "The new member at my father's church."

"Excuse me?" Matthew says.

I picture the brother that was standing at the back of the church a few months ago to the man I saw standing out on my lawn. *Is it the same person?* I'm not positive, but I have a sneaky suspicion that it is. Suddenly, I'm impressed with this man's boldness and I start laughing.

"Should I be concerned?" Matthew asks.

"No. No, not at all. I actually think that I'm going to enjoy this little game." My answer doesn't seem to ease his concern.

"I tried to run the number she called," he tells me. "But it turns out to be a burner that this Kwame bought at like either a gas station or convenience store."

"So what, you think he's a professional or something?"

"I don't know what he is, but we're on to him now. It's just a question on whether we can figure out what they got cooking up before they make their move. I don't mind telling you that I'm uncomfortable about this. I think we need to go to the police. What if she succeeds?"

"She won't."

"But if she does?" He insists.

"If she's that good, then she'll deserve inheriting my money. But she and her sloppy boyfriend aren't that good. Believe me."

Matthew settles back again and calmly braids his fingers together.

"When you followed her, where did she go?"

He pulls out a small pocket memo pad and flips through his notes. "She just did a little window-shopping on Rodeo Drive and drove around. For a minute I thought she picked me off, but I'm not sure. I think it was a good idea to bug her cell."

"If there's one thing women like to do is talk on the phone."

"Mind if I toss in my two cents?"

"Sure, knock yourself out."

"Cut your losses. Kick this chick to the curb. It's just not worth all this frustration. You have an iron-clad prenuptial. She's not going to walk away with much. But if you die . . ."

"Not going to happen. That bitch is *not* going to get the best of me."

"Still, I think that you should take the necessary precautions—she's not in your will, is she?"

"At the moment."

"Change it, in case she succeeds."

I frown. "I'm offended that you have so little faith in me.

It's not like she's the first wife that I've had to get rid of—that *we* had to get rid of."

"True." Matthew draws in a deep breath. "But one dead wife is one thing. Two turning up dead is quite another. It's going to raise questions—about *both* deaths. I don't think it's worth the risk. My suggestion is either file for divorce or turn what we have over to the proper authorities."

"But what's the fun in that?" I ask.

"Excuse me? She's plotting to kill you."

"Yes, she's plotting to kill me on a tapped phone." I prop my elbows on the desk and lean forward. "No, Tracy and I are going to see this through. And maybe you're right. Maybe we don't need to kill her . . . we just need to get rid of her punk-ass boyfriend, bring her to the body, and let her know just who she's fucking with. I bet her fast ass will settle down then."

"So . . . you just want to scare her?"

"I want her to submit!" I slam my fist down again. "She belongs to me, goddamn it! She either plays by my rules or she will never play another game again."

"But—"

"But nothing. I want you to find out who this Kwame is, what he does, where he stays—everything. You got that?"

Matthew huffs out a long breath. "All right. You always did like taking unnecessary risk."

"Taking risks is how I got rich. You could learn a thing or two from me."

"Believe me, I am. Like never give up my playa's card and stay away from gold diggers."

"Sounds boring. Everyone needs a little excitement in their lives." My gaze falls back down to the *Hollywood Gawker*. Now that I think about it. Trey Hamilton and I seem to have that in common.

"We'll stay on her, but unless she meets up with him soon . . ."

"Don't worry. I know where he'll be tomorrow. Come to my father's church. He'll be there."

Matthew stares at me, puzzled. "Are you sure? Why would he go there?"

"Because he's a cocky sonofabitch, that's why. He'll be there. Trust me."

36

Kwame

"Welcome to Cali!" I stretch out my arms at LAX's baggage claim and wrap them around my cousin with a big grin on my face. It doesn't go past my notice that my boy looks like shaken.

"I can't believe that you convinced my ass to get on a damn plane, man. If God wanted a brother to fly, then he would have put wings on him."

"Point taken." I pat him on the back a few times, then we break away. "I appreciate you coming out here on short notice."

"Anything for you, my man. If you got a problem, then I got a problem. You feel me? We're family."

I bob my head, definitely happy to hear that shit. "Let me help you get your stuff, man." We turn toward the carousel and quickly spot his bags and then stroll our way out to the parking deck.

"I take it that since you been out here for a hot minute that you found Tracy. Is she working some stripper pole or something?" He laughs.

"Not funny, cuz. You're talking about my wife."

He tosses up his hands. "Sorry. My bad. I see that she still has you wrapped around her finger."

"If that's your rude way of asking if I still love my wife, then the answer is yes. If you want to know if I'll do anything to make or keep her happy, the answer is yes again." I toss his bag in the back of the new Mercedes I paid cash for with Omar Fines's money.

"Whoa, dawg. You rolling like this?" Mike steps back and does a quick inspection. "How did a brother come up this damn fast? You got connects out here already?"

"Naw, man. I ain't slanging or nothing like that."

"Then you must be jacking, because you ain't going to convince me that you rolled up on something legit that has you stacking the kind of weight it'll take to scoop a ride like this."

"I'm not jacking, either," I boast, climbing into the car.

Mike drops down into the passenger seat and I reach over to the glove compartment to show him my papers. "This shit is all me, cuz."

He glances at the papers and then tosses them back at me. "All right, I give. What's the deal, and please tell me you brought a cousin out here so that he can get in where he fits in, too. You know I got twins on the way."

I frown. "Lakathy is pregnant?"

"Naw, two of my chicken heads are due on the same day."

"Man, you're a fool." I start up the car and roll out.

Mike just shrugs and then tips his shades down while he takes in the scenery outside his window. "So this is the big sunny state, huh? I don't see what the big deal is."

"Stop fronting. You know this shit looks way better than what's popping in Detroit."

"What? Are you turning Judas on me, man?"

"I just call it like I see it."

"Huh-uh." He turns in his seat so he can look at me. "I'm still waiting, you know. Or you going to tell me you hit the lottery or what?"

I shake my head, still loving the fact that I have him hanging in suspense. "Nah, man. My baby helped me get this car."

"Who? Tracy?" He glances around the leather interior. "*Your* Tracy?"

"The one and only."

"Sheeeiiit. All right, I'm game. What I got to do for her to break me off a little cheese?"

Smiling, I glance over at him. "Help me kill her other husband."

37

Jaleesa

BRIJETTA HAMILTON ARRESTED
AT HUSBAND'S MISTRESS'S CONDO

I squeal at the headline Andy holds up at my door. "Ohmigod!" I snatch the *Hollywood Gawker* out of his hand and stare at the picture of Brijetta in her silk nightgown being shoved in the back seat of a police car. "Now, this is priceless."

"Giirrl, this soap opera is turning into one ghetto hot mess," he says, switching his hips as he enters the apartment. "My phone has been blowing up all morning. I got tired of telling everybody no comment, so I decided to come over and get the 411 straight from the horse's mouth."

"I take it that I'm supposed to be the horse in this scenario?"

He clamps his mouth shut and pretends to twist a key to lock his lips.

"All right. I see how you do." I shake my head and then glance back down at the paper. "All joking aside, I think the bitch really is close to losing her mind."

Andy plops down on my couch. "What happened, chile? Why did she come up here in the dead of night in her Victoria Secrets? Was Trey up in here?"

"No, not yet. Give me a little more time with that one." I

wink over at him. "Last night he said something about being in love with two people."

Andy's eyebrows jump up at that. "Last night? So he was here?"

As much as I want to rock his world with something that juicy, I have to shake my head. "Phone. We've been doing pillow talks for the last couple of weeks."

"Pillow talk—without the sex? Interesting."

"Nah, I've just been really trying to get to know him, you know?" I shrug as I join him on the couch. "Be there to listen when he needs a friend."

"Uh-huh. The one-two step of stealing a bitch's man. Yeah, I feel ya. So how did the missus end up over here trying to clean your clock, if you haven't made it to third base yet?"

"She caught us on the phone."

"Shut up!" He leans in close. "Were you two talking nasty?"

"Not even."

Andy frowns. "You know for something that's supposed to be the scandal of the year, it's lacking some real juice."

"He asked me if I've ever been in love," I confess, wiggling my eyebrows.

"Shut up!"

"I'm telling you. It's just a matter of time before Trey and Jaleesa Hamilton are going to be the next power couple running this town."

"Jaleesa Hamilton? Don't you think that the current Mrs. Hamilton might have something to say about that?"

I roll my eyes. "Puh-lease. That bitch needs to chill out and take a Valium. Clearly, she is not cut out for life in the fast lane. Every little thing sends her over the edge. Trey is getting sick of it."

"And what? He told you this?"

"He didn't have to. I can sense it."

"Uh-huh. Don't be offended if I remain skeptical. You don't exactly have a good track record on these things. Remember that time you thought Jamie Foxx was going to plop a ring on your finger after meeting him at some wild party, only for his ass not remember ever meeting you."

I hit him over the head with the *Hollywood Gawker*. "Why do you have to bring up old news? Besides, you're no better. You used to think that Trey Hamilton was gay."

"Whatever, heifer. Everybody's gaydar is allowed to be off at least once."

"Uh-huh. Well, I'm right about this. Brijetta knows that she's losing Trey. Why else would she straight flip out and show up here, trying to bang my door down? If everything was all good in the hood, there would be no need to worry about his ass straying."

"And . . . he still hasn't slept with you," Andy says, jumping up and heading to the kitchen.

"Yet!" I holler out to him while he digs through my refrigerator only to come up with bottled water. "Shit. What time is it?" Glancing around, I check the small clock on my end table and bounce up. "I got to head out," I say, folding the paper. "Mind if I keep this?"

"Sure. Plan on framing it?"

"Something like that. Right now I have to head out to Malibu to Kent Webber's place. We're mapping out a career plan for me." I shake my head. "Maury certainly never did that shit."

"You're moving up." He heads back toward the door. "I guess I'll turn my cell phone back on and continue with the 'no comments'; unfortunately, it's still a little spicier than the truth."

"Not for long!"

An hour later, I exit my condo and push my way through the largest group of paparazzi I ever had.

"Ms. Love, how long have you and Trey Hamilton been having an affair?" one of them yells toward me.

"No comment."

"Are you worried about Mrs. Hamilton making good on

some of her threats last night?" someone else shouts. "Will you be filing for a restraining order?"

"I'm not afraid of that woman!" I stop to glare at them. "But I'll do what I have to in order to protect myself."

They shout more questions, but it's clear if I stop to answer all of them I'll never make it to where I'm going. I push up my shades and toss "no comment" for the rest of the way to my celebrity conscience Hybrid and then roll out. During my ride to Malibu, I have to admit, I'm feeling damn good about life. I have my career on track, Trey Hamilton on the hook, and his crazy wife on lockdown.

Silly trick is going to show up at my door and act the fool. I chuckle under my breath. When I get in the neighborhood of where I'm going, I pull out Kent's instructions and then wind my way up a path to a gorgeous white palatial pad that is positively breathtaking.

"Now, this is what's up," I whisper, parking next to a black Porsche. "Isn't that Trey's car?" I climb out and walk to the back and reread the license plate: TRYHMLTN. For a guy who claims to be low-key, I don't get the vanity plate. A bigger smile stretches across my face. *Wonder why he's here.* I quickly trot up to the front door and knock. After a full minute, I try again.

What the hell?

I cup my hands around my eyes and try to see through the glass. When I don't see anything, I start walking around the house; because most of it's glass, I'm sure that I'll be able to spot Kent and Trey if they are in here. *Maybe they're down on the beach.*

I'm still mulling that possibility when I reach the far right wing of the house. "Damn, you can even see into the man's bedroom." I chuckle at the house's risqué and open nature. But then I see bodies in the bed. Two bodies.

Two *male* bodies.

"OH. MY. GOD!"

PART IV

When the chickens come home to roost . . .

38

Sinclair

"*Let me go!*" *I kick and scream as Omar wrestles and drags me down a dark corridor. Tears stream down my face as terror grips me.*

"Don't you want to see your husband, Tracy? Huh? Don't you want to give him one final kiss good-bye? Or maybe you prefer to join him?" Omar gets a good grip around my waist and then hoists me up and continues to drag me like a rag doll into an even darker room.

My screams hit a whole new octave and then someone clicks on a light—which looks more like a mini spotlight for a body slumped over in a heap on the floor.

"C'mon, Tracy. Time for one last reunion." Omar grabs the back of my head and forces me to look.

My gaze rakes in the familiar form and then finally lands on the face. Kwame!

I scream and bolt straight up in bed.

Across the room, Omar sits in the cream-colored chaise, watching me and sipping on a whiskey sour. "Bad dream?"

His calm indifference to my brief hysteria unnerves me more. For a few seconds we just stare at each other, as if suddenly realizing that the other is a complete stranger. My dream, still very fresh in my mind, definitely has my paranoia at an all-time high.

His thin smile never wavering, Omar sets his drink down on the small reading table next to the chaise and stands. "It's a good thing you're up, anyway. We don't want to miss morning church service."

With that cool announcement, he turns and strolls to the adjoining bathroom for his morning shower. When he shuts the bathroom door one last chill races up my spine. *It's not a dream. It's a vision.*

The minute I hear the water come on, I whip the sheets back and race out of bed to dig my cell phone out of my purse. But before I can pull up his code contact info, the bathroom door opens again. Jumping, I turn and try to hide the phone behind me while Omar's gaze zeroes in on me.

"Calling someone?"

I open my mouth to answer but not a sound comes out. He stalks toward me and I instinctively step back, but at least I manage to find my voice. "I was just checking to see if I need to put it on the charger."

Omar holds out his hand and I hesitates for only a second before handing over my phone. Our eyes lock for a long moment, but then he finally looks down and sees that I hadn't attempted to contact anyone just yet, but he covers by saying, "One bar left. You better charge it up." He hands the phone back.

With a weak attempt to smile, I scamper around him to my vanity table and hook the phone up to the charger. I feel like I'm walking on eggshells while his gaze continues to follow me. No matter how much I try, it's impossible to try to act normal or recall my usual poker face.

"Hey, why don't you come join me," he suggests, cocking his head toward the bathroom.

I glance up like a deer caught in headlights, mentally screaming for my drying tongue to start working. But when it doesn't, he approaches me again, this time taking me by the hand and leading me toward the bathroom.

"You know there's nothing like having sex before church service—other than having sex in church." He chuckles at his own joke while seeming to not notice—or not care that I'm not exactly hyped about joining him in the shower.

My brain scans every excuse in my mental Rolodex for why I don't either feel like going to church or taking a shower, but every fiber in my body is telling me that it's better to shut up and get my ass in the water.

Omar closes the door behind us. "It's been a while since we have taken a shower together. What—probably a year?" He starts peeling the spaghetti straps from my nightgown. "That's waaay too long." He leans down and starts placing small kisses along my shoulders. "Mmmm. Nice."

I close my eyes and grit my teeth. Any other time, I'd be able to fake this, but I can still hear my screams echoing in my head while Omar cups and squeezes my breasts.

"You taste so good," he pants, finally locking his mouth over one unpuckered nipple. He licks and sucks for a while, trying to get my body to respond, but it doesn't work—and again, he doesn't seem to mind. Omar lifts his head, still smiling, and unties his robe.

It's a shame that a body that ripples with such fine muscles and chiseled abs is sabotaged by the package that swings in between his legs.

"C'mon. Let me get you clean."

He takes my hand again and opens the glass door. I step into the large stall and welcome the steady drumming of the hot water from overhead. Omar wastes no time taking some liquid soap and lathering me up. His black gaze seems to deepen with intensity as he watches my expression while he slides his hands around my curves or slips in between my legs. We're playing some kind of game and I wish that I knew what it was.

Could he know? And if he did, how did he know?

My emotions bounce all over the place while I try to conjure up some type of performance for his ego. I don't think he's buying it, but one never quits in the middle of a play. Then suddenly and brutally, he whips me around, bends me forward, and rams his cock straight into my ass. Shocked, I gasp out and flail my arms back.

"All shit. Now this is what I'm talking about."

Now he's moaning and groaning louder than I was a few minutes ago. I, on the other hand, am gasping and panting in shock. Before too long, Omar's pulls out and splashes off all over my back.

"Damn, baby. That shit was good." He plants a kiss on the back of my head and then tells me it's my turn to wash him. I turn and look at him, still feeling violated.

"What the fuck did you do that for?" I sputter.

He grins. "What? You didn't enjoy that? I thought it was hot." He winks and smacks me on the ass.

I'm still smarting two hours later when we're sitting in our regular pew at the Power of Prayer Ministries. Reverend Fines is jacked up on the Holy Ghost today because he's running all across the stage, up and down the aisle, and even spins around like a bottle top.

I keep sneaking angry looks over at Omar, but he continues to look serene and satisfied, watching his father do his thing. A couple of times, he turns and catches my stare and smiles. With that, I'm just left to turn and fold my arms.

"Right now, it's time to testify," Reverend Fines announces. "If you've been blessed, then you must testify. Even if you're still going through something, you must testify in order to break the chains that bind you. Can I get a witness?"

The church shouts, "Amen," and a whole lot of hands are raised and waved in the air. Instead of asking people to come on up to him, he walks out with a mic in his hand, choosing members at random and instructing them to give their testimony. For a crazy moment, I think he is going to stop next to me, but then lets out a relieved breath when he walks on by.

However, that relief is short-lived when the microphone is shoved in front of Kwame, sitting in the back row.

"What about you, my brother?"

"Um. I—uh."

"C'mon, brother. Don't be shy. Everybody has a testimony."

Omar, along with the entire church, turn their attention to Kwame. I, on the other hand, am wishing, hoping, and praying the floor would open up and just swallow me whole right now.

"Well, I guess—"

"Start with your name," Reverend Fines interrupts and then gives him the mic again.

"I am, uh, Kwame Franklin."

"And what's your testimony, Brother Kwame?"

"I don't know if I really have a testimony."

Sitting next to Omar, I close my eyes. *Why the hell is he still coming here?*

"Everyone has a testimony," the Reverend encourages.

"Well, I recently got out of prison. I served a dime back in Detroit on a drug-related incident. I guess I'm grateful for surviving that." He tries to give the microphone back.

"And what brings you out west, Brother Kwame?"

Don't answer it. Don't answer it.

"Actually, I came out looking for my wife, Tracy," he says rather cocky. "I heard she came out this way a while back. Don't get me wrong, I understand that she never wanted to be playing wife to a brother locked down—but you know I came out here to see if I can win her back. God willing, I will."

"Amen," the church cosigns, then half the congregation starts applauding—the half that was women.

I, on the other hand, am too afraid to open my eyes. When I finally do, I steal a look over at Omar, who positively looks like he's ready to kill.

He knows.

39

Brijetta

"Thank for coming and getting me, Momma," I say, plopping down in her own old Ford Escort and struggling to get the door shut while hordes of photographers snap away. One of the most humiliating things is that I'm still in this damn nightgown and looking a hot mess. I can't believe that I had to sit in that damn jail, nice as it was, for over forty-eight hours because it was the weekend.

"It's all right, baby," Momma says, though she is clearly rattled by how rude these people really are. "I don't know how you guys put up with this craziness." She starts the car.

"What? You don't find this glamorous?" I ask, succeeding in getting the door shut.

She presses her lips together and tries to pull away. If anything, I'm glad that she's finally getting a snippet of what I have to go through and not just think that it's all about limitless credit cards and big mansions. "I don't understand why Trey couldn't come down and get you."

"I'm sure that if I knew where to find him, then maybe he would have. I called the house and his cell phone more times than was allowed, but he never answered. Amaya is off on weekends, so you were my last choice."

"Geez, thanks."

"I'm sorry, but you know what I mean." I fold my arms and stew in my anger. As much as I don't want to, it's time for me to face some facts. Trey is a liar. Trey is a junkie. Trey is having an affair with Jaleesa.

Tears surface and they feel like battery acid as they drip down my face. I'm so fucking tired of this shit. Tired of the back and forth. Tired of fighting and tired of crying. But I'll be damned if I know how to get off this damn ride.

"You're not going to sit over there and start crying, are you?" Momma says. She never has been one for watching people feel sorry for themselves.

"No," I lie, not bothering to wipe away the fat drops rolling down my face. I can tell that she wants to say something, but for once in her life, she takes one look at me and lets it go. When we arrive at my estate, she gasps to see that there are even more photographers lined up at the gate.

"My word. Are they multiplying?"

"All cockroaches do."

She rolls down the window and I tell her the pass code. Slowly, the gate opens and Mom slams on the accelerator. When we climb out of her car, she looks both shaken and concerned. "Do you need me to stay? I can, um, fix you something to eat or try to call around and find Trey."

"You can stay if you want, but I'm in no hurry to see my husband anytime soon." I turn away and march up to the front door.

Momma quickly rushes up behind me. "You're not thinking about doing something foolish, are you?" she asks. "I mean, I understand you being a little upset, but I'm sure that Trey has a good explanation for not coming to get you."

"Really? Like what?" I push in the door and enter the quiet house.

"I don't know. Maybe he's on the set today."

"And you think filming is more important than bailing your wife out of jail? Riiiight." I toss my keys on the foyer table and head toward the staircase. "I need a shower."

"Well, maybe he didn't know that you were in jail," she offers.

"Mom, the world knew I was in jail," I say, still marching up the stairs.

"Baby, I don't know. But I just can't imagine him choosing not to come get you. Trey is a good man."

That does it. I freeze in the middle of the staircase, turn, and glare down at my mother. "No offense, Mom, but you don't know what the hell you're talking about. You know absolutely *nothing* about Trey."

"Brijetta—"

"NOTHING!"

She jumps.

"The whole world has him on a pedestal. They think just because he's handsome and charming that they know him! No one sees his dark side. No one cares to. But you know what? I see it! I see it every fucking day when he lies to my face—or when he's freebasing, snorting, or shooting up. I've lost count of how many times he's OD'd or when he turns violent or suicidal. But let him tell it, he doesn't have a problem. Let him tell it, I'm the one that overreacts. I'm the crazy one! Well, I'm sick of it. TREY HAMILTON IS A CRACKED-OUT JUNKIE WHO DOESN'T KNOW HOW TO KEEP HIS DICK IN HIS PANTS!"

Momma gasps and flutters a hand to her mouth like I'd just told her that God didn't exist.

"How do you like that headline?"

Behind her the front door bursts open and Trey rushes into the house. "Oh, thank God you're here."

I fold my arms and glare down at him.

Momma looks like she doesn't know what to do. I've clearly spun her world on an axis, and hopefully she'll stop looking at her son-in-law through rose-colored glasses. "I, uh, think that I'll just leave you two alone," she says, backpedaling.

Trey turns his Hollywood smile onto her. "Thanks, Momma Kate. I appreciate you bringing B home."

Momma nods, but she doesn't say anything as she waltzes past him to get out of the door.

Trey looks awkward as he waves to her before closing the door. Turning around, he looks up to me and opens his mouth.

"Save it," I tell him. "I really don't want to hear it." I resume my march up the staircase, knowing full well that Trey was going to be stupid and follow.

"I know you're mad, but I was coming," he says. "I got stuck in traffic."

"What part of 'I don't want to hear it' don't you understand?" I shout, storming into the bedroom.

"At least let me explain," he went on.

"NO!" I jump and turn around. "I don't want you to say *anything!* I don't want to hear your voice! I don't even want to see your lips moving, because whatever is coming out of it is just a big-ass pile of bullshit." Those damn acid tears return, making me feel like a weak bitch again.

"Brijetta—"

"NO!" I press a hand against my forehead and try to squeeze the tension out of it, but it's not working. "Look, we need to face some hard truths here, Trey. This shit isn't working. Not by a long shot. And I'm . . . I'm tired of being the bad guy. I'm tired of being the bitch that feels like she needs to listen in to your calls, or discover drugs stashed all over the house, or read about you screwing your costars. It's too much. It's. Too. Fucking. Much!"

At my words, his face falls while he takes a step back.

"Don't you see that?" I ask. "I feel more and more like your mother or your nurse than I do like your wife. How is that fair? Are you running around seeing about me like that? When was the last time you had to sit up in here worried about my benefit? Ever walked in here and found my ass not breathing with a needle in my arm? Ever catch me in the middle of the night talking to another man? How is any of this fair?"

"It's not," he croaks.

"I sat in jail for two days. I couldn't find you. My *mother* bailed me out. My *mother!*"

Silence.

"This is broken. This marriage is broken and I don't see how on earth we can ever fix it."

"Please, B. Don't say that." He starts toward me, but I back up. I watch tears pool in his eyes and it only makes me angrier.

"DON'T! Don't you dare start fucking crying on me. You have no right. NONE. I'm the one that's been wronged. Everything in this house has always been about *you*. What you want. What you need. I'm sick of it. SICK. SICK. SICK." My tears fall fast and free, and despite my anger, I allow Trey to wrap his arms around me so that I can drench his shirt with my tears.

"It's going to be all right. Shhh." He kisses the top of my head.

Before I know it we're lying on the bed. I'm curled neatly under his chin while he continues to hold and kiss the top of my head. Eventually, I fall asleep, but when I wake, I feel more exhausted than ever.

"You're the last person I want to hurt," he whispers.

I'm not even sure that he knows that I'm listening.

"I don't know why I keep screwing things up, I really don't. I just know that you're the one right thing I've managed to accomplish in my life." He kisses my head again. "Don't give up on me. Please don't give up."

"Are you sleeping with her?" I whisper, letting him know I'm awake.

"No."

I draw in a deep breath, but I'm not sure that it's relief or that I even believe him. "Are there *any* secrets you're not telling me?"

Silence.

"Tell me now. I can take it. It might hurt, but I can take it if you tell me now."

There's another brief silence before he answers, "No. No secrets."

40

Kwame

"You didn't tell me that your ass found religion in the joint," Mike says, tossing back a beer at Posh, a swanky little nightclub off Sunset Strip. The place was sort of a throwback to the 90s—a lot of Tupac and Biggie is bumping from the stereo system.

"Naw, you got the wrong understanding," I tell him.

"What? That wasn't you getting all GQ'd up yesterday to head out to church?"

"I went to church, but it isn't because I found religion. Tracy goes there."

Mike chokes and nearly spits out his beer.

I chuckle and pat him on the back. "If you can't hold your liquor, cuz, maybe I should take you to Chuck E. Cheese or something."

"Very funny." He grabs a bar napkin and wipes his face. "I fly out west and find out the whole world has flipped upside down. Tracy's balling out of control, you're rolling in a Mercedes, and now Tracy is running her heathen self up in somebody's church. Next thing you're going to tell me is that God is the one telling her to snuff out her husband."

"Nah, that'll be the Benjamins that is doing that."

"It usually is," he chuckles, then tries for another swig of beer. "So when are we going to do this, man? And how much you talking about breaking me off?"

"How does fifty large sound to you?"

"Seventy-five sounds better."

"Seventy-five it is." I reach for my own beer while Mike's mouth damn near hits the bar.

"Damn, it's like that? Shit. Maybe I should have said a hundred."

I shrug. "Maybe you should have."

Mike shakes his head and drains the rest of his beer. "Does Tracy have any more illegitimate husbands we can take care of?"

"She better not." We laugh.

"So what? You've been hanging out here, watching her play wife to some other dude? Man, that doesn't even sound like you."

"More than just watching."

"Blackmailing."

"It was never about the money. If I rode through here and told everybody that she was a phony, what would that have gotten me? Nothing but a quick divorce. But if I hung around, remind her how good it is when we're together, then I knew that nature would take its course."

"And the money?"

"Hell. At first I didn't think that she would do it. Figure she'd call my bluff. But hey. I've only spent a small portion of it. When we finish this job, it'll be our money."

Mike shrugs his shoulders. "Whatever, man. I never could figure you two out. I'm just here to make this paper and get the hell out of this bougie-ass city. I don't think that I've seen a set of real titties since I got here." His head turned just as a Rihanna look-alike strolls past us at the bar.

We toss back a few more bottles before I peel a couple of more bills off the fat knot I keep in my pocket. Neither one of us is really fit to get behind the wheel, but since it's not really all that far back to the hotel, I don't really give it a second thought.

"You want to plan this shit out when we get back to your room?" Mike asks.

"Yeah. Cool. I figure it's best that we plan this shit and leave Tracy out of it. The less she knows the better, you know what I mean? This brother being such a high-profile brother, if people start looking at her sideways, we aren't stuck on relying on her acting skills in front of the cameras."

"I hear ya." Mike bobs his head. "But you know what will really help me think tonight?"

"What?"

"Some weed. You got a connect out here? This dry spell you got me on ain't cool."

I laugh. "Yeah, all right. I met a cat that can hook us up. He doesn't like strangers, though, so let me drop you off at the hotel, make a run, and come right back."

"Done deal." He claps his hands and then rubs them together. "I knew that you'd hook me up."

A couple of minutes later, I pull up to the front of the hotel, reach in my back pocket, and hand over the key to my suite. "Be back in a few."

"All right. I'm going to hold you to that." Instead of climbing out of the car, he sort of rolls.

I can't help but laugh at him, even when I pull off. My drive over to this cat, Ceasar, I met a few months back only takes about ten minutes. I get enough trees for me and Mike to smoke for at least a week before heading back. At the hotel, I toss my keys to the valet and then head on up to my room. When I get there, I knock and then wait.

"Yo, man, Mike. Let me in." I knock again. *Now, I know his sorry ass didn't go in there and fall asleep.* I have to walk all the way back down to the front desk to ask for another key to my room. When I return, I'm ready to cuss Mike out. But when I enter the room, I get the surprise of my life.

41

Omar

"So it's done?" I ask, smiling and tucking the phone beneath my ear.

"Yes, I got him," Matthew confirms. "We can proceed as planned."

"I always knew that I could depend on you," I tell him, then disconnect the call. Instead of getting up to leave the office, I lean back in my high-back leather chair and braid my fingers together. I want to take a few minutes to just soak in this moment. On my desk is the small file Matthew has managed to pull together on Kwame and *Tracy* Franklin—husband and wife.

To say that I'm pissed would be a complete understatement. The woman I *thought* I was married to for the past two years doesn't and never existed. She had completely fooled me, and that shit doesn't just happen every day. Being in this business you have to stay one step ahead of all the liars, schemers, and straight gold-digging hos who swarm this town like a venereal disease. But in the end, I'm weak, just like any man when their vision of a perfect woman strolls by them. And perfect was exactly what I thought when Sinclair gave me that first smile at this small club in Chicago. Was she rough around the edges a bit? Yeah, but in a way, it was part of her charm.

Maybe her slick act was also perfect timing, seeing how we met within just a few months of my putting a bullet through my first wife's head, which from time to time I regret. But in my opinion, the bitch got what was coming to her. Her numerous affairs and her insufferable arrogance had gone too far and had pissed me off one time too many. The lesson that I thought I'd learned from that fiasco of a marriage was to stay away from women in the business, because the minute their star starts to shine . . . they start thinking they are running things. *I* made Zayna who she was. *I* was the one who hooked her with all the right people and invested in her when no one in this town would give her the time a day. The early years were great. She knew her place and certainly knew what would happen whenever she stepped out of bounds.

But when the millions poured in and other people started whispering in her ear, suddenly I was just the dirty old man slash sugar daddy that she thought she could talk to any old kind of way. I put my foot on her neck a couple of times, forced her to start showing up at her precious Hollywood parties with pounds of makeup to cover the ass beatings she deserved.

Then came the cheating. Not once, not twice—but with a whole lot of men she would sneak and see whenever she traveled without me. Giving our growing conflicting and busy schedules, it happened a lot. That's when I put Matthew on her ass. He kept me informed of everything that was happening. The way I see things, I warned her that I didn't believe in divorce. The only way out of our marriage is through the coroner. It looks like Sinclair or Tracy needs to learn that shit, too.

42

Jaleesa

"I KNEW IT!" Andy hooted at me from across our table at The Ivy. Across the street, as always, the paparazzi click away. "I knew that brother had a little sugar in his tank. Didn't I tell you?"

He holds up his hand and I roll my eyes as I give him the high five that he's waiting for. "Now, don't start getting a big head. Nobody likes a know-it-all."

"Translation: Your ass was *wrong,* future Mrs. Jaleesa Hamilton!" That proclamation tickles him some more, so I have to sit here and wait for him to get all his gloating out of his system.

"Are you done?"

"Naw, girl. I'm going to be laughing about this for the rest of the day. Whoo." He plops back in his chair and shakes his head.

"I'm not going to lie, I was stunned shitless." I see a waitress walk by. "Can I get an orgasm over here?" I smile, getting my usual kick out of that order.

"So what did you do after you saw them all hugged up in the bed?"

"After I put my eyes back into my head, I took my ass back up to the front door and rang the doorbell until I woke them up. When Kent finally opened the door, the official story was that Trey came over and spent the night on the sofa after his fight with his wife.

Andy stretches his brows at me. "You think the missus knows?"

"Hell no," I say, chuckling. "Not the way she's been getting buck wild about me, and I ain't even fucking her man."

"Not from lack of trying."

"True. But if you want to know my two cents—"

"Don't I always?"

I lean in close. "I think Brijetta's woman intuition is beeping, but she's misreading the muthafucka. She *knows* her man is cheating. She knows something ain't right in the kitchen, but I'm the red herring. No way does she believe Trey is on the DL. And frankly, I wish, I hope, I pray that I can be a fly on the wall when she does find out."

"You and me both." Andy snickers, reaching for his drink just as mine arrives.

"I think she's going to take bat-shit crazy to a whole new level. Further than that stunt she pulled at my place. So basically while she was trying to bang down my door, Trey was banging Kent's back door."

"Ha!" Andy rocks back in laughter, drawing a few more stares our way.

"I should have pulled out my camera phone and snapped a picture," I admit, regretfully.

Andy cocks his head. "Uh-huh."

"What?"

"You're sitting over there trying to plot on how you can be the one that drops the boom on Brijetta."

"And have it not be traced back to me," I add. "If the shit backfires on me, then I don't want my new and wonderful agent to take it out on me."

"Very shrewd."

"You say that like it's a bad thing." I laugh. "In the meantime, we keep denying the rumors or saying no comment and when the truth comes out, I can still come out smelling like a rose when someone like Perez Hilton blasts him out of the closet."

"This definitely sounds like you already have a plan."

"I just want that bitch to get what's coming to her. I should have sued the hell out of her ass."

Our waitress returns with Andy's light pasta salad. He looks at me. "Not eating anything?"

"Can't. I'm trying this new six-hundred-calorie diet," I huff, watching him take his first bite. The minute he chomps down, my stomach growls indignantly.

Andy just shakes his head at me. "So what's the real deal between you and Brijetta? A few months ago, you two were friends. And whatever happened with you and Sinclair? Now you hardly even mention her."

My eyes start rolling again. "Sinclair and I are another story—and one that I don't want to get into."

Andy's brows jump. "Is it as juicy as it sounds?"

"Juicy and strange. One day you'll have to read about it in my memoirs."

"Bitch."

"I love you, too." I ignore another stomach growl. "All that matters now is that I don't have to take your advice about moving to New York and doing boring-ass theater work. My star is on the rise, and I'm going to do everything I can to make sure that it stays that way."

"All right, boo. You do you. But now that Trey Hamilton won't be on your arm for the film's wrap party, who are you going to show up with?"

Just then I glance up to see Spencer Reid walking to a table. When he glances over and catches my smile, I think I've found my answer. "Looks like I'm going to have to go back into the recycling bin."

★　★　★

The last day of filming ends at three. The entire cast and crew stand around the set and watch as Trey Hamilton says his final line straight into the camera in front of the green screen.

"AANNND CUUUUT!" the director shouts.

Everyone erupts into a thunderous applause while I stand off to the side smirking at out handsome superstar. *Gay! Damn!* I shake my head, still reeling from the hot mess I'd stumbled into. It's absolutely hilarious watching both him and Kent try to cover shit up.

I'm still cracking up. This shit is priceless. Trey may think I bought that story, probably because he's a drug addict, but Kent knows I didn't buy that shit. Not for a long shot, which is why, I believe, those auditions he had lined up are now done deals and I'm committed to film projects for the next eighteen months—I love Hollywood bribes. But a bitch like me is still thinking of one thing and one thing only: revenge.

I continue to watch Trey shake hands and hug people while he heads in my direction. I have to hand it to him; even knowing what I know, he still has the innocent Boy Scout thing going on for him. Maybe I've been wrong about him. Maybe there is an Oscar in his future.

There's a palpable silence growing over the crowd as if everyone is waiting to see if we'll hug or shake hands. I'm certain that there are a few cameras aimed and ready to be leaked to the tabloids. I smile, ready for my close up, when Trey suddenly hangs a right and starts shaking hands and hugging another group of people.

No the hell he didn't. I try to pass the shit off, but there is little I can do but turn and start saying my good-byes to the others on the set, too. The whole time my face is tight and heated.

43

Sinclair

The last thing I feel like doing is attending a damn wrap party, but once again, Omar doesn't want to hear or is accepting any of my excuses. For the past few days, I have hardly been able to even take a piss without him hovering above me, and when he's not here, the cameras are zoomed in on me. Leaving the house doesn't help or work, either, since I keep seeing that same BMW stalking me like a part-time job. But the kicker has been my missing cell phone. I've looked everywhere for it so I can try to warn Kwame that I believe Omar is on to us. I only had his contact number stored in my cell's address book.

Now, I came up the mean streets on the south side of Detroit. My point being that it takes a lot to scare my ass—and I am terrified of the man I'm forced to lie down next to night after night. I almost prefer that leather belt to this creeping eye-balling and his whispered questions.

"What are you wearing tonight?" Omar asks, while slipping on a clean black shirt.

"Just a cocktail dress," I answer, brushing the back of my hair up so I can pin it into a bun.

"Which one?"

Damn. Is he the fashion police, too? "It's the blue Chanel I bought a couple of months back."

"Show me."

I glance back at him through his reflection in the mirror to see if he's serious. He is. Swallowing another piece of my pride, I stand up from my small perch and walk into the walk-in closet to retrieve the dress. Then like a saleswoman at a department store, I hold up the dress so that he can inspect it.

"No. Do you have something that is a little more conservative?"

"Say what?"

"Conservative," he repeats, looking at me like I just got off the short bus. "Do you ever buy anything that doesn't have such plunging necklines? Do you even know how to be modest?"

"I don't understand," I say, my voice edging with attitude. "When I bought this, you said that you loved it."

He looks me dead in my eye. "A lot has changed since then. Hasn't it?"

I'd love to think that he's just referring to Clevon, but I know better. "Look, Omar. Maybe I should just stay home?"

"Why? Do you have something else planned—expecting company maybe?"

My voice continues to harden. "Of course not."

Omar cocks his head while a thin, crude smile cuts across his lips. "Find something else to wear."

"No." I clamp my jaw tight and throw the Chanel dress down on the floor. I fully intend to finally stand up for myself, but for an older man, Omar is on me so fast that I barely blink before he's right there knocking the taste out of my mouth. My head snaps back and the next thing I know my face is hitting the floor.

"I said find something else to put on," he hisses.

With my head pounding and stars blinking before my eyes, I try to crawl away. "No."

"Don't. Give. Me. A. Reason," he warns. "You're going and

you're going to wear something appropriate to the occasion. Do I make myself clear?"

I don't answer while I continue to crawl away. For that, Omar delivers a swift kick to the right side of my ribcage and completely flips me over onto my back. It seems like it takes forever for oxygen to revive my lungs, and while I wait for that small miracle, Omar steps over me and into the closet. When he returns to me gasping on the floor, he holds up a black dress with a bateau collar. It looks more appropriate for a funeral; but more importantly, it's the dress I was wearing in my dreams.

"I like this one," he announces with a straight face. "Wear this one."

Glaring up at him, I hiss, "You're crazy."

"And you're a slut. Makes us an interesting couple, don't you think?"

Cutting my eyes away, I glance at the bedroom door, but I can feel him daring me to make a move. He wants me to fight him. It'll give him a reason to beat my ass. Why didn't I leave when I had the chance?

Greed.

My vision blurs beneath a rush of tears, but I finally manage to pull myself off the floor. Pressing my fingers against my bottom lip, I glance down at a few pearl drops of blood.

"Do you have something else smart to say?"

Silence.

"I didn't think so." He thrust the dress at me and I accept it. "Now hurry up. You won't like it if you make me late." Omar gives me another crude smile and then resumes getting dressed as if nothing had happened.

Inching toward the bathroom with my ribcage busted in, I can't even get myself to look at him. I just know that I need to hurry up and just get this night over with. Tomorrow, I'm getting the fuck out of here hook or crook. Money or no money.

After washing up, I quickly cover the bruise that's quickly

darkening the right side of my face with an extra layer of makeup and finishing powder before stepping into the modest black dress Omar picked. But before walking out of the bathroom, I catch sight of a new pack of razor blades I'd open just yesterday. I glance back in the bedroom to make sure that Omar isn't looking and quickly stash one in the palm of my hand. When I get to my clutch purse, I slip it in.

A second later, Omar walks up behind me. I freeze while he slowly slides the zipper up. Afterward, we look at our reflection in the mirror. If anyone was to look at us, we look like an attractive couple who couldn't possibly have a care in the world. How could we? We're successful, rich, and beautiful. We're just two more members of the Liars' Club in this damn demented town.

"We better go," Omar says, pressing a kiss against the back of my head.

The moment he walks off I feel the hairs on the back of my neck stand while snippets of my nightmare flash before my eyes. *Don't go.*

At the bedroom door, he turns back toward me. "Is there a problem?"

Don't go.

Heart pounding, I shake my head and then force one foot in front of the other. In the carport, Omar elects to take his black Bentley instead of his matchbox sports car. However, when Omar slams the passenger side door, it feels as if I've just eased into my own tomb. While Omar strolls around to the driver's side, my hand starts to inch toward the door handle, but I'm terrified to make a move and in the end only manage to squirm in my seat.

Omar climbs in behind the wheel and all too soon we're pulling off from the house. The car remains silent. I want to turn on the radio, but I'm too scared to do even that. What the hell? This man has completely turned my world upside down. I'm completely in over my head.

Five minutes into the drive and the car's silence is maddening. I sneak a few looks to the devil on my left and he looks as if there's not a thing in the world wrong. *Keep calm, but stay alert.* However, my fake calmness is tossed out the window when I realize that we're heading in the wrong direction.

"I thought the wrap party was being held at the Tiger House?"

"It is," he answers with a small sigh. "I just need to make a quick pit stop."

"Where?"

He glances over at me. "What? Now you're in a hurry to go to the party? I don't get you, sweetheart."

"You were the one that was in a hurry to get to the party, remember?"

"And now I'm the one that needs to make a stop. So just sit over there and shut the fuck up."

Our gazes clash and duel, but ultimately I settle back in my seat and fold my arms protectively in front of me. Twenty minutes later, we're still traveling in the opposite direction of his precious wrap party. The luxury mansions and sleek metropolitan buildings have now been replaced with old and chip-paint concrete ones. It's definitely not the side of town one should roll through in a half-a-million-dollar car.

Suddenly, we're turning down a bunch of small streets, a labyrinth that just has me lost and confused. At last we pull up to an old brick building that looks like it should be more a part of the ghost town streets of the south side of Detroit.

Omar parks and shuts off the engine.

"What on earth do you have to do here?"

"You'll see."

I shake my head. "I'm not going in there."

He removes his keys. "Don't start that shit again."

"No, I don't give a fuck what you say. I'm not going in there and you . . . You can kiss my ass, muthafucka. For real."

His hand flies toward me, but this time I'm able to block

the first blow and reach for the handle on the passenger door. The second blow is another story. It catches me just upside my left temple and sends my head crashing into my side window. I drop my purse and just barely register the pain because I'm more focused on just getting my door open. But the moment it pops open, Omar grabs the back of my head, snatching me by my hair and dragging me back across the seat, the armrest, and then out of the car from the driver's side.

"LET ME GO!"

My ears ring with his demonic laughter as he then proceeds to drag me kicking and screaming. "SOMEBODY HELP ME! SOMEBODY HELP!"

Omar's laughter only grows as he successfully pulls me into the dark warehouse. "Shut up, TRACY!"

My heart drops.

"That is your name, isn't it? Tracy Franklin—married to one Kwame Franklin from Detroit, Michigan? Or maybe I should say used to be married."

Oh shit! I try to bolt again, doubling and then tripling my efforts to get away.

"Let me go!" I kick and scream as Omar wrestles and drags me down a dark corridor. Tears stream down my face as terror grips me.

"Don't you want to see your husband, Tracy? Huh? Don't you want to give him one final kiss good-bye? Or maybe you prefer to join him?" Omar gets a good grip around my waist and then hoists me up and continues to drag me like a rag doll into an even darker room.

My screams hit a whole new octave and then someone clicks on a light—which looks more like a mini spotlight for a body slumped over in a heap on the floor.

"C'mon, Tracy. Time for one last reunion." Omar grabs the back of my head and forces me to look.

My gaze rakes in the familiar form and then finally lands on the bloody, disfigured face. "NOOOO!"

44

Brijetta

"The last thing I want to do is go to a damn wrap party," I tell Trey.

"I know. I know, B," he says, easing up to me in the chaise in the private library. I had spent the entire day trying to de-stress with hour-long bubble baths, warm tea, meditating—you name it, I was trying it to chill the fuck out. "We don't have to stay that long," he continues to campaign. "We dip in and dip out; it's no big deal."

"If it's no big deal, then why can't you go without me?"

"Do you want to give the tabloids another headline when I show up on the red carpet without my wife?"

"So what? We're going to give them a bigger headline by having me show up on your arm? No thanks. I'm tired of the one-woman circus show. I've given them plenty to print to last me the rest of my life." I turn away and try to plant my nose back into the book nestled on my lap.

"C'mon, baby. Now, don't be like that," Trey says, kneeling before me so that we can be eye level. "The best way to combat these rumors is to show solidarity. Our showing up together will enforce that there is nothing wrong with our marriage."

"Nothing wrong? Are you serious? There is plenty wrong."

He cocks his head and then hits me with those puppy dog

eyes. "I thought that we were going to try and put the past garbage behind us."

"You can handle that freak show all on your own."

"C'mon, baby. Don't do this. You know that I need you."

"You need."

"I *want* you there."

I shake my head. "I don't want to do this. I don't want to do any parties. Besides not being in the mood, that bitch is going to be there."

"Precisely. That why we need to head this shit off."

"What, we're supposed to, like, just stand together and sing camp songs together? Not going to happen."

"B, baby. You're wrong about this. There is nothing going on between us. There is nothing going on between me and Jaleesa. I swear."

"It doesn't even matter at this point. I just . . . I don't want to go," I insist. When it's clear that the puppy dog face isn't working, he reaches back into his back pocket and pulls out an envelope.

I frown. "What's that?"

"A surprise. For you." He hands the envelope to me.

"What's this?" I ask, reaching for it.

"Open it."

I look at him suspiciously while I open the envelope.

His face lights up while he watches me.

Exhaling a long breath, I take the envelope and quickly open it. I pull out a couple of airline tickets and brochures. "What's this?"

"It's our vacation I promised you," he says, leaning forward. "There's two tickets to St. Lucia. It's going to be just you and me . . . and a rehab facility. A real good one, I'm told."

My eyes start to fill with tears. "What?"

"You heard me. We're going to be gone for six weeks . . . or however long it takes for us to get this marriage back on track."

"Six weeks!" I'm not sure that I believe what I'm hearing. "You don't have another picture to do?"

"No, I'm not going to look at another manuscript until we get back. I promise."

Tears instantly pour from my eyes while my hearts leaps with unexpected joy. "Really?"

He smiles back at me. "Really, really."

Unable to contain my happiness, I wrap my arms around him. "Oh, baby. Thank you," I say. "You just don't know how much this means to me." My tears fall faster. The idea of getting away from this crazy city for six weeks or even longer is able to erase all the stress I've failed to relieve today. "When do we leave?"

"First thing in the morning," he says.

"Oooh, Trey!" I squeeze him tighter.

"Does this mean that you'll go to the party tonight?"

"Yes!" It will be hell to stand there in front of those picture-taking leeches, but if that's what I have to do to exchange this hellhole of a town, then damn it, I'll do it.

"We better hurry up. We don't have that much time," he tells me.

We quickly scramble up to the bedroom. I don't think that I've ever gotten dressed so fast in my entire life. It might have had a lot to do with me just being happy. Something I haven't felt in a long, long while. Twenty minutes later, we step out at the Tiger's House off Camden and onto a small red carpet. These sorts of parties are normally low profile, mainly because it's really just for the cast and crew of a film celebrating the end of filming. From here on out, the director, editors, and CGI people will work and produce the final cut. However, on this night, there is a horde of paparazzi on the short red carpet in front of the exclusive restaurant, snapping away.

"Trey! Trey," they all shout. "IS THERE ANY TRUTH TO THE RUMORS THAT YOU AND YOUR WIFE WILL BE GETTING DIVORCED?"

Trey turns on his infamous charm. His bright smile seems to glow under the camera's flashing lights. "No, the rumors are not true," he says, looping an arm around my waist. "Just like there's no truth to any of the rumors about me and Ms. Love."

They quickly hurl more questions—a lot at me, but I just smile and ignore them. We stand there for only two minutes, but it feels more like two lifetimes before turning and strolling into the party. But just then another car pulls up and the reporters start to shout.

"JALEESA! JALEESA! IS THERE ANY TRUTH TO THE RUMORS THAT YOU'RE HAVING AN AFFAIR WITH TREY HAMILTON?"

Trey stops and I instantly know what he's thinking before he does it.

"Don't you do it," I hiss.

Trey slowly turns around.

Standing next to Spencer Reid, Jaleesa answers, "No, of course not. You guys know better than to believe these crazy rumors."

Trey starts back to Jaleesa, pulling me along. I'm trying my best to dig my heels in, but it's not working.

Jaleesa glances our way, her smile is leveled with perfect angels—just like Trey. You can't beat an actor at this game. You just can't.

"Hello, Trey," Jaleesa purrs, then shifts her gaze over to me. "Brijetta."

I try to smile, but I think that it looks more like a grimace. Before I know it, I'm being forced to pose right next to Trey, Jaleesa, and Spencer for the cameras. The photographers go crazy. Questions are still being hurled at us.

"ARE YOU ALL SAYING THAT YOU GUYS ARE ALL FRIENDS AGAIN?"

Hell no.

"Of course, we are," Trey answers. "You guys really shouldn't believe everything you print."

There is a low rumble of laughter from the peanut gallery, but the questions keep coming. Finally, Trey turns with me clinging to his right side and we all stroll into the restaurant. The minute we enter the building, I snatch myself from his side and glare up at him. "How dare you! I can't believe that you did that!"

"Calm down," Trey says.

"Yeah, Brijetta," Jaleesa cuts in. "It's no big deal."

"You," I say, pointing and waving my finger. "Don't talk to me. We ain't friends. We've never been friends!"

Trey eases over to me, and leans down to whisper, "St. Lucia. Just one more night, baby. Do this for me."

From around his shoulder just standing off to the side, Jaleesa gives me this smirk and I swear to God that I just want to rake my nails straight down her face. "I need a drink," I tell him, then head straight to the bar. One night. Just get me through one last night.

45

Trey

Just get through the night. That's all you have to do. Drawing a deep breath, I smile when I feel a light tap on my shoulder. "Hey, Nelsan. Man, how are you doing?"

"Great. I can't believe that my first film is in the can and is starring Trey Hamilton!" He laughs.

My smile stretches just a bit wider for the exuberant screenwriter. "Well, it was an excellent script. Viewers are going to love it."

"I sure hope so. Omar and Spencer have already approached me about penning a sequel and even perhaps a third installment."

"Hey, I only see great things for you," I say while my gaze slowly drifts over his shoulder to track my wife at the bar. When she turns, I hold up my hand to let her know I'll be there in just a second. From across the room I can tell that she's still stewing over that little stunt I pulled with Jaleesa out front. The bottom line is we need to start playing on the offense if this bullshit story about me and Jaleesa is ever going to die down.

Our going to St. Lucia will help as well. And even though the trip is needed to repair some of the damage I've caused in the last few months, Brijetta and I do need to get out of town. Both of us are bucking under the pressures and stress. I have a ton of things I need to reevaluate. Things that I have put off dealing with for far too long.

I'm living under a mountain of lies. There's no denying that now. The oddity of my trying to dispel rumors about an affair with my costar versus the truth of me having an affair with my agent definitely has a *Twilight Zone* quality to it. When Brijetta asked if there was any other lie she should know about, I wanted to scream that my whole life is one big lie. I don't know who I am. I just keep finding myself in positions where I want to be all things to everyone. To my wife. To my fans. To my costars. And to my lover.

Trust me. The decision to go to rehab was not an easy one. And I'm not saying that I have a big problem. I'm just willing to do what I need to do in order to save my marriage. I love Brijetta—every fiber in my body tells me that is true. But there is no denying the love that I have for Kent, either. We've been through a lot together. I owe a lot to him. I know that it pained him deeply when I married Brijetta—and he's hurt every day when he has to see me with her. But there's nothing I can do about it. I need her in my life like I need air to breathe.

I'm thinking that after my little flip out a couple nights ago that I just might have a small drug problem. I was lucky in that Amaya had come by and cleaned up the place before Brijetta had been released from jail or I would have had a whole other set of questions to answer. If I can just kick the drugs, then I think a lot of Brijetta's issues will die down. As for Kent and I, if he could just control his jealousy, then I don't see any problem with us just keeping our relationship on the low. Hell, we've been doing it for ten years.

Just then, Kent drifts into my mind and vision.

"Well, it was good talking with you," Nelsan says, probably because he's picked up that I wasn't listening to him. "See you on the sequel."

"Absolutely," I say, pulling my eyes away from Kent and flashing Nelsan a final smile. I start to make my way over to the bar, but it takes a while with so many people stopping me for short chitchat. The next thing I know, Kent steps into my path and smiles.

"What are you doing, man? You know Brijetta will flip out if she sees me talking with you."

"Hey, it's a party. She can't honestly believe that our paths aren't going to cross from time to time," he says.

"Maybe not. But she will expect me to walk away. Excuse me." I move to step around him, but he quickly blocks my path.

"I need to talk to you," he whispers, then takes a sip of a drink just hanging around in his hand.

"We'll talk some other time." I try to move around him again only for Kent to pull the same stunt.

"When will that be, do you think?" he asks. "When you come back from St. Lucia?"

I blink at him. "How do you know about that?"

"I make it my business to know everything when it comes to you." He flashes a smile that only makes his bruised face look sinister. "You are my number one client, after all."

Annoyed, I huff out a long breath. "I was going to tell you."

"I hope you don't mind when I tell you that I don't believe you."

"Look, it's just a little vacation that I promised Brijetta."

"I love vacations."

"Are you serious?"

"Maybe. I remember before you put a ring on Ms. Plus-size crazy that we used to take vacations."

"Don't start that shit tonight," I hiss, then look around to make sure no one is listening to us. "You promised you'd cut all that jealousy bullshit out if I took you back. Are you saying that you can't do that now?"

"I'm just saying that I don't like it when you try to up and disappear on me. You have a nasty habit of just popping up only when you need me or you're fighting with the missus."

I take another glance around. "Hey, if you want out . . . In fact, it will make it a lot simpler on me if—"

"I didn't say that!" Kent snaps, then reigns himself in.

"I'm trying to figure out what exactly you are saying."

Kent pulls another gulp from his drink and we both flash smiles to a couple of people who walk past us.

"I just want to know how long you're going to be gone," Kent says, amending his tone.

"Six weeks," I tell him.

"Six weeks?" He blinks as if I've said forever. "But I have some projects lined up that—"

"I'm not interested."

"But—"

"It's final. Don't push me on this. I have to go." This time when I go to move, Kent restrains me by my arm.

"Okay. Okay. I'm cool. It's fine. I just want to know these things. You know I don't like surprises."

I huff and shake my head.

"I still need to talk to you."

"Can't—"

"Just for a few minutes. You can meet me upstairs in the cigar room if you think your wife will trip."

I shake my head. "I've been talking to you for too long as it is."

"Come on. You're going to be gone for six weeks. Surely you can give me six minutes?"

I try to resist a certain level of guilt, but then relent because

I was dropping this one on him unexpectedly. "All right. I'll meet you upstairs in the cigar room in about twenty minutes."

Kent's smile finally turns genuine. "All right. In twenty minutes."

"But I can't stay long."

"Don't worry. I know how to make it quick."

46

Omar

"Nooooo!" Sinclair screams.

"What? You thought you and this bitch ass husband of yours was going to get the drop on me? Is that it?"

"OH GOD, KWAME!"

This pathetic bitch struggles and kicks until I finally drop her. She immediately crawls over to her dead husband and tries to pull his head into her lap. "Oh God, baby. I'm so sorry."

That shit cracks me up. "You're sorry? What are you so sorry about?" I ask, walking a tight circle around her. "Sorry that you picked the wrong muthafucka to run your whack-ass game on? Sorry that you got caught plotting and planning to kill me?"

She jerks her guilt-ridden face up at me and my smile just stretches wider. "Yeah, that's right. I know all about it. I got eyes and ears everywhere."

Sinclair starts to whimper again.

"Don't get me wrong. Your ass was good for a while and had me fooled for a couple of years. But your ass got sloppy these past couple of months."

"Omar . . . please."

"Please what?" I bark. "Please let you live? Is that what you're about to fix your mouth to say?" I laugh dead in her face while she lowers her head and bathes her husband with tears.

"Didn't I cut you a break the last time I caught you cheating with that gigolo fitness trainer? Huh?"

"Omar—"

"ANSWER ME!"

Sinclair jumps and then tries to control her terror and . . . and rage. "Y-yes."

"What's that look about?" I cock my head at her.

"You got something to say to me, *Tracy*? Hmm?" I take a moment for our glares to play combat. Then I approach, draw back, and give her an open-handed slap across her face. I feel a surge of adrenaline only edged out with regret for what I want to do to her right now. "Fix your face when you're looking at me," I snap. "I've put up with all that I'm going to put up with. Contrary to what you might think, I've put up with bitches waaay smarter than your hood rat ass. And every one of them had to learn the hard way that Omar Fines is the head muthafucka in charge."

Finally, the rage in her eyes vanishes and there's only fear and terror. The way that it should be. If people didn't fear you, then they didn't respect you. I learned that lesson a long time ago.

"But you're in luck tonight," I spat, releasing her head and stepping back. "Because I'm going to give you a choice." I reach behind me and pull out my 9mm.

"You can either join your late husband here or you can try to convince me that we should give this marriage another try. It's up to you."

Her face blankets with confusion.

"Surprised that I'm even willing to consider sparing your life? Is that it?" I step back and study her. She really is a beautiful woman. But beautiful women are plentiful here in the Golden State. This is all about power. Now that she knows who the hell she's dealing with, I suspect that my little golden bird will stay in her golden cage just the way I want her to.

"So what is it going to be? It's up to you." She's so quiet for so long that I'm almost sure that I can hear her thinking. "Oh, and if you're thinking about going to the police, my man Matthew here"—I turn and Detective Morrison steps out of the shadows and folds his arms—"has the tapes of you and Kwame here plotting to do me in. So if you talk, be prepared to wear matching handcuffs, sweetheart."

Her whimpering stops. She knows she trapped.

"I also want you to know, if you choose to live, I plan on making your life a living hell." I smirk, wanting to adjust my growing hard-on. "And I still expect you to smile and be the perfect trophy wife. You'll continue to live with a modest allowance, and whenever you leave the house, you'll be accompanied by Matthew or one of his people. Are you getting all of this?"

She swallows. "Y-yes."

"Good. Because if not . . . poor Felicia Smith in Detroit is going to get a bullet in her head."

Her eyes widen in more horror.

"That's right. I know everything now, bitch. So what is it going to be?"

47

Jaleesa

Revenge. That's all I can think of every time my gaze drifts over to Brijetta as she and Trey continue to network around the room. I have to admit that the little stunt Trey pulled outside the restaurant took me by surprise, but that's all right. I'll play along for a little while.

"So I heard that Kent Webber has lined you up a few meaty roles with MGM," Spencer says in a lame attempt to make idle chitchat.

"Surprised to see that I'm finally moving up?" I ask, turning to give him my attention. "Not that you ever attempted to try. You didn't even help me land a part on *Defiance*."

"You didn't ask."

"Because you always say no. I didn't bother trying this time." When he opens his mouth, I cut him off. "And don't fix your mouth to say that you would've said yes this time. It'll just insult my intelligence." Spencer and I go back aways. It's never been serious other than the fact that I've performed on his casting couch a few times, only for my ass not to land the part. He's a slick player like that, but it's all good.

After chuckling at me for a minute, he raises his glass to me. "Here's to you going to new heights."

I smile and cock my head. "Thank you." We clink our glasses

together and take a sip of our drinks. I see Kent walking up the stairs.

"I wonder what's taking Omar so long," he wonders aloud. "He should have been here by now." He glances at his watch while his brows dip together.

"Are you afraid that you're going to have to stand up there and give the congratulatory speech?" I smirk, knowing full well how much Spencer hated doing anything that regarded public speaking.

"Nah, I'm sure that he'll be here in time for that." He puffs out a long breath. "It's just not like him to be late. I don't think I've ever known him to be late for anything."

Spencer loses my attention when I see Trey desert his wife at the bar and then start to waltz his way toward the staircase. I lift a curious brow. Now, what the hell is this all about? Spencer continues to talk while I watch Trey. He's still smiling and laughing at everyone, but definitely heading toward the staircase.

"Do you know what's upstairs?" I cut Spencer off in whatever the hell he's saying.

"Hmmm. Upstairs," I repeat. "Do you know what's up there?"

Spencer turns around, thinks for a minute. "I think there's like a cigar room. Though I doubt anyone is up there because we rented the whole place out for the party tonight."

"Oh, is that right?" *Now, what on earth would Kent and Trey want to do in an empty room?* My gaze drifts back down to Brijetta, who's attempting small talk with a few cast members. "Will you excuse me for a moment?" I say to Spencer, smiling. I quickly straighten my shoulders and then make a beeline straight toward the bar. My smile inches wider with every step I take. This is going to be so sweet.

"Hello again, Brijetta."

She turns toward me, the laughter that she was just sharing dies instantly when her gaze locks on to mine.

"Go away. We're not doing this tonight."

"Not doing what? Playing Ali and Frasier again? Well, that seems hardly fair—especially since you're the one that gets to throw all the punches." My voice remains sweet and packed with sugar.

"You wouldn't have to worry about punches if you'd stay in your lane and stay away from my husband."

I wave her off. "Child, please. Your husband is *definitely* safe from the likes of me . . . and any other female cast member, if you want to know the truth."

As expected, her face folds with confusion. "What the hell are you talking about?"

"Hmmm. Oh, nothing. I'm just saying that you had absolutely nothing to be freaking out about. Your husband is not interested in me or any other female cast member on the set." I see someone from the lighting department and I give them a quick smile and wave before shifting a bored gaze back to Brijetta, who is still trying to work out the puzzle I'd laid out for her.

Of course, the silly, blind bitch can't figure it out.

"So what's the next project that Kent has lined up for Trey? Oh, by the way, I have to say that I'm so appreciative of him recommending me to him. You know Maury wasn't doing a damn thing for me."

A flicker of surprise flickers across her face. "Kent is your agent?"

"Yep. What else did you think we were talking about?"

She squirms a bit at my blanket lie.

"But you already know that Kent can work magic with an actor's career. Look what he's already done for Trey." The bartender appears next to me.

"Can I get you something to drink?" he asks.

"Yes, I'd like an orgasm please." I toss him a wink and then refocus my attention on Brijetta. "How long have Kent and Trey been *together?*" I add the extra emphasis on "together," but it just flies right over her head.

"Look, Jaleesa. You may or may not be telling the truth about you and Trey."

"What? You don't believe Trey, either? Hmm. Doesn't sound like there's a whole lot of trust in your marriage."

"I'm not discussing my marriage with you," she hisses. "And I'm not going to sit here and discuss Trey's career with you. If you want to work with that asshole Kent Webber, that is on you. All that matters is that he's out of our lives."

Bingo. "Out of your lives? What do you mean? Trey was out at his place in Malibu just this weekend."

"What?" Deep lines groove into the center of her forehead.

"Oh, yeah. You wouldn't know about that since you were incarcerated. I forgot. Silly me." I smack the side of my face and then the bartender sets my drink down. "Actually, I was surprised to see Trey there so early in the morning. Apparently, he spent the night."

Brijetta stares me up and down. "You're lying."

"Why would I lie about that? Trey and Kent have been *partners* for years. Long before you came along. On top of that, they seems to be *really* good friends. I've never known an agent to be on a set as much as Kent. It's almost like he's Trey's little shadow." I snap my fingers. "Didn't you say that he even showed up on your honeymoon?" I shake my head again. "Weird. Frankly, I think Kent is a bit of a workaholic. I wonder why he hasn't found the right *man* to settle down with."

Brijetta is starting to look a little sick.

"Are you all right?"

She ignores my question and starts glancing around.

"Who are you looking for—Trey?" I join her in scanning the room. "I just saw him and Kent go upstairs." I frown. "Though I don't know why? I'm sure that the cigar room up there is empty. Then again, maybe that's the best place to be alone and . . . discuss business."

48

Sinclair

I'm numb and it's hard for me to process anything that's happening right now. A lot has to do with the fact that I have a gun pointed in my face at this moment. The rest has to do with Kwame's head lying in my lap. Memories of all that we had been through together spin in my head at a dizzying rate. The idea of us being able to survive the mean streets of Detroit's south side only to die in Beverly Hills like this seems like a cruel joke. *You should have left with him when you had the chance.*

I should have done so many things differently. Just thinking about how I was acting just a few short months ago is enough to fill me with such deep and abiding shame that I feel like I'm going to choke on it. The money wasn't worth it. It takes me now staring down the barrel of a gun to realize that. How sad.

"I'm waiting," Omar seethes.

I don't have any doubts that he will pull that trigger, and a small part of me wishes that he would. I'm responsible for this mess. My lies. My stubbornness. My greed.

"Get on your knees," he orders, after seeing I wasn't going to answer his question. Turns out, I can't move either. I don't have the strength. "I said GET UP!" He charges toward me and I brace myself for the blow, but it doesn't help, I'm still sent back reeling. At least this time the pain replaces the numbness that was paralyzing me—as well as a healthy dose of survival kicking in.

"GET UP!"

I stagger, but I manage to ease Kwame's head back down and then climb to my feet.

"Let's try this again. Open your mouth."

My brain is still chugging slow, so to help me out, Omar grabs me by my sore jaw and forces me to open my mouth so that he can shove a gun into my mouth. "Do you want to live or do you want to die?"

Tears leaking down my face, I slowly nod my head, but I still expect him to pull the trigger. After all, did he do the same with his first wife?

"Say it," he says, shoving the gun farther down my throat.

"I—I want to l-ive," I mumble around the barrel in my mouth. More tears fall, and amazingly I start thinking about my mother. My mother. Would she be sad about my passing? Now that Kwame is gone, she's the only family I have. And the only one I'm wishing more than anything to see one last time. I now understand what it's like to make a lifetime of bad choices—to chase after something that you think will make you happy, only for it to give you a temporary feeling of euphoria and then leave you empty.

After what seems like forever, Omar finally removes the gun from my mouth and stares me down for another full minute as if making his final decision. Slowly, anger and rage start to seep back into my veins, but I'm conscious enough to know to try and keep it from showing in my face. He wants a submissive plaything that he can beat and abuse to show his dominance. I can give him that. A little while, anyway—until I can get my hands on my own weapon. Anything will do—and it will happen sooner than later.

"All right" he finally says, reaching into his breast pocket and tossing me a handkerchief. "Clean yourself up." He turns toward his hired hand. "Take care of this muthafucka. Bury his ass somewhere no one can find him."

Matthew, I think his name is, gives him a quick nod and then hops to do his bidding. I forget myself for a moment and clench my jaw. I'll have to figure out a way to take care of this asshole, too. I wipe at my busted lip while I watch Matthew squat down and gather Kwame's body, but then I catch sight of a few tattoos I hadn't noticed but before I can take a better look, Omar starts barking at me, "Move your ass. We have to go."

Reluctantly, I move in the direction that he gestures with only having a second to glance back at my real husband. *Goodbye, baby. I'll see you soon.*

Like a good solider, I march out of the warehouse with my mind set on what I have to do.

Omar is talking shit behind me, but it doesn't matter. I'm calm, cool, and collected.

"Now, get your ass in the car," he says, holding open my door.

Silently, I plop down into the seat and immediately spot my purse lying on the floor. I wait until Omar slams my door before reaching down and picking it up. By the time Omar settles behind the wheel and starts up the car, I've found and palmed my small blade, but cover my action by retrieving my compact and proceeding to repair Omar's handiwork to my face.

"Make sure you fix your hair," he grumbles, pulling away from the warehouse. "It looks like shit."

I fight everything that's holy not to cut my eyes over at him. Instead, I reach up and flip down my visor to take a look at my hair. The idea of our still going to a public event after he'd just spent the last half hour whipping my ass just amazes me. Then again, now that I know that he's a sociopath, I should keep it all in perspective.

Wait for the right moment.

I feel a burning sting in my hand and tell myself to ease up on the pressure of the blade. Chances are that I'm only going to get one chance at this and it's got to be perfect. I flip the visor closed and chance a look to my left. My gaze immediately clashes with Omar's. He's so quiet for so long, I'm halfway convinced that he can hear my thoughts. Remembering that I'm supposed to be submissive, I finally lower my gaze and return to applying powder to my face. But I'm ready to strike.

49

Brijetta

She's lying. She's lying. She's lying.

I repeat this mantra inside my head as I thread through the crowd, but it's not convincing me of a damn thing. In fact, Jaleesa's unsubtle accusations sound more like the most truthful thing I've heard in a long while.

Once I make it to the staircase, my heart is racing at a clip that should land me in the hospital at any second. *Trey and Kent. Kent and Trey.*

How could I have missed the signs? The vicious way Kent always attacked me. The strange way I'd always catch him looking at me. The constant digs about being too fat, my chest was too flat, and my nose was too wide. It was his constant needling that undermined my confidence. Could it have all been because he was jealous?

When I reach the top stair, suddenly I am light-headed. *Breathe. Breathe.* I march past the restrooms and another bar area that's empty. I focus on the large room at the end of the hall marked Cigar Room.

Breathe. Breathe.

But damn it, that was getting too hard to do. Tears are already starting to surface and I'm still a few feet from the door.

But there is a sound I'm starting to pick up even through the din of music and voices drifting from downstairs.

"Ooooh. Awww. Yeeees."

A soft sob escapes from trembling lips. I know that sound. I recognize that moan.

Breathe. Breathe.

I reach the door, place my hand on the knob, and twist it. *He didn't even have the decency or brains to lock the door.* It glides open in slow motion and despite my instructions, I stop breathing. Right up until my gaze lands on Trey with his head thrown back, his face in total ecstasy while Kent's head bobs up and down on his dick. My dick.

The shock lasts for just a few seconds—after that rage takes over.

"YOU NASTY MUTHAFUCKA!"

Trey's head snaps up. "Brijetta!"

"I'LL KILL YOU!" I bolt toward them, hands cocked and then throwing blows like the heavyweight championship is on the damn line. My fist connects against his jaw, his head, his chest. And for Kent's punk-bitch ass, I deliver a swift, hard kick to his already fuck face that sends him howling to the floor.

"YOU'RE A LIAR! YOU'RE A GODDAMN LIAR!"

He struggles to put his dick back into his pants while I'm whooping upside his head. "Brijetta, baby. Please! Let me explain!"

I split his lip on that shit. "DON'T SAY SHIT, MUTHA-FUCKA! NO MORE LIES! NO MORE LIES!"

Trey starts ducking and dodging. But that just makes me throw my punches faster and harder. At the same time, this shriek rips from my soul. Once it starts, I can't stop. It just keeps pouring out of me growing louder to the point that it starts to sound more like a wild raging boar than anything human.

"BRIJETTA, PLEASE! PLEASE! People are going to hear you."

"LET THEM HEAR! LET THE WHOLE WORLD HEAR!"

I'm vaguely aware of footsteps rushing toward us, but I don't give a fuck. When I think about all the lies and promises, I just want to stomp this muthafucka ten feet into the ground. Clearly, the idea of the whole world learning about this affair finally put fear into Trey's eyes.

"BRIJETTA, PLEASE!"

I deliver another right hook dead into his busted mouth. "Keep my goddamn name out your mouth!"

"What the hell!" Someone shouts from behind me. Next thing I know I'm being tugged and dragged away from America's superstar.

"GET OFF ME! GET OFF ME!"

Now it feels like a whole mob is pulling on me. I struggle and fight while the wild boar scream starts to sound straight-up demented.

"Let her go. Let her go," Trey pleads, trying to get over to me.

A few people look at him like he's crazy.

"It's okay," he tries to assure them through his bleeding mouth. "We just need a few minutes to talk."

"We ain't got shit to talk about!" I continue to try and wrench myself free. "As far as I'm concerned, you and your slimy-ass *boyfriend, Kent,* can go to straight to hell!"

There's a collected gasp and few arms loosen just enough for me to jerk free. Of course, I seize the opportunity to get in one more punch, but end up missing because Trey sees the shit coming.

"C'mon, Brijetta," he laughs awkwardly in front of a few hundred questioning gazes. "You're jumping to the wrong conclusions again."

And just like that, I can feel that he'd managed to turn the tide on whether I'm having another tabloid-licious episode. I look around and Kent is a fucking ghost. "YOU'RE A FUCK-ING LIAR! I CAUGHT YOU!"

He shakes his head even though his eyes are begging me to please shut up.

"FUCK YOU! FUCK YOU! IT'S OVER, MUTHA-FUCKA! DONE!" I turn and start shoving people out of my way. "Move, goddamn it!"

"Brijetta!" This fool starts to chase after me. "Please, Bri-jetta. Wait!"

I'm so far past this shit I don't know what to do. "Stay away from me. If you know what's best for you, you'd stay away!"

He catches up to me and starts tugging me on my arm. "Brijetta, please think about what you're doing. Let's just go home and talk about this," he hisses.

"Oh, I'm going home all right. But if you want a piece of sound advice, you better not show the fuck up! I mean it. It's over. You'll be hearing from my lawyer!" I jerk my arm away from him and stomp down the stairs. From the corner of my eye, I see Jaleesa, still sitting at the bar—smirking.

I want to say something, but the only thing I can do is thank her and I'm not about to do that shit. I reach the bottom stair and storm toward the front door. Trey is still begging and pleading behind me. "Get away from me, Trey," I warn, throw-ing the restaurant doors open and stomping down the short red carpet. There is still a number of photographers lined up, and I can see a few eyes bug out when they see us storming out.

"Brijetta!"

"Fuck off!" I snap, and then yell down at the valet at the end of carpet. "Get me my damn car!"

"Mrs. Hamilton! Mrs. Hamilton!" the reporters chant.

"AND YOU ALL CAN FUCK OFF, TOO!" In a blink of an eye, the number of flashing lights double.

"Brijetta, baby. Please. I'm sorry. If you'd just let me explain,"

Trey continues to plea while I'm forced to stand at the end of the red carpet, waiting for a valet to retrieve our car.

"You know what? You sound like a fucking scratched record! I'd done told you I don't want to hear nothing you gotta say. So why don't you go back in there with your friends and try to convince them that I'm crazy? Go convince them that I didn't just catch you upstairs with your dick inside your agent's mouth!"

"WHAT DID SHE SAY?" a couple of reporters ask one another.

Trey turns toward the intrusive cameras. "Back the hell up! This is a private conversation!"

Trey's Porsche rolls to a stop in front of us and I quickly rush around and hop behind the wheel. Trey opens the passenger door and just barely makes it inside before I slam my foot onto the gas.

"Get out," I yell, shoving him toward the open the door.

"No, I need for you to hear me out!"

Racing toward the entrance of the restaurant, I take a hard left, hoping to dump his ass out.

Trey braces himself with the dashboard and just barely manages to remain seated. "What the fuck, Brijetta?"

"I told you to get your ass out!"

"I'm not going anywhere, Brijetta. We're going to talk this shit out!"

I cut another corner and come close to a parked van, which cleanly removes Trey's open door. He jumps and almost lands in my fucking lap.

"What the fuck? Are you trying to kill me?"

50

Omar

"Is that the best that you can do?" I ask, staring over from the driver's seat. It's clear that no amount of powder and lipstick is going to be able to cover up my handiwork.

"Maybe we shouldn't go," Tracy suggests.

"Nah. Nah. We're going," I insist. "Look in the glove compartment. There should be a pair of shades you can wear. We're just going to dip in so I can make my speech and then dip out." My hard, black eyes meet hers again. "And you're going to be on your best behavior, aren't you?"

Tracy swallows, then nods her head.

My lips quirk up. "And when we get home"—I reach over and run a finger from the base of her throat down to her covered breasts—"We're finally going to have some fun . . . just the way *I* like it."

I can feel her body tremble and I continue to get hard as hell.

I smirk. "Yeah, I'm thinking this marriage just might make it." I turn my eyes from her and then place my hands at the ten and two positions on the steering wheel.

"I don't think so, asshole."

I cut my gaze over to her. "What the fuck did you just say?"

Quick as a snake, Tracy leaps over at me and a sharp blade

cuts across my large Adam's apple. "FUCK YOU, MUTHA-FUCKA!"

My shit slices like butter as our car swerves on the open road. I still have enough strength to knock this bitch back to the other side of the car, but she shakes that shit off and lunges at me again while I'm trying to stop the geyser of blood from gushing through my fingers.

She swings at me with everything she has, hitting me in the mouth, face, and head. "WHO'S THE BITCH NOW, MUTHAFUCKA?"

While she's wildin' out, the car is like a runaway train. . . .

51

Trey

"Stop the car, Brijetta!" Trey shouts. "You're in no condition to drive."

She pulls one hand off the wheel to try and smack me again in his head. "Don't tell me what to do, you sorry sonofabitch! I'm done with your ass! Why can't you get that through your big head?"

"Brijetta, I know that you don't believe me, but I love you. I do."

"Oh my God. How the fuck can you fix your mouth to say that shit to me?"

"It's the truth," I insist. "It's complicated and as fucked up at the same time. I know that it hurts you, baby, but that's never been my intent."

"Stop talking. Stop talking. Stop talking," she shouts.

"Please, baby. I need you. Let's—let's just go to St. Lucia and try to talk and work this shit out. I can't lose you, baby. Please, I'm begging you."

"Oh, you done lost me, muthafucka. You better best believe. So carry your ass back to Kent's pad out in Malibu and have yourself a grand old fuck party. Only place I'm going tomorrow after burning your shit is to my lawyer's—and then to the doctor's to get my ass tested!"

Her hatred rolls off of her in waves, breaking my heart. It wasn't supposed to go like this. I had everything all figured out. If I just hadn't gone upstairs with Kent, none of this would be happening right now.

"Brijetta, please. I swear I'll never see him again."

"Fuck that. He can have your nasty ass."

"Brijetta—"

"What are you, a bottom bitch or a top bitch?"

She hangs another left. Tires screech while I try to hold on.

"Answer me!" She turns her head to shout.

A pair of bright lights catch my attention. Another car is rocketing toward us just as out of control as we are. "BRIJETTA, WATCH THE ROAD!"

She jerks her head back to the road, but it's clear we're a half a second away from a head-on collision. "OH MY GOD!"

That's the last thing I hear before the world goes black.

PART V

The aftermath . . .

52

Tracy

Nine months later . . .

I wake to the sound of something beeping around me. More than anything I want someone to shut it off because it feels like I've been listening to it forever. However, when I try to move, nothing happens. *Where am I?* Next I try to peel my eyes open wider, but it doesn't seem to help my blurry vision.

"Tracy? Oh my God. You're awake."

Mom? I finally manage to roll my head to my right side, but I still have trouble making out the blurry person sitting next me and clutching my hand.

"Oh, praise Jesus. He brought you back to me." She leans down and starts washing my face with kisses. It's a bit shocking, but desperately welcomed. I blink a few times and my vision adjusts just a little more. I am able to make out a little of her face, and I'm instantly struck by how well she looks. I guess it was really true. She had managed to clean herself up.

"I had the whole church congregation just praying for you. I can't wait to tell them that our prayers have broken through."

I smile at all the hope and love shining her eyes. And then images start to flash in my mind. Omar . . . the car . . . and . . .

"Kwame," I whisper. His name activates a switch and tears start to gush from my eyes. "He's . . . he's . . ."

"Shhhh, baby. It's all right. Don't stress yourself out." She kisses my face again. "You need to get all the rest you possibly can. Let me just go get the doctor and your husband. Everything is going to be all right."

My husband?

"Mom . . ."

"Shhhh. Don't talk. Rest. I'll be right back." I try to hold on to her hand so I can get more words out, but I'm weak. Her fingers slide from mine easily. I'm helpless to watch her walk away from me. A part of me can't believe that this happening. *It was all for nothing.* Tears splash down my face while both horror and fear twist my fragile nerves into knots. There's no telling the kind of hell I'll have to live through with Omar now. My door swings back open and I try to prepare myself to face that slick devil in an Armani suit.

"Come look," Felicia is saying. "I'm telling you that she's awake."

A small wave of relief crashes over me when I see a blurry white jacket. A doctor. He approaches the bed, sliding on a pair of glasses. When he sees that my mother is correct and that I'm awake, he smiles kindly at me. "Mrs. Fines? How do you feel?"

"All . . . all right, I guess." I try to swallow, but my throat is so dry that it causes me to start hacking.

"Oh, let me get you some water, baby," Felicia says.

I'm still touched by her late bloom of maternal instincts. She quickly pours me a small cup of water from a plastic pitcher next to the bed while the doctor plugs his ears with a stethoscope.

"Breathe in for me," he instructs, placing the cold metal end above my left breast.

I follow his orders, but tugging in too much air only sends me into another coughing frenzy.

"Here you go, baby." Felicia tilts my head up and places the plastic cup against my lips.

I try to sip, but when the cool liquid starts sliding down my throat, I become greedy and try to down too much until I start to choke.

"Easy now," Felicia says. "You have to pace yourself."

After she removes the cup and blots my mouth with a few tissues from the table, the doctor peels each of my eyes open and checks my pupils with a small pen of light. "Mrs. Fines, it is definitely good to have you back with us. Do you recall being in a fatal car accident at all?"

I do, but I shake my head. Instinct tells me that's the best answer.

He nods as if my lie was to be expected. "Well, you were." He looks to my mother. "You were thrown from the car because you weren't buckled in. I have to tell you that it's a miracle that you're even here with us. As for your injuries—they're bad. You've been in a coma for the past nine months. You suffered several broken bones and lacerations. But the good news is that with proper and vigorous physical therapy, you'll heal quite nicely. It might take a year or even longer, but it's doable."

I smile as a second wave of relief washes over me. *I'm going to be okay.* More tears stream down my face. I hadn't even realized that I was even worried about the possibilities of not pulling through this until the doctor started talking.

"As for the other news." He glances up to Felicia. "I'll let your mother talk to you about that."

My gaze swings back to Felicia, who quietly lowers her head.

"I'm going to leave you two alone now so you can talk. I'll send the nurse in in a few minutes."

Felicia just gives me this strange look while we wait for the doctor to leave the room. I already know what she's going to say and I really don't want her to say it. After all, I'd seen Kwame's body earlier that night, so I just assume that the cops have found him within the past nine months.

"Tracy," she begins.

"It's all right . . . Mom." Surprise colors her eyes because it's the first time in decades since I've called her that. "You don't have to say it. Please don't say it."

Her brows dip together. "Hold on. Let me get your husband."

"No . . ."

"Hold on." She rushes out of the room before I can get another word out.

"Damn it." I pull in several breaths, feeling like I'm on the verge of hyperventilating. Then the door swings back open and I can't help but hold my breath and brace for the inevitable.

"Kwame!" By some miracle I sit up. My eyes have to be playing tricks on me. "I . . . I don't understand. How?"

A smile balloons across Kwame's face as he rushes up to the bed. "Hey, you."

"I though you were dead. I saw—"

"Felicia," Kwame says. "Can you give us a few minutes?"

Mom smiles at me again. "I'll be right outside the door, baby. Call me if you need me."

Kwame sits down on the bed next to me while taking my hand into his. "I can't tell you how scared I've been these past few months," he admits. "I feel . . . like I've really let you down and . . ."

"No, it's not your fault. I got myself into this mess. I just don't understand how it's possible that . . ."

"If you thought I was dead, then that can only mean that you saw Mike."

"Mike?" I frown. "Your cousin Mike?"

He nods. "He went missing the night before your accident. I flew him out here to help me . . . you know."

The pieces fall easily together. "Omar had mistaken Mike for you?"

"He must've. I dropped Mike off at the hotel and went out for a quick errand, when I returned he'd just vanished. I knew something went foul, but before I could step to your man, he was killed in that car accident. I guess in the end he got his, huh?"

"So he's dead? He's really dead?"

A long silence floats between us before I remember that private detective that Omar has working for him. "There's someone else," I tell Kwame.

He shakes his head. "No, I figured that Omar wouldn't have done that shit on his own, so I tracked down that dude from the detective agency he had watching you that one time. I got the drop on him—he confessed to taking my cousin out. Guess he thought I was a ghost. I put four bullets in his cranium for that shit and snatched all the evidence he had on us."

"Oh, Kwame, I'm so sorry." I reach up and cup the side of his face. He turns his head and kisses my palm. "Thank you, baby." Next, he leans down and gives me one of the sweetest kisses we've ever shared. But when he pulls back, I could tell there was more bad news. "What is it?"

Our eyes lock. "The other car," he begins. "You need to know about what happened to the people in the other car."

53

Brijetta

THE WORLD STILL MOURNING
THE DEATH OF TREY HAMILTON

I push this week's copy of the *Hollywood Gawker* away from the table and roll my wheelchair over to the tall arch window to stare out to the overgrown lawn. Every day I tell myself that I'm going to call someone to come over and cut it, but I never do. I can't stand for anyone to come around anymore. Not even Amaya. Not even my mother.

Fat tears drop and race down my face as I try to pull in a deep breath. The world blames me for Trey's death . . . even though the police have proved that it was Omar Fines's car that had drifted into my lane. No one cares to hear the truth when the photographers, as well as a restaurant full of people, have blabbed to every media outlet about my state of mind when I'd peeled away from the wrap party. And they're right. I was speeding and Omar's car was speeding. I just don't understand why or how I survived the crash. If one wants to call me living the rest of my life in this wheelchair surviving.

My anger is gone and in return I'm just empty. Twenty-four hours after the accident, Kent Webber up and disappeared. No one has been able to find him. But before he did that, he sat down and penned me a letter validating everything that Trey tried to tell me that night. That his heart was with me and every time he'd tried to end things with Kent, he would bribe and drug or do whatever he could in order to keep him.

He also apologized for all the years that he tried to make me feel like I wasn't good enough for Trey. His actions were out of jealousy. Pure and simple. I wish now that I hadn't burned the letter. I would like to read it again. It was a small nugget that confirmed that my marriage wasn't a complete lie, and now that's gone, too.

For months, the public tried to force law enforcement to bring me up on vehicular homicide charges, but in the end I just got a ticket for reckless endangerment. That's of little comfort. I don't know what to do now. I don't know what my future holds.

The phone rings, startling me out of my depressing thoughts. I make no attempt to go answer it and instead wait for it to go to the answering machine. As soon as the line beeps, my mother's voice booms into the speaker.

"Brijetta? Baby? If you're there, pick up." Pause. "I know you're there, honey. Please pick up the phone." Sigh. "All right, baby. I just called to let you know that Sinclair woke up today."

My head jerks up. I turn the wheelchair around and speed as fast as the electric motor will allow.

"She's all right. The doctors say—"

"Hello," I pick up the line.

"I knew that you were listening," my mother accuses. "You really shouldn't just sit in that big house and mope all day. You need to get out—get some fresh air.

"Mom, what's this about Sinclair? You said that she woke up. How is she doing? Is she all right?"

"From what I've been told—yes. You know I've bonded with her mother when you were in the hospital. She called and said that they're running some tests, but the doctor expects her to make a full recovery."

I sigh with relief. The thought of not being just the sole survivor out of that crash is of some comfort. Not much—but some. "That's good to hear," I say, choking up. "I always did like Sinclair." I clasp a hand over my mouth and the next thing I know I'm having a full blown meltdown.

"That's it. I'm coming over," my mother says.

"No. No. That's not necessary," I tell her.

"I'm not asking anymore. I'm telling you. I'm coming over. And don't bother locking the door because I'll just get the police to knock it down." With that, she hung up.

I place the phone back on its charger and expel a long breath. Next to the phone is a wooden framed photograph of me and Trey. I pick it up and stare at the smiling couple as if they were old acquaintances I haven't seen in a long time. Trey has his arms wrapped around me and is kissing the side of my neck while I'm giggling uncontrollably because I'm extremely ticklish.

He loved me. I know that he loved me.

I press the picture up against my breasts and try desperately to cling to that one fact. But it's hard. I turn away from the table and steer the wheelchair to the French doors and open them for the first time in months. Pulling in a deep gulp of fresh air, I'm surprised at just how much it clears away a good chunk of clutter in my mind. When I pull in another, I swear that I even taste hope. Hope that I will survive this depression. Hope that I'll survive the press. Hope that I'll even trust another man and fall in love.

It won't be for a good long while. But I'll wait.

54

Jaleesa

Six months later . . .

CROWDS FLOCK TO SEE TREY HAMILTON'S FINAL PERFORMANCE

It's like no other film premiere I've ever been to. For weeks now I've been on press junket after press junket with everyone hyping this movie up. With the film opening on Memorial Day weekend, the expectations are for the film to pull well over a hundred million over the three-day weekend. The buzz is high because both the legendary producer and film star both died in the same car crash over a year ago. Add in Kent Webber's disappearance the next day and the town is drowning in speculations that don't appear to be dying down anytime soon.

Meanwhile, I'm the hottest interview to be had. Everyone wants to know what it was like working on such a crazy set. I still get asked about whether there's any truth to whether Trey and I were having an affair. I always give my denial, but with a small smile that hints I could be lying.

In the back of my mind, I know that it's a bit shameful to exploit this situation, but I'll be hard-pressed to find any actress or even actor who wouldn't do the same. The name of the game is to use any and all things to one's advantage in order to survive this crazy town. But if you want to know whether I regret sending Brijetta up those stairs that night, the answer is yes.

Surprised? I'm not completely heartless, especially since word around town is that Brijetta is still walled up in that big old mansion, puttering around in a wheelchair. Believe it or not, some days I wish I could just call her up or drop by to check on her. We do go back a long ways. But I know I can't do that.

That bridge is scorched and it can never be repaired. The same with me and Sinclair, who, last I heard, had inherited a shitload of money, packed up her stuff, and is headed out east to be close to her mother. Strange. Since once I could have sworn she told me that her mother had passed away a long time ago.

Initially after the accident had been reported back at the Tiger House that night, in my hysteria, I'd blabbed that I'd been the one to send Brijetta upstairs to check on her husband. Minutes later, she had flown into a rage and the rest was history. I wish I could take back the admission, because ninety percent of the interviewers wanted to know why I'd sent Brijetta up those stairs.

Brijetta's accusation hurled at Trey that night also made the circulation. Was Trey Hamilton gay? Again, I would never say yes, but my smile did. Some days I feel like it was my fault that Trey and Omar were dead, and then there were others when I felt that I had nothing to do with Brijetta driving the way she was that night or, for that matter, how Omar and Sinclair were driving.

But there were some Trey Hamilton die-hard fans who didn't see it that way.

"Jaleesa!" a reporter from the E! network shouts and waves me over. I brighten my smile and approach. "How excited are you tonight?"

"Very! Can you believe this crowd?" I sweep my gaze around.

You would've thought that this was the night of the Oscars or something. There are so many stars; a lot of them had nothing to do with the movie, but want to be seen at the most talked about event. The streets are chock-full of Trey Hamilton fans, holding up posters, cheering and crying.

"Critics are already raving about the film," the reporter says. Rumors of a posthumous Oscar nomination for Trey Hamilton's performance. "Word is that Spencer Reid and Nelsan Reynolds are ready gearing up for the sequel. Are you signed up to do the next film?"

"Not yet." I hold up my crossed fingers to the camera.

"You were a Kent Webber client, weren't you? Any idea where he's disappeared off to?"

I shrug my shoulders. "Your guess is just as . . ." From the corner of my eye, I swear I see Kent strolling down the red carpet. "Well, I'll be damned." My smile brightens. Clearly, Kent Webber had finally come out of mourning. Thank God. I haven't been able to find the right agent since he disappeared. "Kent!" I hold up my hand and wave toward him.

The reporter and the camera man in front of me turn and zoom their cameras on Kent Webber, who was now steadily making his way over to me. He drifts easily between stars and security. But when he gets to within ten feet of me, I see him reach into his jacket. Then, in slow motion, I watch as he pulls out a gun, aims, and then fires.

I feel my body jerk back once. And for a brief moment, I wonder what just happened. People start screaming and then running. I glance down for a second, surprised to see I'm standing in a pool of blood. When did that happen?

"IT'S YOUR FAULT HE'S DEAD!" Kent shouts.

My gaze shifts from the pool of blood and back up again.

Kent smiles as a team of security guards rush to tackle him, but he squeezes off two more shots. And I'm still wondering what happened when the world goes black.

THE LIAR'S CLUB

LAYLA JORDAN

About this Guide

The following questions are intended
to enhance your group's
reading of this book.

If you enjoyed *The Liar's Club*, don't miss

Sweet Little Lies

by Michele Grant

Coming in February 2011 from Dafina Books

Here's an excerpt from *Sweet Little Lies*. . . .

1

Days Like This

"Christina girl," my grandmother used to say, "timing is everything . . . and yours is always a day late and dollar short." Grammy Vi was freaking prophetic.

As I sat on the tarmac seated next to a testy black man whose last name I didn't know and first name I couldn't remember, I had to wonder at the circumstances that brought me here, to this moment. Thinking back to five days ago, I asked myself the following questions: Would I have been more lucid and less homicidal if I'd drunk my morning coffee first? Would I have been more rational if I hadn't been caught standing there with wet hair, trying to hold on to the post-shower sex glow? Would it have made a difference if this hadn't happened three days before my wedding?

I'll never know. Here's what is known: It was Wednesday, a warm, sunny late summer morning. The kind of morning you only get in the Bay Area. The sun was beaming through the last of the fog, with a slight breeze coming off the water. The wind softly rustled the teal silk drapes I had hanging across the one open window in my bedroom.

All was right in my little piece of real estate on Harbor Bay

Island. Alameda was literally a hop, skip, and jump from San Francisco, nestled on an island and backing up to Oakland. My 2 to 2.5 house wasn't huge, but it was big enough for the two of us that we would live here after my wedding in a few days. The best thing about the house was a view of the Bay Bridge, with San Francisco twinkling like a magical jewel beyond. My bills were paid, my man was near, and my spirit was happy.

I woke up late, a rare treat. I had taken the rest of the week off to prepare for my wedding. My fiancé, Jay, was spooned to my back, his arm possessively wrapped around my waist, his thigh wedged between mine. Another rare treat since he traveled so frequently. I lay next to him for a minute just . . . living. Black love, y'all. I smiled to myself before I slowly eased out of his hold and headed for the bathroom.

Midway through my shower, the etched glass door opened and he stepped in. Very quickly, the shower went from Rated R (hot and sudsy) to Rated X (wet and steamy). We went from zero to sixty and back to zero in fifteen minutes time. Another few minutes of actual showering and I stepped out to face the day. I silently apologized to my ruined hair, yanked on the fluffy robe and slippers before padding toward the kitchen.

So it was 10:02 AM, according to the coffeemaker. I stood pouring my expensive Guatemalan whole beans into the grinder when Jay said his first real words of the day. ("Like that right there, baby," didn't count.)

"Listen, sweetheart, about the wedding . . ."

I paused in the pouring of the beans and ever so slowly turned my head to look at Jay. Jay, my (yes, I know) fiancé. I paused because I knew the tone. That hesitant, *I hate to tell you this* tone. I had heard the tone before.

Twice before, to be exact. The first fiancé used the tone in the car on way back from my final wedding gown fitting. Cedric wanted me to listen while he explained that he accidentally married his college sweetheart a month before our wedding. Accidentally. Boy's night out, ran into her. One drink led to another, which led to Vegas, which led to me calling 175 friends and associates with the news assuring them that, yes, I would be sending those thoughtful gifts back and, no, we were not just going to have a big party, anyway.

The second fiancé used the tone at a charming Italian restaurant on the Bay across the wharf from Jack London Square. Perry wanted me to listen while he explained that he was confused about his sexuality. His what? I shrieked! Yes, his sexuality. He had been living a lie and wanted me to know (two weeks before our wedding) that he wasn't sure who he was or what he wanted. Well, if he didn't know, I certainly had no clue. He was kind enough to call half of the 125 friends and associates.

So, yes, when my third—THIRD—fiancé stood naked in my kitchen with that look on his face and tone in his voice . . . I froze before biting out, "What about the wedding?" I had a tone of my own: cold, suspicious, pissed off.

He paused before answering. Jay was a 6'1" dark chocolate bodyguard-build kind of brother. Square-jawed, former Marine, short cropped fro with a razor sharp line, laser-beam eyes so dark brown they appeared black. A nose that would've been Grecian had it not been broken twice before, and lips that would look pouty on anyone not so unapologetically masculine. Not an ounce of fat on his faithfully maintained body. Well proportioned, he was a man who moved stealthily on his long limbs, large feet, large hands, large well—everything. As I said, well proportioned. When he smiled, he was an engaging teddy bear of a man. When he didn't he was the kind of brother who seemed intimidating, even frightening. He stood there looking like a Zulu king in need of a loincloth. But right now, he was the one who looked scared, "Now, Chris, let me just say—"

I put down the beans, no need for $15.95 of imported goodness to get ruined. I decided to employ a little psychology. I walked over to him calmly, put my hands on his broad chest, and smiled encouragingly. "Just tell me, baby. Whatever it is, it'll be okay. Just say it all at once; I'll just close my eyes and listen." I closed my eyes.

He sighed and relaxed slightly, rubbing his cheek against my forehead. "You're so sweet. The thing is . . . I'm really not Jayson Day. My real name is David Washington. I'm an undercover operative with the NSA, and I've been out here on assignment for the past two years. I shouldn't have let things get this far; but when I met you, you were just so sweet and sexy. I couldn't help myself."

I opened my eyes slowly and took a step back. "What are you talking about, I had your background checked! You work corporate security for TeleTech and you grew up in Oakland! I've met your parents, for Christ's sake!"

He gave me a look of smug amusement that did not sit well at all. Not at all. "I know, they told me someone was checking my cover. I thought it was cute. Those people you met were actors. The thing is, baby, I would marry you in a heartbeat but . . . I'm already married."

I stood with my mouth open trying to figure out what to digest and what to reject. Cute, actors, NSA, already married, WHAT? "You're what?"

"Um-hmm, married—with two kids back in Denver. Daughters: Dina and Daisy. They're seven and twelve." Why he felt the need to share details was lost on me.

"Kids?" I really did not know what to say.

"I can show you pictures . . ."

The word *pictures* was still floating in the air when the doorbell rang. In the middle of crisis situations, I tend to go on autopilot. I just take the next logical step to get to the next logical place. So for no other reason than autopilot, I answered the front door. Yes, I did. I forgot I was rocking the robe, with my wet hair turning into a Chaka Khan fro and my naked fiancé (ex-fiancé?) standing in the foyer.

"Parcel servi—" The young black delivery guy paused at

the sight that we presented: Me, cute of face and slight of body, 5'5", a cocoa-colored and petite package wrapped in a huge fluffy pink robe, matching slippers, and a scowl on my face as I cut the side-eye to the dark chocolate naked guy. Eyes the color of milk chocolate that were thickly lashed and normally tilted up with good humor were currently squinted and shooting virtual fire. Bow-shaped lips normally painted a shade of peach were bare, naked, and pursed.

"Hey." I released my death grip on the door handle.

To his credit, he recovered quickly. "I have some more packages for you, Ms. Brinsley. Looks like more wedding gifts. A few of these require an adult signature. If you don't mind my asking, are you okay?" This guy had been delivering all manner of packages related to the wedding for over ten months now. He was a cute, dreadlocked, kind of baby-faced, toffee-skinned, tall guy probably in his mid-20s and I didn't have a clue what his name was. On the occasions when I was home for his deliveries, we made small talk about the weather. I said clever things like, "Working hard out here in all this rain?" He would smile all flashing dimples and twinkling sage green eyes and reply, "Gotta earn a living." And now, he was bearing witness to one of my top ten worst life events . . . okay, top five. I was determined to maintain a shred of dignity.

Before I could respond, Jay . . . David . . . Jay/David spoke up, "Man, do we look okay? Can't you just leave those and go?"

Why was he speaking to my delivery guy? Why was he speaking at all? "Don't speak to him that way. At least he's concerned about my well-being. As a matter of fact, just don't speak at all."

Delivery Guy shuffled from one foot to the other, clearly wishing he was anywhere else than here. I could relate. "Ms. Brinsley, are you okay?" I found it interesting that out of the two men in the room, the one I WASN'T supposed to marry this week was most worried about my well-being. Duly noted.

Forcing a smile, I reached for the pen. "Sure, why wouldn't

I be?" I signed the e-signature box with a flourish before handing it back to him.

He read what I wrote, paused with brow raised, and read it again. "Did you mean to sign this 'Just shoot me now'?"

My lips twisted. "Does it matter?"

Making a sound that was a mix between a snort and a laugh, he headed to the rear of the truck. "I guess not."

I kept my eyes on Delivery Guy. Just looking at him was soothing to me. He was a lean, corded young man. Skin like toasted almonds. And he hadn't just broken my heart. I watched in detached fascination as he lifted packages and placed them on a dolly. Without turning my head even an inch in his direction, I hissed out instructions to Jay/David, "Put some clothes on and get out."

"Christina . . . we need to talk about this," Jay/David said.

Finally glancing in his direction, I adopted my "disgusted" pose. Hand on one hip, size 7 foot tapping, head tilted ever so slightly to the right. "Think you've said enough."

"I don't want you to think that this, what we have, isn't real."

Was he kidding me with this? He wanted to talk about what was real when quite possibly everything he had said to me for close to three years was clearly a damn lie. "Oh, it's real. It's real jacked up."

"Christina, I really wanted to marry you."

I didn't want to hear another word. Not one. More. Word. "But you're not going to . . . because you can't . . . riiight."

"Would you rather I didn't say anything and let you live a lie?"

"I would rather you hadn't lied for the past two or three years. For all I know, you're lying now. As a matter of fact, of COURSE you are lying. Undercover Brother . . . puh-lease! Give me some credit. You could have at least come up with something believable. Why not just feed me sweet little lies? You don't want to marry me, so be it. What was this, some sort of elaborate con? I don't know what to think. I don't know what to do with this. What I *do* know is that you waited until three days—THREE DAYS—before our wedding, but exactly fifteen minutes after you made sure to get you a little morning nookie to drop whatever this is on me. Go put some clothes on your lying ass and get out!"

He made a move to reach for me and probably realized that any point he was going to make would be far more effectively delivered when he was clothed. Turning, he walked hurriedly back to the bedroom.

My house was a semicircle with the kitchen, office nook, and dining area on one side; foyer, living room, and half-bath in the middle; and two bedrooms and two baths on the other. It was designed and decorated to maximize the view of the Bay. But it also meant that from the front door you could pretty see everything going on in the house.

Delivery Guy wheeled the dolly to the front door and peeked in nervously before tapping on the door frame. "Uh, you want me to bring these in or leave them out here?"

What to do with the wedding presents? It was all too much to process. "Might as well bring them in, uh, what's your name?"

He shot me a look at the moment I realized it was stitched onto his uniform. We spoke simultaneously. "Steven."

Shrugging, I gave a wry grin. He would have to forgive my lack of attention to detail. My life was in the process of going to hell in a handbasket . . . again. "Sorry, Steven. Can you just set everything on the table?"

"Sure." He transferred packages with the haste of one dying to be done and on his way. It occurred to me that this was as awkward a moment for young Steven as it was for me.

Jay/David came back out with some sweatpants hastily yanked on, pulling a T-shirt over his head. "You ready to talk?"

"I'm ready for you to go." Funny, in a not so humorous way, how your entire world can tilt in the blink of an eye. Not twenty minutes ago, I was wrapped around this man planning to have years and years of the same. Now I couldn't stand to look at him.

"But I think we should . . ." When he took a step toward me, I put my hand up in the universal back-up-off-me sign. Poor Steven stood there with a "What the hell have I walked into?" look on his face.

"Jayson, David—whatever your name is! Please!"

"Christina, I know you. If I leave without trying to fix this, you'll never let me back in."

"You don't need to get back in here, you need to get back to your *wife* . . . and Dina and Daisy, was it? Whatever, I can NOT believe this. "

He looked at me, face all pitiful like I should be concerned about making him feel better.

I looked at him, mad as hell, wondering how this happened to me . . . again.

Steven took the last box off the dolly and turned toward the door with understandable haste. I lived here and I was ready to be somewhere else my damn self.

Jay/David reached for my hand, only for me to yank it back. He reached again, encircling my wrist and tightening enough to hurt. "Jay, that hurts."

"Just listen to me for just one second." Meeting his eyes at that moment, I realized that I had no idea who he really was and that made me panic.

Hissing at him, I tugged again. "Let me go."

Steven stopped dead in his tracks on his way to the door. He let the cart handle drop to the ground, turned, and stepped to Jay/David all in one fast motion. "Man, I think you oughta just go."

Jay/David looked incredulous. I was a little stunned myself. But Steven took a no-nonsense posture—chest out, legs planted firmly slightly apart. Looking back and forth between them, I noted the contrasts. Whereas Jay/David was broad and thick, Steven was all taut lines and sleek muscles. Jay/David had about twenty-five more pounds on his frame, but Steven was about two inches taller. While Jay/David looked like he'd seen military combat, I'd lay odds Steven had seen street combat. Personally, in a dark alley, I wouldn't have wanted to piss either one of them off. They stood staring each other down like Serengeti lions from an Animal Planet documentary.

Jay/David's nostrils flared and he snarled, "Punk, don't make me—"

"What?" Steven asked, raising his chin and flexing one hand.

Yanking my wrist away, I stepped in between the men, "Fellas. Separate corners. Both of you can go."

They stepped apart from each other a step at a time. Jay/David picked up his keys from the table. Steven lifted the dolly handle off the ground where he'd left it.

"I'll be back." Jay/David said, before storming out the back door.

Steven reached into his back pocket and handed me something. Looking down, I realized it was a handkerchief. I tilted my head and looked at him. "Why—"

"You're crying." His voice was soft and gentle. He exited my front door, closing it with a quiet click behind him.

Reaching up to touch my face, I realized it was true. I had tears streaming down my face and I hadn't even known. "Thanks," I said belatedly to the empty room before sinking into my easy chair to cry in earnest.